**Life had its strange ways, presenting him with a chance to love her as he should've loved her centuries ago…**

He must learn how to bear a lonely life. As Kate had said, what kind of life could he give her? Of course, she'd referred to Phantom and Christine, but Kate might as well have spoken of him and her. Yes, he could provide for her, but not give her his heart, and love without heart just wasn't love.

A corner of clear plastic case sticking out of the pink wrapping on the passenger seat caught his eye. Kate had the CD in her hand when she left the car. She'd put the soundtrack in her purse. How had the case found its way back to the car? Perhaps she left it behind to make sure he would return it. No, she wouldn't do such a deceitful thing. She had promised she believed him when he'd said he would see her again. He placed the CD inside the glove compartment. He opened the door and set one foot on the concrete. Emina's ethereal whisper stopped him from exiting his car.

'*The CD is a guarantee you'll pay Kate a visit.*'

His heart ceased for a few beats, pain stabbed at his chest. "Emina, my dove. You must not interfere."

'*You promised me, Matthias.*' Scolding in her tone made her voice louder.

He sank against the backrest. How could he keep his vow when he spent every moment thinking of what life might've been had she lived? "That is one promise that will have to go unfulfilled. I can never love another."

'*I will not cross over until you fulfill my dying wish. And there's a matter of karmic debt you created during your time with servant Kate. It must be repaid with this Kate. The imbalance in your life goes back over three centuries.*'

He raked his fingers through his hair. Karmic debt, the concept of compensating for the ill treatment of an essence during its past life had to be repaid to the reincarnated soul was not new. Emina was right. Her wish was selfless. She had thought of him and their children, wanting him to find someone who'd love them and who they'd love in return, and reclaim the balance in his life.

*'Open your heart and you'll see there's room for love. Kate is not just another woman. She loves you to a fault.'*

"This Kate is not the same woman I love—" He clamped his mouth shut before his tongue could complete the word. Preposterous to think he had loved a servant. "You saw me kiss her in the car?" Blood rushed to his head. What would she think of him?

*'You should be ashamed for allowing your stubbornness to get the best of you. Why are you turning your back on her, on love?'* Her whisper faded, and he strained to hear the last few words.

"I'm not stubborn. It's a sense of propriety. Stay with me, love. Let me explain. Don't leave." Desperation edged his voice and closed his throat. *'With you gone, I fear the beast is stirring inside me,'* he confessed, despite his qualms. By not admitting the fact he hung onto a false hope that he imagined the urges and the voice every time he succumbed to desire for Kate.

Warmth spread over his chest. Emina's whisper echoed in his mind. *'The beast is part of you, has been for centuries. Without it, you wouldn't be where you are today. Once you allow yourself to love Kate, the entity residing in you will be placated.'*

Her voice faded. He waited. Had she gone or chosen to give him her famous silent treatment?

Kate Rokov's grades are plummeting. She needs to get the voice out of her head, or she will flunk her finals in college. Matthias Zrin, a three-centuries-old immortal, born into an aristocratic family as Miles Rusinic, is enthralled with Kate. It is his voice preventing her from sleeping and her stubbornness is testing his limits. He wants her to write down his story to settle his late wife's Earthbound spirit. His tragic love story has become Kate's obsession since fifth grade during her summer trip to Rusinic Castle. Their coming together settles the old spirit and breaks an ancient curse and, in doing so, a flame spanning over three centuries reignites and burns with wild desire. In this tale of two life times and desire versus emotional need, both know some dreams will have to wait for the right time, but the magic between them is impossible to withstand.

## KUDOS for *Rose of Crimson*

In *Rose of Crimson* by Zrinka Jelic, Kate Rokov is attending college in Ontario Canada. Kate begins hearing voices in her head and discovers that an immortal wants her to write his tragic story of doomed love and betrayal. Once she agrees, he reveals himself to her and begins giving her visions of his early life three hundred years ago. And of course, Kate falls madly in love with him, but how much chance does she have with a three-hundred-year-old immortal? After all, she's in her early twenties, a foreigner in a strange land, fighting discrimination and bullying, and running from her great-great-grandmother's curse. A prequel to Jelic's *Bonded by Crimson*, the book reunites us with the main characters, combining contemporary and historical into a touching, heart-warming, and heart-breaking love story. ~ *Taylor Jones, Reviewer*

*Rose of Crimson* is the first book in Zrinka Jelic's *Crimson* series. We get to see the characters before *Bonded by Crimson* starts, when Kate is still in college and first meets Mathias, only she thinks his name is Miles. He contacts her telepathically, explains that he's a three-hundred-year-old immortal, and asks her to write his tragic story of love, revenge, and murder as she fights to break her great-great-grandmother's curse, which was caused by Miles in the first place. Kate pretends she can't hear him, so to get her attention, he starts humming in her head until the poor girl has no choice but to give in and do what he wants. Jelic has crafted a heart-warming story of forbidden love. I like the way she blends the contemporary and historical scenes into a well-written saga spanning three hundred years. ~ *Regan Murphy, Reviewer*

I was given a copy of Rose of Crimson by the Author Zrinka Jelic in exchange for a honest review. I really enjoyed this novel. When I was first approached, I was thinking to myself "Great another Vampire story" and not in a good way. I found Rose of Crimson very refreshing in its approach. The novel didn't revolve around the Paranormal but around the love story and Kate's present life, I loved that! ~ *Sara, Boundless Book Reviews*

This story will keep you reading if you want to find the answer. Beautifully written, enthralling, and very romantic. ~ *Trish Jackson, Author*

# Rose of Crimson

ZRINKA JELIC

*A Black Opal Books Publication*

GENRE: PARANORMAL ROMANCE/HISTORICAL ROMANCE

This is a work of fiction. Names, places, characters and incidents are either the product of the author's imagination or are used fictitiously, and any resemblance to any actual persons, living or dead, businesses, organizations, events or locales is entirely coincidental. All trademarks, service marks, registered trademarks, and registered service marks are the property of their respective owners and are used herein for identification purposes only. The publisher does not have any control over or assume any responsibility for author or third-party websites or their contents.

# DEDICATION

*To Miljenko and Dobrila ~*
*may your love story live forever.*

# Chapter 1

Guilt seared Matthias like a branding iron, but he soldiered on. Wrong of him to sneak into Kate's place, and having to shield her mind from seeing him poked hard at his conscience. His methods had yet to produce any results. Perhaps he should try a different approach. No, not this close to breaking through her defenses, he must persevere despite stabbing remorse.

He leaned against the wall and scanned the familiar unit. Not much to look at, nothing posh. A bulb on the range hood cast dim light over the basement flat. Kate's neatly stacked books sat on the small table. In two steps, he closed the distance to the round plastic surface and picked up the thick text, *Developmental Math,* yellow sticker under the title read USED. The glossy pages flapped under his finger as he flipped through, he admired that she had not scribbled inside, but placed neon sticky notes at the edges. She wouldn't lessen the value of her textbooks. She planned to sell them once she graduated and, if in mint condition, they'd be appraised higher.

Matthias put the volume back. Kate would be done with her school come May and he still had not made much of a progress with her. Stakes were high should he not succeed, Emina's spirit would never settle. No. Failure was not an option. But he visited Kate for entirely different purpose than to fulfill his promise he had given to his wife on her deathbed.

The apartment door flew open, hitting the wall and taking him by surprise. He leaped backward with a start. Kate stormed in.

"Wicked, we totally got you this time." The roaring laughter of the blockhead, Potter, reached Matthias just as Kate stepped onto safe ground and slammed the door of her unit.

Fury burned its way through Matthias's nostrils while she picked slimy paper balls out of her hazel brown hair. Again, she'd ducked her head when she should have reported the two pranksters to the building manager. Matthias clenched his fists and couldn't understand her passiveness when it came down to her mischievous neighbors.

Those two scalawags wouldn't bother her anymore. *Not his Kate.*

"Why don't you report them?" he growled through clenched teeth, temper seeping through his voice.

Kate didn't look in his direction. She removed her coat and boots and put on her fluffy pink slippers. What had made him think she would act differently this time?

He clamped down on the urge to wrap her in his arms, moved out of her way, and flattened his back on the wall as she shuffled toward the chair. Just because he decided to stay invisible, didn't mean she couldn't bump into him. "Ignoring me won't make me go away. You should know that by now. When will you answer me?"

She dropped onto a chair. Corners of her mouth dipped down and tears glistened in her eyes. Matthias crouched in front of her. His heart tore. How he hated to see her like this, exhaustion etched on her face, dark circles under her eyes. If she'd only open up to him, he'd make all her fears stop. But she was strong willed and kept ignoring him.

She got to her feet and wiped at a tear hanging from the little star shaped scar on her chin. The reminder of her clumsy childhood she always hid had not marred her face. It only added to her perfection. He was going to kiss that spot. Someday.

After rummaging through the fridge, she pulled out a clear container with leftover pizza, and then placed two slices in the microwave.

Matthias tracked her as she poured a glass of water from the filtered pitcher. "What did the doctor say?"

Her hand holding the glass stopped half way to her lush lips. She huffed. Would she answer his query? "Like I'll tell you."

His heart missed a beat, a hint of joy kindled in him. After a year and half, she finally acknowledged his presence. "Did he diagnose you with tinnitus?"

She snapped her glance in his direction—only took her eighteen months to do so. Her green eyes seemed to settle on him and narrowed as if struggling to focus. But her wandering gaze assured him she couldn't make him out. He waited on Kate's answer, which wasn't forthcoming. "You were afraid to talk about your true symptoms, weren't you?"

Kate turned away from him and faced the sink. "When will this stop?"

"When you stop ignoring me." Matthias's voice came out heavy with need.

She plugged her ears, shook her head, and mewled. "Stop talking already and leave me alone," she snapped and left for the bathroom, locking the door. A second later, the sound of running water drifted from the shower.

With his hand on the doorknob, he fought against the urge to follow her there, to admire her nude perfection.

The building walls shook as the door of the unit above hers slammed shut, snapping him out of his desire. He scurried to the apartment's door. Through the peephole, he caught a glimpse of Chris Miller's camouflage green pants at the top of the first landing as he stormed out of the building.

What, did the boys have a fight over the last beer? A smile stretched his lips. With Miller gone, this was a good opportunity to get Potter alone—the right time to pay him back for how he treated Kate by scaring the socks off the boy.

ひつひつ

The voice ceased and Kate's rage calmed under the warm shower. She came too darn close to giving in to her hallucinations. Ignoring the voice in her head was her last defense. No way could she allow her mind to slip. *Hearing aid or surgery*, the options the doctor had given her pressed on her mind. At twenty-four, neither appealed to her, nor would they, no matter her age.

She turned the shower off, stepped out of the tub, and wrapped herself in a purple bathrobe. Silence greeted her outside the bathroom. The quiet state was temporary. The voice would return. Always had.

Her dinner overheated and she sat at the table with a glass of milk, waiting for the slices to cool off. The doctor couldn't help her today. It wasn't tinnitus that bothered her day and night. It was the alluring voice of a man. The paranormal would be Dyane's expertise. She'd have answers to all this, but Kate couldn't ask her. After all, it had been Kate who had stated that renewing their friendship would only work if they didn't speak about ghosts.

That Dyane claimed to see them pop up everywhere spooked Kate.

What the heck? If her friend could cure her, it was worth a try. She grabbed the cordless receiver and dialled the overseas number.

Kate was about to hang up after four rings when Dyane answered, sleep making her voice harsh. "Hallo."

Kate cringed, darting her glance at the clock on the stove. With six hours difference, eight o'clock in Toronto meant it was only two in the morning in Croatia. *Well done, Kate.*

"Hallo?" Dyane sounded a bit more awake.

"Dyane, it's me, Kate. So sorry. I wasn't paying attention to the time difference."

"Kate, sweetie, don't worry. I'm glad you called. How are you?"

"I'm all right." Kate bit her lip. Dyane would detect the tremble in her voice. "I don't know. Things are different here. Dumb students are popular, not the smart ones."

"Oh, honey." Dyane huffed. "The same idiocy is catching up in our schools. A hunch tells me you're not calling me because of this."

Kate drew in a sharp breath. A knot in her chest seemed to loosen with her friend's words. "You're right."

A long silence followed on Dyane's end. "And you're not calling about that two timing, good-for-nothing son of a—"

"You'd think I'd call overseas because of him?" Kate snapped. The boy, for she could never refer to immature male as a man, was not worth her effort of dialing the thirteen digit European number.

"I think you'll find this last bit funny." Dyane laughed. Of course, gossip was the main past time activity in their small town. "He's gone AWOL. Two girls claimed they were preggers. Turns out the bimbos lied to get him. But they were after his daddy's money."

"Still a skirt chaser, I see. Flashing his dad's money made him popular. Nevertheless, who in their right mind would want to waste a moment on him?"

Silly question. She had wasted an entire year on that idiot. His sweet babe, he'd called her and, once she'd succumbed to his persuasions and slept with him, he discarded her like yesterday's trash. Never again would she let a man make a fool out of her.

"Listen, we talked enough about him. I called about something different."

"I know," Dyane said. "Well, since you're calling in the dead of the night, there must be some sort of problem. I've sensed this would happen to you." There was a pause from the other end of the phone. "Kate, there is a powerful male presence around you. I know we agreed on no reading fortunes, but I had to find out. I did a spread."

Kate winced at Dyane's words. "I just want us to be as we were. Don't like this pretending. It won't change the fact you have a special gift."

After another long silence, Dyane sighed. "So do you, but you keep ignoring your gift. Someday you'll come to your senses. I'm glad you're not mad that I read your future in Tarot cards."

"How can I be mad? Tell me, what did you see?" Dyane already mentioned trouble, just how much of a disturbance was there?

"A King of Wands was in your spread, a very determined man is hanging around you, but he's not letting you see him until you acknowledge him. He will test you. Do you have trouble sleeping?"

"Why do you ask?" Kate gasped. Dyane was right on.

"The Moon was right in the middle. It predicts troubling rest, but at the end was The Chariot. You will win this. Tarot cards don't lie."

Kate swallowed the lump forming in her throat. An entity was testing her and she'd have to find the tactics. "I'll win? How? Some days I'm sure a man's voice is in my head, yet sometimes sounds like he's near me, but whatever the case, he's here."

"He wants you to listen to him." Dyane yawned.

"The voice seems to want me to converse with him. So far, I've been ignoring it. God almighty, the entity is persistent." Guilt stirred in Kate, she should let her friend return to bed. "Fine, I'll listen to him. Once. Now go back to sleep. I've kept you talking long enough."

"Spirits can be tenacious. Sorry I'm not much of a chatty cat at this hour. If cards in your spreads change, I'll send what comes up via email."

"Sounds good. Say hi to everyone for me. Except the fool." Kate's words rushed out before Dyane could hang up. The unspoken rule never to mention her ex-boyfriend's name remained enforced. "And, Dyane?"

Dyane sniffed. "Yes?"

"I wish you were here. It would make everything so much easier."

"Honey," her friend croaked. "You'll graduate this spring and then you're coming home, right?"

Kate pushed back tears. Nothing would bring her more joy than the fact she'd be going home after her graduation. "Not exactly."

"Why?" Dyane's whisper pressed heavy on Kate's mind.

"I had to take out a loan and must repay it. Plus, my mom thinks the old curse won't reach this far." The hex imposed by long dead Great-Great-Grandma could go to Hell. It was the money, or rather lack of it, that prevented Kate from returning home.

"Oh, Kate, I'm so sorry to hear that. Maybe this one time you could ask your dad—for money."

The despair in Dyane's voice shattered Kate's hopes. God forbid she could approach her father for help. "No, let him keep every penny of his inheritance along with the house and land."

"Hang in there, sweetie. Things will turn out for the best."

A breath of a smile pushed out of Kate. "Thanks, I needed to hear that. Bye."

A sudden, heavy thud on the ceiling caused her to jump and spill milk from the glass. Damn Potter and Miller's rudeness up there. As if a voice in her head wasn't enough torture. All of a sudden, she'd lost her appetite and tossed her dinner in the garbage bin under the kitchen sink. After gulping down two capsules of a sleep aid, she slipped into her bed and tugged the blanket to her chin. All she wanted was to face the three tests tomorrow well rested and not haunted.

Under the warm covers, her tension eased and her eyelids drooped while she slipped into the dreamless sleep.

The smooth, masculine voice pierced through Kate's sleep, waking her in the darkest part of the night. With a heavy head, she rolled to her side and glanced at the clock on her nightstand. Three-thirty in the morning flashed in bright red numbers on the display. Just great. Would she ever sleep through one single night?

The pill had let her sleep exactly four hours. Or was it the ghost, since the darn medicine lost its effect too fast? Without sufficient sleep, she ran the risk of failing the exams. She flipped to her side, wrapped the pillow around her head and moaned.

"Why can't you leave me alone?"

She was awake now. Experience told her the voice

wouldn't let her go back to sleep. The down duvet crinkled as she kicked the cover to the side.

Rubbing her sore eyes, she tapped her feet on the hardwood floor until her fluffy slippers tickled her soles. She floundered in the dark basement flat to the kitchen counter and hugged the coffee machine. The appliance was timed to start brewing at eight o'clock, but she needed a big cup of java right now. With her hip braced against the edge, she yawned again as the first drops dribbled into the pot. Freshly brewed coffee wafted to her, exorcising the last bit of sleep from her eyes.

*How many twenty-four-year-old females can say they hear voices in their heads?* Kate shuddered. It had to be the stress of the workload. No ghost, no tinnitus. This thought set her at ease better than facing a future wearing a hearing aid. Another three weeks until the end of the fall semester, then she'd put her brain on the shelf and not think of school.

With her fingers digging into her scalp, she braced her elbows on the Formica countertop. The possibility of landing a teaching position after graduation was slim. A wise person would have dropped out of the program while still ahead, but she wasn't a quitter.

The coffee machine finished brewing with a loud gurgling noise and a big puff of steam. Armed with a mug, she snatched the pot and poured. Black and bitter, just like her life since she'd moved to Canada. With all the tuition, textbooks, rent, and food expenses, she had managed to stretch her scholarship fund for two years. A year ago, she had been forced to take a student loan. Heck, by the time she graduated, she'd be working just to pay it off.

The worn-out cushion of the sofa that had come with the apartment sank as she lowered. Her body formed around the familiar lumps. The screen on her laptop lit as soon as she moved the mouse and the Google page loaded.

The first sip of coffee burned inside her mouth, she smacked her lips. Her sore eyes adjusted to the piercing light of the screen. The possibility she was afraid to face pressed on her mind. While hugging the mug in her hand she typed *S-c-h*, into the search engine. This was insane. If she really was schizophrenic, there would be other symptoms, not just a voice in her head.

An invisible hand brushed hers and the cursor moved backward, deleting the three letters she had typed. "You are not schizophrenic."

Her heart dropped, her spine went rigid. All she could do was grip her mug and hold her breath. He was here. Only a ghost could come through the door bolted with three locks. The sincerity in his voice and Dyane's advice convinced her she should listen and try to communicate with him. But she was afraid. Of what, she didn't know. No more touches came from him and her body relaxed.

Scolding herself for getting so messed up over nothing, she rose from the chair and turned toward the small television. Late night programs had become her best friend since this insanity started.

A click of the button on the remote and the picture appeared while laughter from the audience filled her small apartment.

A rerun of *Saturday Night Live* wasn't to her liking so she continued surfing. Gosh, basic cable, thirty-seven channels, and nothing on but commercials.

"There is a voice in your head." The announcer's voice blared out as she zapped to the next station.

She frowned, cocking her head. "You got that right."

"Don't ignore it. Listen to your inner voice." Golden pizza crust appeared on the screen. "Call five-three-six-double o-double-o now..." the advertisement went on as she flipped to the next channel.

She snorted. A pizza commercial came so close to curing her illness. But even they said to listen to her *inner voice*. What she heard was a man's muttering, definitely not *her inner voice*. So far, she tried everything except listen. Even the blaring music from the headphones and hours in the gym had stopped working. By now, it was obvious she wouldn't get rid of the murmur. So why not try and see if she could cooperate with the voice? Then she'd tell it to leave her alone.

She crossed her legs, closed her eyes, and inhaled deeply. Her heart pounded with anticipation. *Okay, here goes nothing.*

"I'm listening," she said with a quivering voice.

Nothing happened, just as she'd predicted, but the hushed whisper didn't cease. She opened one eye and placed her coffee on the table. After mustering some courage, she cleared her throat and spoke louder, "I said I'm listening."

"And it's about time." The deep male voice answered in her native Croatian.

She sprang to her feet, her eyes refused to return to their normal size. Her breath caught as her chest tightened. "Wha—where y—you—" she stuttered in the same language, scanning over the dark interior. "You can hear me?" Okay, she had asked for this, but she had never expected the darn thing would work.

"Uh-huh." Air brushed her neck, as if someone breathed the answer.

Her hands clutched the couch for support, and Kate leaned against the armrest. "Potter? Miller? Is that you?" Her voice trembled.

"You really think I'm one of those dickheads?" A dry laugh resonated with disappointment. "My name is

Mat—Miles. I'm Miles." The voice came from behind her this time. A cold air brushed her bare shoulder.

"Please don't touch me." Fear gripped her, yet the smoothness of the man's voice had an unexpected calming effect on her frail nerves.

"I know you are afraid now, but don't be."

Cold fingers wrapped around her arm. A shrill scream ripped from her. She yanked her arm away and backed against the wall. "What do you want from me?"

"I'm sorry. I don't want to scare you. I just want you to listen to me, to understand." His voice came from a few feet away.

"Understand what?"

"You are the only one that can help me." The despair in his voice almost had her convinced.

"How?" she breathed.

"By listening. Things have happened in my life and it's too late for me to right them, but someone needs to know."

Her glance drifted toward the phone on the corner stand. With a slow step backward, she approached and grabbed the handheld from the cradle. Her shaky fingers dialled the number of the police but, in the next instant, she pushed the off button. What would she tell them, that there was an invisible intruder in her home? Sure way to get lectured on how pulling pranks on emergency services was a serious offence. "Why can't I see you?"

"You will see me soon." From the sound of his voice, she determined he was standing behind her.

Her heart seemed to steady. "Are you a ghost?"

Heat must have come on and pushed the cool air from the ceiling vent. Or could it be he brushed her bare arms with a feathery touch.

Miles's soft laugh embraced her. "To be a ghost, I'd have to be dead."

She rubbed her arms. "You're saying you're alive?"

"For all intents and purposes, yes."

Unsure if she should be annoyed or sympathetic, she turned in the direction of his voice. "Do you see the light? You should go into it."

"There's no light," he whispered close to her ear. "I'm not dead."

She took a long step back. Her heart thudded and, despite the warm air blowing down on her, cold shivers raked her spine. What kind of trick had he pulled to make himself invisible? "Please leave me alone. And stop this incessant whispering in my head."

His invisible fingers tucked a strap of her camisole back on her shoulder. His action did not freak her out. "I can't leave you, but if you paid attention, you'd notice that the sound has ceased."

She cocked her head, listened, then relaxed her shoulders. There was no humming in her ears. Joy filled her and she couldn't suppress a smile, liberated from the sound that had kept her up at night and filled her waking hours to the point she had thought she was going insane. "It's gone. Oh, thank God."

"Had you opened your mind earlier, you wouldn't have gone through all the torture." The voice took on a cheerful tone, invisible knuckles brushed her arm.

Goose bumps rose on her skin. Was she an idiot because she seemed to enjoy his soft touch?

"Now you expect me to do something for you or the humming will return. Right?"

Excitement filled her as she anticipated his caress again. Or could it be the mystery that was building? Stupid of her to get all giddy. He could inflict that God-awful humming in her ears and take her back to the miserable time.

At least she now knew nothing physical was wrong

with her, however it seemed there was only one cure for this kind of ailment. Do what he wanted.

"Something tells me I won't have to do that again." A husky tone laced his whisper.

# Chapter 2

Kate dug her fingernails into her palms. The loneliness must be getting to her at this dead hour or she wouldn't imagine the incoherent whispers had taken a deep masculine tone. Impossible, she wasn't that lonely or loony and she had been conversing with him for the past twenty or so minutes.

He seemed less threatening and that smooth voice of his eased the tension between her shoulders.

A spark of curiosity ignited to a full blaze. She must find out more about him. "Need *me*? What for?"

"To tell my story." There was no mistaking this time as his fingers raked gently through her hair, making her chest heavy and spinning her mind. How could he have known she was a sucker for head massages? He moved his fingers down her neck and shoulders. *Yes, dig in right there and loosen up the knot.* Damn, this was good. She must stop him or she'd write down the complete saga.

He eased the pressure on her skin. "How does that kink in your shoulder feel? Better?"

"It's almost gone." Bless him, the man worked magic on her in more than one way. "Hey, how did you know I had a kink in there?"

"You rubbed that spot before." Now he brushed his fingers over her neck.

Hmm, what else had he seen her doing? Oh no, those few times she'd stepped out of the shower and realized she'd forgotten to hang a fresh towel and ran to the linen closet wet and naked. Heat rushed to her cheeks, she sucked her lower lip between her teeth. The invisible visitor remained silent. Perhaps he hadn't been in her flat during those incidents.

"So, what's your story about?" She arched one brow, tilting her head under his pressing fingers. Of course, everyone had a story, so why was she surprised an undead ghost consulted her to tell his tale?

"You'll find out soon enough." A tickle ran along her arm once more. "And it can't be told in one night."

Wonderful, that was what she got for sticking her nose in the paranormal stuff in the past. Now he'd cling around her for who knows how long. She had hoped to be rid of him, preferably tonight. The feel of his caring touches returned to her mind. From what she gathered by his closeness and the touch of his big hands caressing her neck and shoulders, he must be tall and, she imagined, quite muscular. Oh, if she could only see him, but she quickly shook the idea away.

Why was she so accepting of this disembodied voice? Though she struggled to remain as calm as possible, from the literature on the subject, the best was to keep one's fear in check in the presence of a haunted soul. Yet, her curiosity sprouted and spread through her veins like weeds. "Listen, Miles." She exhaled. "You sought out the wrong person. I have to cram for my exams and I have term papers due. Can't you find someone else?"

"No." He demanded, "I can't let you go. I need you to write down what I can't tell anyone anymore."

She gasped. He wanted to confess something. A murder he committed long ago. Or had he been murdered and wanted to point out his killers? Either way the dial on her curiosity gauge turned up to full volume, this had Agatha Christie written all over it. If the crime took place long ago, what was she to do with the evidence? There she went again, letting her imagination run wild.

The absence of his touch left her wanting for more. "I've seen your school papers. You are a good writer."

"What, were you standing over my shoulder the entire time?" Of course, he had. She shouldn't be surprised. Chances were, he'd seen her running for the towel. The fact that he hadn't mentioned it told her he was a true gentleman. "College assignments cannot compare to what you're asking me to do. There are so many other skilled persons for sure. So, why me?"

He rolled out a low chuckle. "You will see as the story unfolds."

She wobbled her head. Okay, he piqued her interest. He had a secret to uncover. Perhaps she could do this. Kate dragged her hands over her face, folding them over her mouth and nose. What was she thinking? Where would she find the time to squeeze in this assignment? No, she couldn't. That was a stupid idea.

"Don't fret." The couch cushions lowered. He had said the truth. He was here in body and mind. "I'll guide you along."

"Fine," she said, then bit her lip. "No, wait. I'm too busy. I can still get my grade point average up."

"I'll help you with that too. Come. Sit next to me on the couch."

Reluctantly, she stepped to the sofa and tapped the other end, to make sure she wouldn't end up in his lap, then lowered, clasping her knees with her laced fingers. "What do you know of my studies?"

"In three centuries, I've graduated from many schools."

She felt her chin gently cupped.

*Three centuries?* How could he still live unless he was an immortal. If only. Once she believed in the alternate world co-existing with this one, and in her mind's eye, it seemed less ugly than the reality. She lowered her lids as his thumb pressed over the scar on her chin. An unexpected shiver shook her as he traced her lips. "Are you trying to seduce me?" she whispered. "I'll do it under one condition."

Disappointment shattered her bliss the moment he let go of her. "I'm sure we can come to an agreement. I can pay you for your time. Name the price."

*He's got money? A secret stash he buried centuries ago. Stop fantasizing.* Yes, she could use the money, but a strange premonition told her not to accept his offer. It seemed he wasn't here to harm her or he wouldn't be striking deals with her. "I don't want your money, but I do have to study for exams and you will not bother me on those days. Once your story is done, you will leave me— *for good.* And I mean it. You're not to come back. Ever."

Silence filled the air.

"Hallo?" she called, turning her head from side to side. "Are you still here?"

He cleared his throat. "That would be two conditions, but it's a fair deal."

A deal? How much of a bargain did she get? But if this was the only way to get him out of her head, then so be it. "Promise?"

He huffed. "Put your pinky up."

She almost choked on a snort. "A pinky swear? That doesn't hold any merit."

"It does for me. Put it up."

*Hmm, this should be interesting.* She stuck her finger

up and his twined around hers. He tightened the hold tempting her to do the same. In a swift motion, their linked pinkies pulled apart.

"There, my promise is sealed. I'll leave you for now. Get some rest. Tomorrow we'll begin." His voice drifted toward the door.

"No, not tomorrow. I have exams. Did you forget our deal already?"

"No, your exams are later today. Tomorrow is Saturday, no classes."

With a loud inhale, she glanced at the clock. Twenty minutes to five. She could get another three hours of peaceful sleep and face the demanding day, but after such an experience, she'd spend the few hours tossing and turning thinking about him and his story. Returning her gaze at the opened door, she nodded. "Tomorrow then."

"Make sure you lock up behind me." His voice came from the small foyer, growing fainter on his last words. After a few seconds, the door closed and she wondered if he was really gone.

Tension left her and she let out a breath. In two long strides, she closed the distance to the door and bolted the three locks, checking them over and over. They worked properly. *God all mighty, what's happening?*

All of a sudden, she felt alone in her small apartment. She had to admit the voice was her only companion. Though she should hope for Miles to stay away because he gave her the creeps, a small part of her hoped he wouldn't. A grunt crept to her lips at the absurdity. What had he done to her? She must sort through her confused feelings.

Still, those caresses couldn't have been accidental. Even if they came from some sort of ghost, the mere thought of those intoxicating embraces stirred butterflies in her stomach.

❦❦❦

The illuminated face of the digital clock by Kate's bedside provided enough light for Matthias to watch his beauty sleeping. He pushed on the worn-out armrests of the equally rugged beige recliner.

He stepped to her cast iron bed. Kate's chest in her pink camisole rose and lowered with her even breaths. A mental image of an awkward teenager, hiding the retainer and thick glasses behind a curtain of hair, appeared before his eyes. It had been a long, hard trek, and although she couldn't see herself as beautiful, she had grown into a gracious young lady, just as he had foreseen.

The struggle she had put up to ignore his whispers for over a year had shaken his faith. But now that he had broken through her defences, another fear crept into his mind. He'd have to reveal all the details, bring all of the ugly past into light.

Kate stirred and rolled to her side. With a brush of his knuckles on her cheek, he smoothed away a few strands of her hazel-colored hair. A faint smile stretched her lips while her eyes remained sealed.

"Sleep," he whispered, putting her in a deeper state of slumber. "Dawn is near." He wanted to lie down next to her warm body, hug her to him, love her. Instead, he clenched his fist then, in two heavy steps, he returned to the chair.

While the first blush of dawn had appeared in the east, the light of the day wouldn't come through the small windows of this basement apartment for at least another two hours. She hadn't slept well in months all because of him. He could have imposed his story on her through dreams, but once she awakened, the visions would fade fast and would be forgotten before she sipped her morning coffee. She would have shrugged it off as a weird dream. So much for the awareness of mortals, their fickle mind couldn't make any sense of disconnected images generated in their dreams. His story had to be told, not inflicted through sleep visions.

He should reveal his identity before his story unfolded. As his beloved Emina had always said, the truth would set him free from the start, but Kate's reaction worried him. His tragic love story had become a local legend, but the details of the tale he was about to reveal, and the history of Kate's ancestry, would come to light. No, he should let her discover his being on her own. It wouldn't take her long to figure out who he was. Numerous tourists passed through his castle, oooed and aahed listening to the curator retell the folktale, but none was as fascinated as Kate. With a bit of luck, he'd be deep into his story by then and her natural curiosity would drive her to continue putting his words on paper.

"Are you here?"

Kate's calm question startled him. She propped up on her elbows and stared toward the chair he sat on. Pins stirred inside him. As much as he revelled in her emerald green eyes, their very sight brought back painful memories. "My apologies. I didn't mean to wake you this early."

"It's all right." She sat up, swung her legs over the edge of the bed. "You let me sleep the whole night. I can't remember the last time I slept more than a stretch of four hours."

"Then you must be well rested and eager to begin." But the dark circles under her eyes suggested she could use an hour or more of sleep.

Arms stretched above her head, she yawned, got to her feet and straightened. "Not before my first cup of coffee. Want some?"

"Coffee?" His voice, ridden with startled pleasure

about her newly found ease around him, sounded foreign to him.

"Oh, right. I forgot you're a ghost." She palmed her forehead. "Silly me."

He opened his mouth to explain once again that he, in fact, wasn't a spirit, but he closed it fast. If the ghost theory was a plausible explanation for her, then he'd let her think so until he convinced her otherwise.

"I would love a cup, thank you."

A funny frown appeared on her face. "You would?" She wobbled her head as if contemplating the possibility. "Why not? I guess even ghosts have to get a caffeine fix."

Leaning against the wall, he waited for her to brew their beverage and fill two cups. Since he had invaded her thoughts, she had spent a lot of time in the gym, exhausting herself so she would sleep. Guilt stung him, but he had to admit the hours of exercising resulted in a mouthwatering body, begging to be caressed. He regretted his thought as soon as a part of his body responded to it. Pangs of conscience stabbed at him. No woman since Emina's death provoked such reaction in him.

"I'll put the cup on the table for you."

She turned, her unrestrained breasts under her nighty almost brushing his chest. His hands instinctively reached for her. He balled them into tight fists. Damn, three centuries of gentlemanly upbringing forgotten in an instant.

Soon, he would have her. For all of God's creations, where had that thought come from? It hadn't been a year since his wife passed away. What kind of spell gripped him? Kate's resemblance to her ancestor sparked him. Centuries later, the young servant's soft smiles and longing gazes still danced fresh in his mind. In fifteen years since he first met this Kate, his beast had not awakened, but the possibility forever griped him with fear.

The plastic patio chair scraped against the vinyl floor

of the tiny kitchen pulling him out of his lustful thoughts. Kate placed the mug down on the round table top, then gestured. "Have a seat, or float, or whatever you ghosts do. I'll get myself decent."

She scurried to the bathroom. From the aroma wafting to him, Kate brewed strong, hearty coffee. He raised the cup and inspected the plain, blue mug. After the first sip, he smacked his lips. Yep, coffee was to his taste.

Perhaps he should reveal his appearance, but not his true looks. Something Kate would find attractive. But no. He'd come here to set the truth forth and starting with a deceitful appearance was not a good beginning.

A few minutes later, she emerged wrapped in a purple bathrobe. Her long hair pulled in a neat twisted bun.

"I see you can manipulate things," she said, approaching the table.

"Huh?" He shook his head.

She pointed to his mug.

He gasped, realizing all she saw was the cup hovering in midair. "Yes, as I explained I'm not really a ghost."

"All you said was 'I'm alive.' And not in those exact words."

Her attempt to mimic his voice coaxed a chuckle out of him. "Maybe I'm an angel."

Her face beamed as she slowly raised her chin. "A guardian angel?"

"Sorry, I shouldn't confuse you even more." He shrugged. Remorse stung him. "I'm neither a ghost nor an angel. But I'll try to explain the details of my existence through the story."

"Sometimes my curiosity gets the best of me." She wagged her finger, leaning over the table. "As long as you leave me alone on exam nights we should get along."

"I haven't forgotten." He returned to his seat, while

she re-filled her cup and brought the carafe to the table. "When are you writing your next exam?"

"Wednesday." Steam rose from the liquid as she topped off his beverage. "Third period."

"You've got time. I'm positive you've already crammed all of the material for the test." The promise to help her study flickered in his mind. Kate wouldn't accept his assistance during the test, but he'd be there nonetheless.

Gathering the terry robe around her hips, she plopped onto the chair. "I did, but I'd like to go over the material once more. Or twice."

"Fair enough. I'll leave you alone until then, but I can't leave such a good cup of coffee." After blowing on the hot surface, he slurped. "Before I go, I think you may want to see me."

A smile lit her face. "I do."

"Close your eyes then."

"How am I to see you with my eyes closed?"

"I'll tell you when to open them."

Still holding the carafe in her hand, she obeyed. "Let me see you then."

He stood and stepped behind her chair. Hesitating briefly, he couldn't help from slightly altering his appearance before he released his hold on the part of her mind that would allow her to see him. "You can open your eyes now."

She slowly tilted her head to glance over her shoulder. A gasp escaped her. Her chair flipped as she sprang to her feet. "My God, you are my angel."

He narrowed his eyes, his heart fluttering. She recognized him—after so many years.

Her glance darted at the cabinet next to her sofa. She chewed on her lip, as if trying to recall something.

"I'm sure I put it in here." She walked to the

nightstand and pulled the top drawer out, then rummaged through its contents. "Ah, here it is."

She returned to the table with a scrapbook in her hand. Flipping through, she stopped on a page with a faded red rose and turned to him. "Roses are notoriously hard to press, especially if they are in the full bloom, but this one turned out pretty good."

With shaky fingers, he traced the pressed blossom. "How old do you think this rose could be?"

"I remember it like yesterday." She flipped a few pages of her scrapbook then stopped at a Polaroid photo of a childhood moment captured in time. She stood by the rose bush in the courtyard of his castle, nowadays was a tourist attraction. "The summer of 1998 was so hot. I was plastered to the polyester seat of my dad's car, but I didn't care, I wanted to see the castle Rušinić. I scurried into the courtyard. For some reason all I could smell was this sharp twinge of vinegar." She wiggled her nose before continuing. "My mom got scared thinking I suffered a heat stroke. Then you stepped out through the door behind me, dressed in a traditional costume. There was a festival going on in the village so I assumed you dressed for the occasion. I was only eleven years old at the time, but I'm sure it was you I saw. I don't remember that scar on your temple, but you combed your hair differently." A sheepish smile bloomed on her face. "I never stopped thinking of you. How on Earth did you find me?"

"I was always with you, Kate," he breathed, glad she didn't turn away from his scarred face. He must remember to project the same mark every time he was with her. "To you this rose is fifteen years old, but to me it is over three centuries old."

She returned her gaze at the rose and tilted the scrapbook under her nose. "What?"

"We saw each other through time. Some kind of a

time tunnel, I'm assuming. What else do you remember?"

Her lips parted as she stared at him. "I remember your crystal blue eyes, but mostly the sadness in them and it seems the sorrow only deepened with time."

The tremble in her voice and the truth of her words tore at his heart. Time couldn't heal every wound. "Two more people were with you that day. Did they see me too?"

"No, my mother still insists I hallucinated from the heat and that I picked the rose." She shook her head. "I could never prove you gave it to me."

"You didn't hallucinate and I'm pleased you thought of me all these years." Matthias lowered his gaze to the book on the table and flipped back to the page with the rose. He smiled at her inscription ~ *From my secret angel.*

"Don't read that." She slammed the book closed, catching his fingers. "As I said I was just a silly kid then. My dad says I need to get my head out of the clouds."

Her cheeks blushed, but her soft smiled lingered. He pulled his fingers out from the pages. "Dads are not always the wisest. I should know."

She refilled his cup and topped hers. "Since you're here, why not give me a hint of this famous story of yours you want me to record."

"I thought you'd guess by now." If she had a clue, she was damn good at not showing it. He couldn't read any hints in her thoughts. He should prolong their chit-chat, until she became acquainted with him, used to seeing him.

"A thought did cross my mind. It's hard not to guess, when a tale from that castle is a local legend and I'm so fascinated by it. I can hardly wait for you to start."

"I knew you'd guess. First." He paused, contemplating whether or not to ask the burning question so soon.

"Tell me if you know anything about your great-great-grandma Kate."

Her eyebrows arched. She scrunched her lips and tilted her head toward the ceiling. "The old hag who cursed her family?" Kate lowered her eyes to his. Another shy smile stretched her lips and she averted her gaze to her cup. "Sorry, I'm still trying to adjust to seeing you. Why do you ask about her?" A shudder shook her chin. "She's long gone. Something like, three centuries ago, though I can feel her presence around me. I don't know if she's watching over me or waiting for the right moment to kill me."

# Chapter 3

Matthias shifted in his chair, loosening up his rigid spine. Kate's words had stung him. The walls of her small apartment closed in on him. Over the centuries, he'd feared his actions had driven servant Kate to depression, but he never believed she'd inflict evil on anyone, least her blood or that her power would extend beyond her grave. Three hundred years later, her deceased great-great grandma haunted her descendants and caused fear. He should have been long gone too, yet here he was. Perhaps finding this Kate would settle her old grandma's spirit.

He must not make the same mistake he did so long ago. Suppressing his feelings for her would take more than he had in him.

The picture of her ancestor surfaced. Tears had soaked her face. God, how had she begged him not to marry her to someone else. Before he could speak again, he cleared his throat. "She cursed her family?"

"Not the entire family, just the women. I grew up hearing the stories of her powers from beyond." Color drained from Kate's face, she took a sip and lowered her drink to the table. "But stories like that can't be true. At least I believed so. Then a drunk driver slammed into the car my little cousin was in." A few strands of her silky hair came loose as she shook her head. "There's no other explanation, but the curse. You see, in three centuries, there were less than ten girls born alive in my dad's family." Kate leaned over the table and lowered her voice to a whisper as if to prevent her ancestor from hearing. "I'm the only one she allowed to live this long. My mom seems to think she wouldn't kill her namesake, but I'm not so sure I should be counting my blessings."

Heavy weight pressed on his chest. This was not the servant Kate he had known. "How did she kill them?"

"For the most part, the girls were still-born." Kate waved her hand. "I know it sounds silly to think the old hag had anything to do with it from beneath. One of the girls died of tuberculosis a month before her wedding. I and my cousin, who is now confined to a wheelchair and needs constant care, were the only females born after the Second World War."

His intentions had been noble when he had married Kate off. She had become a mistress in her own right, ruled the entire household and the estate. Others had served her. Never had he believed his actions would cause a cataclysm of this nature. "Why would she do this?" He took a sip and the hot beverage went down hard.

"Oh, the story has not changed much as it was told through the generations. Basically, she was madly in love with her master who, I suppose, didn't return her love. Or maybe she got a little carried away, who knows? Whatever the case, Conte Adalberto got rid of her." She shifted. After taking another sip and licking her velvety lips, she continued, "But you dodged my question. Where does this interest in her come from?"

"Conte Adalberto," he whispered, staring into space.

"Now that is a name I haven't heard in a long while. Why would you think she served him?"

"There were some guesses that she came from the Castle Rušinić." Finger pointing at him, she smiled. "Why are you avoiding my question again?"

Damn, she was demanding. This wasn't going to be easy. She already had his last name, another minute and she'd guess who he was. "What was your question?"

"Don't play dumb. You heard me." A sharp wince and her widened eyes confirmed she was hot on a trail of a realization. "You were dressed as an aristocrat when we saw each other across time and if she worked as a servant in a castle somewhere in that part of Dalmatia, you could be her master. Right?"

Matthias released a breath he held in his cheeks. It would be so easy to go along with her story and blame the ravishing of her ancestor on his father. After all, the man's reputation had preceded him. The conte had taken all females who came through the castle. Servants, chambermaids, field hands—made no difference to him. But besides the fact he'd despised the man, Matthias was here to set forth the truth.

"No, I'm not him." He dragged the words out through his teeth.

"Hmmm…come to think of it…" She tilted her chin, and bit her lip. Her eyes rolled left, right, then she slowly raised her head as realization flashed on her expression. "Wait, didn't the conte have a son, Miljenko?"

Darn! It didn't take her half as long as he had hoped. Suddenly, the very floor beneath his feet seemed unstable. "I've shortened the name to Miles."

With her eyebrows knitted and mouth agape, she stared straight at him, or through him, he could not tell. For a moment, she seemed petrified. But her sensitivity for the paranormal had her well seasoned for encounters.

Only, this would be her first real one. Her brow relaxed and her smile replaced her previous expression.

"I don't believe this," she whispered. "The famous Miljenko Rušinić is here, in my basement flat. And drinks coffee with me."

A chuckle escaped him. She hadn't sprung to her feet and run to the bathroom to lock herself in, nor did she ask him to leave. Not that he would have, but all the same, he'd have a hard time convincing her to hear him out.

Clearing her throat, she must have gained her composure because her voice steadied when she asked, "So what business did you have with my great-great-grandmother? According to the legend, you only had eyes for Dobrila."

"Let's leave the details for when we get into the story. And please, call me Miles. Miljenko died long ago." His heart steadied too, he seemed to be on a firm ground now. Perhaps keeping some details from her would be wise, but she loved to read romances, even if she'd never admit it. At the very least, he'd make the story romantic.

"Now, I really can't wait until we start," she cooed.

He had hoped that would be the case, and it seemed his wish was granted. "But I'm a man of my word. I will leave you to your studies now."

"No, don't go just yet," she blurted, grabbing his wrist. A sheepish smile appeared on her face and she released her hold. "You know I had kind of a crush on you since the day I saw you."

Unbelievable! Kate had just admitted what he had known all along. He struggled to keep from grimacing. The mere thought made him uneasy. He shifted, wanting to touch her.

Her whisper carried a hint of relief as she continued. "I felt a presence around me since those days, but never mentioned the idea to anyone."

With her finger pressed to her lips, she fixed her gaze at him. "Dobrila's father shot you in the head? I thought the story said he shot you straight in the chest."

"Yes, the bullet from his flint pistol hit my temple." He pointed at his scar tissue. "And second time in my chest. Still, I hope you like what you see."

"I do." She tilted her cup and set the blue dish down. "Empty. And we drained the whole pot."

"I guess that's my cue. I will leave now and come back after your exam." A heavy feeling pressed on his chest. He swayed. If she asked him to go, he would, but he didn't want to.

"Actually." She paused, putting her hand up. "I'm having fun talking to you. It's always quiet in here. Unless those idiots upstairs play their hip-hop tunes. And it's nice to speak to someone in our native tongue." Her cheeks blushed, and he couldn't help but think she was embarrassed to admit she enjoyed his company.

She continued to wind her hands when he placed his fingers on hers. "You have no idea how happy you made me by accepting my presence."

After a moment of silence, her fingers wrapped around his and steadied. Perhaps he should ease her into his tale. "Since you are itching all over to get into my story, why not start?"

Her head tilted toward the tiny window. "May as well. It seems we'll have another cold and snowy day." She turned to him, eyebrows arched. "Will it take long?"

He let go of her hands and stood. "I'll keep it short for the first time."

"Come to think of it, there is a novel about your tragic love already."

With slow steps, he rounded the table and crouched in front of her. "The ending is not true." He grimaced. "And I don't like how it was written. After three centuries, only the bones of the story are left, but the Devil is in the details, as the saying goes."

She squared her shoulders. "I'd love to get the meat of the story. There's even a stage play. Have you seen it?"

"I tried," he said, laughing. "When the actor who played me stepped onstage—" chuckles stifled his words.

"What's so funny?" Kate laughed in confusion.

"Well, I tried to keep my face straight. I really did, but I couldn't. I never looked that ridiculous. Oh, you should have seen the faces of the people in the audience. If Emi—I mean, my wife didn't kill me then..." His voice trailed off as the laughter left him and amusement abided.

The smile vanished from Kate's face. "Are you still married?"

"No." He cleared his throat. He had said too much already. Damn, Kate was so good at easing him off and he let his tongue lose. In three centuries, he had not called his wife by her mortal name. It'd be hard, but he must ensure to always refer to Emina as Dobrila. Emina's story would have to wait. "Let's leave that for another time."

"You are so secretive." She leaned toward him. "I like it."

*And soon, my dearest, you'll discover all of my secrets.* Those long lashes encircling her eyes lowered as he caressed her neck. How did he get smitten by her? His demon had quieted almost a century ago. Its urges had driven him to Kate's great-great-grandmother. But this young woman in front of him had a different effect on him. The kind he felt for—Emina. No it couldn't be. He'd love his late wife forever and no other would take her place.

He straightened, taking his position behind Kate's chair. "You should relax so we could begin."

Her head wobbled and the tension relaxed in her neck and shoulders under his massaging hands. "This isn't going to make me forget everything I studied for the test, is it? Just a warning, I'm a sucker for massages. I could get used to this."

"No." His whisper came out husky even to him. He could get used to having her young vibrant body under his fingertips. "This works on a different level." He stopped his hands. "Now, close your eyes and open up your mind. We shall start our journey through a different world."

◌◌◌

Kate lounged in her favorite chair. With one leg dangling over the edge, she savored the sight of a man sitting across from her. Daylight chased away the darkness from the corners of her apartment to reveal the lavender highlights in Miles's jet-black wavy hair. She still struggled to grasp the whole idea that the very ghost of Miles Rušinić occupied the seat at the other end of the table. The corners of his lips curled ever so slightly. If soft lines didn't appear around his eyes, she wouldn't know if he smiled or not.

After sharing the whole pot of coffee with him, his demeanor had failed to convince her he was an apparition. Since he had shown himself, his form had taken on a solid presence.

As a ghost, one would think he should be transparent and hover about, but then it might have been the media planting this idea into her head.

"You said it's complicated that I've heard your voice for over a year." Kate eyed him sideways, marvelling in the strong lines of his beautiful face. "You materialize in my front room, you can read my mind—yeah, I'd say it's complicated! I believe I am owed an explanation before we begin."

"You were able to hear my voice only because you have a very strong mind. And then we are connected through your ancestor, which helps the matter a lot."

"Ah right." She laughed softly. "Seems like everything falls into place with Great-Great Grandma Kate's curse. So, you lived in the same time as she did, some three hundred years ago. What are you? A ghost? An angel? A God, perhaps?"

"You think too much, Kate. Why don't we just get started with the story and I will explain everything at the right time?"

This was not the answer she had hoped for. How long would it take him to tell his tale? Looking at his warm blue eyes, she suddenly hoped for an eternity. Wait, what was she thinking? She had a paper due and needed time alone to study. Also, to finally be rid of the alien voice in her head seemed like a wonderful thing. "Okay, let's begin." She snorted, frowning at his folded hands. "The sooner we get this over with, the better."

With his lips pressed to a thin line, Miles cocked his head. Could her words have hurt his feelings? Kate cleared her throat. "I mean, what do you want me to do?

"As I said, close your eyes and open your mind." He reached for her hand, but she pulled them to her lap fast. "This won't hurt a bit. Trust me, Kate."

Yeah, right, trust a ghost in her flat. It took some effort to do as he directed, but the way he said her name, whispered actually, touched her core. "Closing my eyes is one thing, but I don't think I can open my mind so easily."

"Focus on my voice." The chair scraped the floor. She peeked through her lashes. He pulled closer.

She shifted, uneasiness pressing on her gut. What if

he inflicted her with the vision of a murder or a nasty memory, something she wouldn't be able to get out of her mind ever again? The thought alone caused her to do the exact opposite, close her mind, but she couldn't ignore his smooth voice. "I'll try, but can't promise this will work."

"Have some faith." His soft plea instilled her with ease, but her shoulders refused to relax. "I mean you no harm."

*Good to know.* She always paid extra attention to details, no matter how insignificant they might appear. He may think his Freudian slips had escaped her. A ghost wouldn't lie, he'd want to get the truth out and get something off his chest so that his soul could rest in peace. So, who was he really? More importantly, what was he? Then there was the small matter of his touch. Or rather the way her body reacted to his touch. She couldn't stay oblivious to the sensual shivers he raised in her when his hand came in contact with hers. To her own surprise, she found herself craving more of those caresses.

His low chuckle made her open one eye. Had he heard her thoughts?

"No peeking," he said with a mocking grin, "or I'll have to blindfold you."

Heat seared her cheeks as she squeezed her eyes shut again. An image of him planting sensual kisses on her neck, while white stars ignited behind her blindfolded eyes appeared. She shook her head and sent the fantasy away, and focused on the task at hand.

"Listen carefully," he said. "You must concentrate or this won't work. Once we establish the connection you will see the same thing as I. Kind of as if you're watching a movie."

"Wait one second." She raised her hands to stop him from whatever he was about to do and popped her eyes open. The last thing she needed was a selection of pictures to play over and over in her head. Wasn't his voice enough, and for the last two hours, his image occupied her thoughts? "How do I stop it?"

"Just tell me to stop and I will." His eyebrows twitched as he nodded. But it was the softness in his voice that convinced her to close her eyes again and lean into the chair.

"Are you ready?" Anticipation edged his whisper and tried to get hold of her too.

Feeling a slight tightness in her stomach, she inhaled deeply. She was as ready as she'd ever be. Seconds ticked away and he remained silent. What was he waiting for? With her eyes squeezed, she had surrendered to the darkness.

"Do you see anything?" He finally broke the silence.

"Huh?" she croaked. "I thought you wanted me to close my eyes."

Miles gave an exhausted sigh. "I meant could you see any visions yet, silly."

Unable to hold back her chuckles, Kate shrugged in mock defense. "I know, I know. Just kidding." She was relieved when some of the tension between them eased with the bantering. "So, what exactly am I supposed to see?"

"It's not working." Soft sounds came from the tabletop, as if he drummed his fingertips. "We may need a physical connection. Put your hands on the table."

Could this be his attempt to touch her again? It made no difference. He wanted to hold her hands and her heart rejoiced. Without hesitation, she obeyed and his tender fingers curled around hers.

His thumbs tickled her knuckles. "Look deeper."

She shook her head in frustration. "What's there to see, but darkness?"

"Let's try something different. Can you hear any sounds?" He gave her hands a soft squeeze, setting her heartbeat to a faster rhythm.

"No, nothing." Other than his sweet voice which she couldn't get enough of. *What? Where did that thought come from? Just a few minutes ago, I wanted to get rid of him.*

His finger-play on her knuckles ceased. "We must be patient. Perhaps if we sit in silence for a while…"

Kate licked her dry lips. Amazing how the sound of his mellow voice distracted her. She could hardly concentrate. Maybe he got a sneak peek into her thoughts and therefore suggested to be silent.

Though she'd much rather keep listening to his words, his theory made sense. Her nerves slowly stilled and she stopped fumbling.

"Can you feel anything?" he spoke again.

She waited. There was something. "I think so." Yes, definitely a cooling breeze on her skin.

"What?" A demanding tone crept in his hot whisper.

A tuft of her hair came loose from her clip and brushed her neck, as gentle as Mile's touches. "I feel a breeze."

"Good, good. Concentrate on that." A hint of smile in his voice ensured her the vision was right. "Can you hear the wind now?"

She leveled her head and raised her voice. "Yes, I do hear it. It's howling now. It's not a breeze anymore, but a gusty sirocco. And I hear something else, too."

He must have put his weight on the table because the top wobbled. "You don't need to yell, the storm is not real. Is it waves crashing on the rocks you hear?"

She nodded, fighting to keep her voice low. The storm felt every bit real. "Yes, it is. And I feel rain drops on my face, but I still don't see anything."

This whole new experience sent shivers through her, but she sucked her lower lip between her teeth and suppressed the feeling.

"Try to get into my head." Pleading reflected in his voice.

A silent chuckle escaped her. "*Me* get into *your* head? It's the other way around."

"Don't break the concentration," he demanded. "Keep searching your mind for visuals and you'll be able to see what I see."

"Yes, I think I can." She smiled, nodding as the first picture emerged in her mind. "I see gray clouds hovering low over a vast sea."

The wide sleeves of his shirt floated in the wind. She burst into a short laugh. "What is this you're wearing? Puffy sleeves with lacy trims." She scanned the outfit down to the ground where a few grass blades grew among rocks. She wore a black vest with golden buttons, red velvet trim, and pants reached just below her knees. Though ripped and dirty, the white of her hose contrasted to the black bow, which decorated her shoes. Miles had spoken the truth she experienced everything from his body. "I think you need a fashion upgrade, you're dressed like some aristocrat of yore." Her voice trailed off and she raised her hands to her face. Though white and soft, they were still man's hands. He had all the makings of the blueblood.

This was a vision from his young days. The waves crashed against the rocks on a sun-bleached beach. "Where am I?" she thought out loud.

"You're seeing the world through my eyes. As for my wardrobe, that was the fashion of the times and I was eighteen summers old. But what I'm wearing is not important here. Pay more attention to the whole scene. What do you feel?"

"Okay." She tilted her chin and allowed the moment to take her. In an instant, her chest constricted as anguish overwhelmed her. "Oh my God," she whispered through her tight throat. "You're about to commit suicide."

"Stop talking and listen to my thoughts." His voice came from afar. Her mind spun as the vision pulled her in deeper.

At first, guttural growling filled her ears. She strained to make sense of the sounds then words became apparent. Kate struggled to keep her eyes closed. Her lids wanted to pop open as frightening, awful, feral and disturbing thoughts of a gutted and dismembered female body filled her mind. Miles's thoughts came through broken, as if he was sending vibes on the wrong frequency. Kate slid deeper into the moment. There was a conversation going on, an argument, but with only one person involved. She sensed Miles fought against another entity inside him. A spirit he desperately tried to placate. Suddenly Kate read his mind like the words written on blank pages.

He wouldn't, couldn't kill her. Kate, his childhood friend had become more over the years and had served him well. He had found relief from the demon's urging when he had inflicted pain on her. And if the beast required him do it again he would, but he had not the sense of a killer.

Dobrila. No. He must not think of her. Not now. Their love would have to remain a secret. What if the fiend inside him caused him to harm her as he found the pleasure in hurting Kate? Miles would not be able to live with this burden. But it wasn't only his demon. The quarrel between their families had been going on for almost a century. What he wouldn't give if he and his beloved weren't born into the altercation?

Kate felt a new surge of determination flooding the

spirit of Miles. To hell with the brute clouding his sanity. To hell with their feuding families, forbidding him to love Dobrila. And to hell with the beast's urges to kill Kate in a most gruesome way, making her suffer in pain. None of this would have happened if he never existed. And there was a way to stop this hurt. The only way.

One final scan over the swells of the choppy sea. A white crest formed on a wave approaching the sharp cliffs.

He picked up a rock the size of a large sack and hugged the mass to his chest. With his back turned toward the sea, he inched his feet toward the ridge. All he had to do now was to lean backward. His chosen wave was just beneath him. It was time to let go.

Without further ado, he took the plunge, hoping the strong sea would crush his body to the boulders in a moment. The sleeves of his shirt flapped in the wild wind. One…two…three…four seconds it took for his body to fall some fifty feet. The wave gripped him and icy waters pulled him under. Muffled sounds of stones scraping along the bottom by the force of the sea filled his ears. As salt water poured into his nose and mouth, filling his lungs, his urge for air became unbearable. He wanted to propel himself to the surface and draw in a long breath. Instead, he hugged the stone tighter. Pain ripped through him as his head met the sharp edge of the cliff. His blood tinted the water around him red. Darkness closed in on him. In a second, all his hurt would leave him and his heart would beat one last time.

All his previous deaths felt the same. Would he stay dead this time?

జ్ఞజ్ఞ

The vision stopped. Filled with sadness, Kate

searched the darkness behind her eyelids for more. No, he couldn't have died or there wouldn't be much of a story to tell here. There had to be more. She jolted back at Miles's continuous finger snapping. "I said that's it for today."

Blinking, she adjusted to the light while questions swarmed. Why did he choose the memory of him dying to begin with? "But—we just started. And you killed yourself, you goof. Why? I gathered that life was tough, but how were you to fix things? Who was this Kate you hurt? My great-great-grandma? Why did you hurt her? What did you mean by if 'you'd stay dead this time'?"

"Save your questions." He put his hand up in a stop-right-there gesture. "I shouldn't have kept the first vision so long. We'll continue on Wednesday. What time are you going to be back?"

"I don't know." She shrugged. Again, he avoided all her questions. She should get angry but curiosity pre-vailed. If only she could keep him talking to her in this human shape. What would she do if he left and didn't come back? With this short peek into his soul, he wove a connection between them. He couldn't just walk out the door now and leave. Afraid he would again cease to a faint voice in her mind if she pushed too hard, Kate re-strained from shooting more questions. "I have field placement in the afternoon. God, that teacher always keeps me doing her job. I hope to be here by six."

He rose slowly. "I'll be back then. Good luck on your test." Scrambling into his black leather jacket, he opened the door. "Make sure you lock up after me."

She grabbed the knob as his hand slipped over hers. His fingers wrapped around her hand. He raised her hand and his lips brushed her knuckles, the intensity in his crystal blue eyes held her under the spell, then he pressed a soft kiss to her hand. The tilt of his head made him appear so sexy, she could leap up and kiss him. Instead, she sighed while he stepped into the hallway and headed for the stairs.

Her knees quivered while she turned the locks and leaned against the door. He'd just kissed her in most gentlemanly way. What was the matter with her? Had she'd been on her own for too long? *Expect nothing and you shall not get disappointed.* But she stopped believing in her mantra and, without her notion, so many things were unclear.

# Chapter 4

Kate faltered her steps on the way to her locker. She glanced from left to right. Snickers and wry looks coupled with whispers in the hallway didn't escape her. The entire year she had managed to avoid becoming a target of hot gossip, but as it seemed, somehow she got on the radar. Gosh, she thought she had left high school behind when she matriculated to the Ryerson's College, but most of the full time university students seemed mentally stuck in their teenage years.

She continued down the corridor, reached her locker and spun the combination on the padlock.

"Hey, Kate." Andrew shoved his bag into the locker next to hers.

"Hi." Kate cast a friendly smile at the skinny guy with the baseball cap. "Ready for the test?"

"Yep. I studied like crazy the whole weekend." His dark eyes shrunk with his grin. "You?"

"Same here." Kate opened the compartment and squeezed her backpack in. Her weekend's adventure with Miles could hardly pass for studying, but she had managed to glance over the chapters once.

Andrew was a nice guy and friendly toward everyone, so she decided to ask. "What's this snickering all about?"

"Don't pay any attention to it, Kate." Andrew took his coat off and un-wrapped his scarf. "We're here to get our diplomas and get the hell out of this place."

Kate grew suspicious. She may not know Andrew well, but she knew this academic type wasn't into any kind of gossip. If he knew what everyone sneered about, this must concern either him or her. "You know something, don't you?"

"Well." Andrew wobbled his head, most likely contemplating whether to tell her.

"Just spit it out, Andy," Kate urged. "Whatever the news, it could never be as bad as last spring when I dragged the strip of toilet paper stuck to my shoe all the way to the auditorium."

"Fine. I overheard Amanda talking in the cafeteria. Apparently, Coach Kowalski has a sweet spot for you."

"Coach—" Kate swallowed a lump. This bit of news was the last thing she expected. "Who?"

"He's a head coach of the hockey team." Andrew waved his hand. "Amanda is pissed. She's all into him and hangs around the arena with her minions most of her spare time to chat him up."

The door clattered as Kate shut the locker. "Oh God, and now she thinks this coach is sweet on me?"

"And here she comes." Andrew leaned with his back against the locker and crossed his arms over his chest.

A girl in black tights approached with two equally large friends in tow. Did they really think leotards and tank tops became them? Kate waited. For these chicks, all it took to forget why they approached her was a couple of boys. Not today. Darn, guys always hung around them. They hoped to get lucky and these girls never disappointed them.

"Listen you—you—Ruckus." Amanda frowned, waving her meaty finger in Kate's face. "I've been working the coach for months and you think he'd like you just because you're so—" Her eyes roamed up and down Kate. "Athletic. I'm warning you, hands off. He's mine."

"Amanda." Kate raised her hand, searching for words this simpleton would understand. Since the very first day, Amanda had proudly announced to the entire class she enrolled in the college because of her search for a rich husband. "First of all—" *Your roots are showing.* "My last name is Rokov. I don't know this coach or whoever started the stupid rumor. Second, the coach is a member of the faculty. He wouldn't dare get intimate with students in any way." If he had no scruples, chances were, a hockey coach wouldn't choose either of them, the plain Kate nor fake Amanda. A long sigh of exasperation escaped Kate. Her adversary would never comprehend this, and she was wasting her breath trying to explain it to the phony. "He's yours, for all I care." *And you really should remove the chipped nail polish.* "And while I'm at it, the leggings are meant to be worn with long tops, or it appears as if you ran out of the house and forgot your pants."

The frown on Amanda's face turned grotesque. "Who are you to give me fashion advice?"

One of her minions chuckled. "It does look like you're not wearing any pants."

"Shut up, Simone," Amanda demanded. "We only let you hang out with us because you pay for stuff."

Kate shook her head. Amanda's attempt at a British accent was like nails on a chalkboard. "What's up with the accent?" Kate asked.

Amanda flipped her hair in some super-model gesture. "I'm British."

"You are? Since when? This morning?" Kate gave

her a once over. "Weren't you Jamaican yesterday? All your uncles are black, remember? In fact, you claimed to be Native American, and before that you were Italian, and before that you were Russian. Strange, since you abhor foreigners."

Amanda shrugged and narrowed her eyes. "You stay away from my man. *Capisce*?"

"Argh." Kate turned away from the gossip-loving trio and continued toward the classroom, Andrew in tow. With any luck, she wouldn't have to deal with Amanda and her troopers. It wouldn't be easy avoiding the popular trio. Tripping and shoving would become daily treatments. Taking her usual seat in the middle of the classroom, Kate scanned over a few students who showed up for the test. Miller sat near the door, his face grim. She'd bet anything, it was him and his dumb friend who started the gossip. Potter especially, the man hated her with a passion for no apparent reason.

A few more students entered, followed by Professor Campbell. His brown leather briefcase rubbed his pants as he strutted straight to the front of the class and did a quick head count. "Eighteen. There should be twenty-five of you taking this test." With his hands propped on his hips, he leaned against the desk. "We'll give the latecomers five minutes. Any last questions?"

Silence fell over the small crowd. The door swung open and Amanda and her minions strolled through the doorway. The smell of coffee wafted from their extra-large cups, served with two helpings of cream and sugar—the famous Canadian double-double.

"Ladies," the professor croaked, tapping his finger at the sign on the whiteboard. "No food or drink in the classroom. Leave your cups outside the door."

Their mouths opened wide in a grotesque expression, but they obeyed.

"You have seventy minutes to complete the test." The professor distributed the papers, face down then paused by Miller. He continued, "I don't want to see anything on your desks other than calculators."

A flurry of activity followed as everyone shoved their papers and textbooks inside their bags or onto the floor.

After taking his seat in front of the class, the professor glanced at the clock on the wall behind him. "You can begin."

Sixty minutes later, no one had finished. There were a few questions Kate had to re-read and think about, but this last one caused her anguish. Shoot, she couldn't guess. Of all the given choices, there wasn't one she would pick. It could be *D*, dare she pick it, or *B*, or any of them. She poised her pencil ready to circle *D*.

'*If you choose* D, *it will be your fourth incorrect answer. Read the question again.*' Miles's voice startled her.

With her forehead resting on her hand, she hissed, "Miles, what the hell are you doing here?"

'*Shhhh, you don't have to speak. I can hear you in your thoughts. But you don't have much time.*'

Erasing the circled letter, she directed her thought to him, '*This is still cheating, you know.*'

He must have been here the whole time, watching over her shoulder. Though it seemed no one else suspected an entity standing next to her and giving her the answers. '*I'm not giving you the answer. I'll lead you to it. Consider my thoughts your own. No cheating then, you see?*'

Her cheeks heated. How much of her other thoughts did he catch in the past? Fine, she could live with a small nudge in the right direction. '*Okay, I'll read the question again, but I'm still not getting it.*'

'*Look at the graph. You took the value from the wrong curve.*'

"Five more minutes, class." The professor's announcement caused many sharp hisses and rustling of papers.

A realization struck her. She quickly circled answer *B* instead.

'*Great, now recheck questions eleven, seventeen, and twenty-six. But don't get everything perfect or the professor will be suspicious.*'

'*Nobody's perfect with this professor. He'll find a way to mark me down.*'

'*I'll see you tonight.*'

Miles's voice ceased and Kate returned her attention to the questions he had pointed out to her. Yet again, he was right. They were tricky. After a quick correction, she gathered her stuff and delivered the test to the professor.

Miller cast her a desperate look on her way out of the classroom. A glance at the exam in front of him confirmed he was still on the first page and the three first questions were incorrectly answered. That was what he got for trading study time for partying. By now, he should be well versed in the concept of "opportunity cost."

"Kate," Andrew called and she halted, turning to him. "How did you do?"

"Fine, I think." Kate shrugged, but a slight guilt stung her chest. She had a little guidance from a supernatural being, but who would believe her if she admitted it. Anyhow, he had promised he'd help.

Why was she trying to justify her acceptance of his aid? No one judged her or suspected she cheated. It wasn't as if she'd never aced a test before. Anyone else would jump at the opportunity.

"How about you?" she asked Andrew.

"It's hard to tell, but I'm positive I'll pass. I've got to

run to my next class." Andrew tapped her arm. "Are you coming over for Christmas?"

Kate frowned. She craved the comfort of family and friends during the festive season but, chances were, she'd sit alone in her apartment. "I don't want to impose on your mom. I'd feel like an outsider."

"Come on, my mom loves you. I'll have a few friends over. You know you're welcome." Andrew glanced at his wristwatch. "Think about it. I'm late already. Bye." He scurried down the corridor.

Kate ambled to the cafeteria and took the corner table with one chair. Thinking of Andrew's invitation, she un-wrapped her bagel. Maybe she should go. She'd be safe with him. He wasn't interested in her, at least not in a sexual way. He checked out guys on the campus with interest.

"Kate!"

She almost chocked on her sandwich as Miller's voice came from behind.

He'd pulled a chair to her table and plopped his heavy body on it before she could even swallow.

*Yeah, have a seat, why don't you?* She scooted her chair away from him.

"You don't mind if I sit here, do you?" His tight smile revealed short, uneven teeth.

She scanned the cafeteria for his worthless friend. Miller and Potter must be up to something nasty to embarrass her again. But when she couldn't spot Potter's face in the crowd, she cut Miller a sharp glance. "What do you want?"

The red-faced guy in front of her pursed his lips, eyeing her bagel. Kate tugged the food closer to her. "You're keeping me from my lunch and I don't have the time nor do I feel like chatting to you."

Miller cleared his throat, looking out the window,

than back at her. "You're like super smart and I—" He lowered his eyes. "Well, I need help."

*Aha! Payback time.* "Really? You called me a stupid cow. So why should I help you?"

"Because I can pay you ten bucks for an hour of tutoring." His face turned red as he leveled his wintry blue eyes with hers. "If I don't graduate with this class, my dad wants me out. He's a school principal and he'll get me a custodian job. I don't want to work in some mediocre position for the rest of my life. I can still get my grades up and pass."

*I doubt it.* But ten dollars an hour was tempting. Kate scratched the side of her neck. She could use the money. While she had him working, she would study too, earn a few bucks, and take care of two problems at once.

"Tomorrow, fourth period. Meet me in the library." She paused, thinking of pumping him for information. "But first you tell me who started the crap about me and a particular hockey coach."

A grin spread on Miller's face. "You won't regret this. And about the rumor, Potter said the coach made himself invisible last Saturday night and came to our apartment." He choked on his snorts. "Apparently, he's a vampire." His laugh ended with a coughing fit. "Don't worry about Potter," he said with his fist pressed to his lips. "I kicked him out. He eats my food, drinks my beer, and owes me money."

Miller continued on but Kate's mind drifted. An invisible visitor in the apartment one floor above hers? The same night she had made first contact with Miles. This couldn't be a coincidence. Was Miles—a vampire? Her heart jumped to her throat as a realization hit her. This could explain his need for secrecy, the fact that he didn't want her to see him right away. Was what she'd seen his true appearance? All the while they talked to each other she'd never spotted any oversized vampire fangs behind his lush lips, fangs that could tear her throat out. Oh, God. An ice-cold shiver trailed down her spine. Miles would call on her again. Tonight.

Fresh snow crunched under Kate's boots. The steam of her breath was visible in the frosty arctic air. Her gym bag bounced on her hip as she scurried from the bus stop, across the parking lot to the front entrance of her apartment building. Going home where Miles would visit her in a few minutes wasn't the smartest idea, but she had nowhere to hide. She stepped inside the hallway. Potter scrambled to his feet.

"Jeez." She jumped with a start.

He took a step back and tripped over one of his over packed boxes. "Stay away from me, wench. I'm moving out. Happy?"

With the keys rattling in her hand, she skittered down the stairs. Yes, his eviction made her happy, but she had never exchanged a single word with the moron and she wasn't about to start now. She'd check her mailbox later, when the building was Potter free.

"What's the matter?" His sneer bounced off the walls from the staircase above and urged her to unlock the door to her unit faster. "Cat got your tongue?"

Darkness fell early in December and engulfed Kate's apartment. The stale smell of morning's coffee lingered in the air. At the flip of the switch, the ceiling light revealed the empty apartment. She dropped the navy-blue sack by the front door. Two hours in the gym did little to ease her anxiety. The more she told herself there were no such things as vampires, the less she believed it.

The shrill ring of the phone in the silent apartment

rushed the goosebumps down her legs. Could it be Miles cancelling his appointment? Wouldn't be the first time a man shunned from her. Unless, of course, they had an ulterior motive to stick around and if he was a vamp then he wouldn't leave until he fed on her.

She plucked the cordless phone from its cradle on the corner stand and plastered the piece to her ear. "Hello."

"Kate," Dyane said with relief in her exhale. "Finally I've got you home."

Kate's spirit rose with her friend's voice, even if she was half the world away. "Dyane, oh, I'm so glad it's you. Do you have news for me?"

"Yes, but first I need to hear about you. Did you make the contact?"

"I did and at first I was happy about it. You'll never believe who the ..." What she should call him? He'd established he wasn't a ghost. The vampire was yet to be determined, so that left an immortal. "Well, if I tell you he's Miles from the tragic love legend, would you believe me?"

"Cards can't reveal details. Your fascination with him made my guess easy." Determination in her tone sliced through the line.

"Did you do another spread?"

"Several. In fact, I'm doing one right now." Cards flipped and cracked under Dyane's fast fingers, then a hiss came from her end.

"What?" Kate snapped. She didn't like Dyane's tone so far, but intrigue got the best of her.

"The three cards keep coming up in every spread. Two of Cups, you're in love. Three of Swords, the harmful intrusion of the third party and separation is imminent, and The Wheel of Fortune. The situations in your life will come to a close, but the new opportunities will replace them."

Kate rolled her bottom lip in a grimace. Her in love? Preposterous! Since she'd made the contact with the owner of the haunting voice, her perception of him had changed, and she'd developed admiration for the legendary Miles. Arguing with Dyane was pointless and a waste of time. If cards said Kate was in love, to Dyane it meant it was fated.

However, the three cards had not produced the answer she hoped for. She'd have to ask straight out. "Can you tell me if he's a vampire?"

"A King of Swords came up too. It only means he could appear unapproachable, unfeeling, and cold because of his remote countenance. What makes you think he'd be a vampire?"

The one Tarot card described him better than anyone ever could. The sadness in his eyes could only be due to a great loss. "Some rumors I heard in school and unexplainable events. I put two and two together and concluded he might be a blood sucker."

"I don't think he is. However, Four of Swords did come up once. It could mean he fought many inner battles, but in his case the swords on the wall represent many lives he lived."

Sadness pressed on Kate's mind, spread shivers through her. He had committed several suicides, only to be revived by the creature residing in him.

"I'll have to go now. He'll be here any minute."

"Okay, keep me posted on the situation. I know overseas calls are pricy and we can only talk for a few moments, so email me."

"I will. Say hi to everyone." Kate ended the call and replaced the phone on the cradle.

Gnawing on the nail of her middle finger, she paced in front of her small sofa. Dyane's words instilled little confidence in her. What if Miles was a vamp? What could a vampire want from her? Blood what else. Then why hadn't he sucked her dry and left her carcass behind for someone to find days, weeks or even months later? No one visited her place. Chances were, she wouldn't be found until someone reported an unbearable stench coming from her unit. Miles was strong compared to her. She wouldn't put up much of a resistance. She stopped and stared at the locks on her door. No amount of locks or bars on the two windows would keep him from getting to her.

If she moved out, maybe she'd get away, but for how long? Just when she thought she was safe in his presence, he turned out to be a vampire. It seemed her only way to survive this was to do what he asked. She examined her chewed nail. Darn, she'd made the cuticle bleed. With her hand shoved in her jeans pocket, she resumed her frantic steps.

He'd be here any moment. The battalion of butterflies rose in her stomach at the thought of him. What was wrong with her? The man would want to suck her blood and she turned mushy thinking about him. So what? If he intended to kill her, she'd be in his embrace at least for a few minutes. Maybe Tarot cards did tell the truth. She was in love. Nah! Dumb thought. Dyane had planted that seed in her head.

The front door opened. "I'm here," Miles announced as he stepped into the apartment, a large paper bag in his hands.

She froze. Fear threatened to overtake her reasoning, but his arrival tightened her abdomen. God he was gorgeous.

"I thought I should just come in now that you can see me, so I—" The smile vanished as he approached her. "Kate, what is the matter? You didn't turn this white the first time you talked to me."

Her dry tongue stuck to the roof of her mouth, but she pushed the words out. "Are you a vampire?"

With a heavy exhale, his eyes closed and his ebony hair shook with his head. "Let's sit down."

# Chapter 5

Kate stared at Miles. With each breath, her resolve to discover the truth about his long existence grew deeper. She couldn't sit down and discuss this over a dinner, no. Not when her stomach churned at the very thought of him as a creature of the night who sucked blood from unsuspecting maidens.

The slow appearing smirk on his face told her he read her thoughts. He pulled the chair out and lowered to the seat. "You watch way too much television."

At his offhand remark, her eyebrows shot up her forehead. "And whose fault is that?"

He shrugged. "Yours."

Her mouth hung open. *The audacity of the man.* "Mine? You're the one who kept me up most nights with your murmuring."

He winked, his little smile widening. "I expected you to open up to me much sooner."

She threw a kitchen towel at him. "Your approach was somewhat unconventional."

He caught the cloth and balled it in his hands. "And if I came to you with my claim, you'd agree to help me without questioning my sanity?"

She rolled her bottom lip. He had a point, damn it. "Okay, you win, but you still didn't answer me. Are you a vampire?" The demand in her voice surprised even her. Would a vamp joke with her before he sucked the last drop of her blood? How would she know? It wasn't like she bantered with one of them on a daily basis.

"I—" He extended one hand out. "I don't know myself."

Wide eyed, she couldn't take her gaze off him or steady her heart. "How can you *not* know?"

He scratched his jaw. "All I know is that I don't have fangs."

"But you do crave the blood?"

"I did." He nodded. His expression showed a mixture of sorrow and shame, but the two simple words he spoke filled her with dread all the same. "Almost a century ago." Leveling his eyes with hers, he continued. "Can you imagine what it was like to crave something so badly but not have the means to get it?"

She scanned over her scarcely furnished apartment. "I can."

"I wasn't referring to wealth. That didn't prevent me from getting blood. It was someone's cruel joke of leaving me fangless." Leaning toward her, he gave her his seductive little smile. "But you are not poor, I know what poor is."

"You do?" Her curiosity sparked. "Weren't you an aristocrat?"

He waved his finger. "Ah, but you're forgetting something, my dear. When Dobrila and I started our lives together, we couldn't go back to our families. As far as they knew, we were dead and buried. We had to move away and live on the streets."

Miles and Dobrila had mingled with the bottom of the society?

Kate couldn't picture them as common and homeless people. "How long had you lived like that?"

"Thankfully, only a month or two. But I still have fond memories of those days and the importance of having a few friends in low places. Why are we standing here and talking?" He placed the brown bag on the table. "I brought us dinner. Hope you like Chinese."

Her shoulders relaxed. He wouldn't bring her food if his intentions were to harm her, not unless he planned to fatten her first. Therefore, she couldn't be too cautious. "You're not going to kill me?"

"No." Annoyance filled his tone. His brows furrowed. "Where did you get that idea?"

With her hand crumpling the hem of her shirt, she nibbled on her bottom lip. Why not let him sweat the truth out? "Did you visit Potter the same night you came here?"

The realization flashed in his blue eyes. The fabric of his coat crumpled as he crossed his arms.

"So that's what this is all about." He waved his hand and chuckled. "I was having some fun with the oaf. But—" He raised his finger. "—I prevented him from playing another sick prank on you."

"Well, thank you," she said, tucking a strand of her hair behind her ear. "Nonetheless, the whole school laughs at me and some coach."

"Damn." He took off his coat and draped the heavy parka over the chair. "I never thought my joking with him would go so far. You have my word the rumors will stop."

"No need." She put a hand up. The last thing she needed was having him get involved in the students' affairs whose mentality never left high school. "I found rumors stop on their own if I don't pay any attention to them. Just let them run their course."

"You're making it sound as if they are some sort of virus," he said through his laugh.

His laughter relaxed her and she chimed in. "Oh, they are."

"I'm glad we cleared up that misconception." He pointed at the bag of food on the table. "Are you hungry? Let's eat."

She winced at the sharp pain caused by her chewed nail and yanked her hand out of her pocket.

"Don't worry, there's nothing breaded and deep fried in here." He ceased pulling the takeout containers out of the bag and grabbed her wrist. "You're bleeding." His voice reflected a hint of concern as he got to his feet, moving closer. "Let me take care of this."

The way his hand gripped her wrist, she didn't have a choice but to follow him to the bathroom. *Will he lick my wound?*

Opening the faucet, he shoved her hand under the cold water. "Did you do this to yourself?"

"Ouch, my finger stings." Her instinct urged her to pull her hand out of his. Instead, she flipped the light switch on when he tightened his hold. "You want to play a doctor now?"

He grinned not taking his glance from her finger under running water. "I'm not playing. I've been a doctor for centuries."

"I thought Miles had not lived long enough to complete any schooling." As soon as she spoke those words, she regretted them. He was here in body and soul, so he could have become a doctor during his very long life.

He shut off the water and pulled the towel from the rack. "You're right, Miles's life was cut short," he said. He patted her hand and opened the medicine cabinet above the sink. "Do you have bandages?"

"There should be a box." With the door in between

them, and mirror facing her, she cringed at her reddened face. Though she'd probably never get used to him hearing her thoughts, it was nice to have company. Okay, so he wasn't a ghost or a vampire, but he was a man and his musky scent sent heat spreading through her.

"Good, you have antiseptic cream. This should do." He spread the white ointment, dressed the wound. "Stop biting your nails. It's a nervous habit."

She gave him a mocking grin. "Will do, Doc."

"So, are you hungry?"

"In a little while. Hope you can hold off." With any luck, he didn't hear her stomach rumble, but she couldn't eat just yet. He was right, her nerves needed to calm a bit more.

He took his seat at the table. "Then let us continue with the story."

She sat facing him, and extended her hands to him. "Shall we hold the connection again?"

A tiny smile stretched his lips as he stared at her in silence. He must have read her mind again. She was the one who itched to hold hands with him and it seemed he wanted the same. With his wrists resting on the table, he twitched his eyebrows in invitation to place her hands in his. Warmth flooded her when his fingers brushed hers. What would it be like if he was to touch all of her? Oh, she better not think of that.

"Concentrate." His soft tone ensured that he had heard her last thought.

She closed her eyes and the vision began to play in an instant. Perhaps it was her eagerness to continue with the story so getting into the mind trip had not taken as long as the first time. He lay face down on the pebble beach. "You were so young!"

His fingers fumbled. "Pay attention to my thoughts, not my looks."

❧❦❧

Shrieks of a seagull had seeped into his conscious-ness. With a start, he opened his eyes and raised his head. A crab crawled in front of his nose. This close, the crus-tacean appeared to be a giant. He scanned his surround-ings. The storm had passed but the clouds continued to loom. Steady waves rushed to the shore.

With a long groan, he rolled onto his back. Pebbles dug into his flesh. His head throbbed. The intensity of the pain ensured him he had returned to the world of the liv-ing. How long had he stayed dead this time? The demon inside him quieted as it always had after a suicide. The revival process must have taken energy out of the animal. But the beast would awaken again and control him.

A thought occurred to Kate. She contemplated whether to speak and break the concentration, but she itched to get the question out. "Is it possible you were unconscious and the sea spit you out?"

"No, I died." The solemn tone in his whisper touched her core. "Pay attention to my thoughts again."

They sat in silence for a stretch. With the demon pla-cated, she couldn't detect any of Miles's thinking. In-stead, she paid attention to his actions.

The ground spun as he staggered on his feet. Every muscle protested in pain with the slightest move. His groans filled the silence. He scanned to the top of the cliff he had jumped off. It was a long way up. No one would come searching for him in this wilderness.

Putting one foot in front of the other over the rocky terrain, his joints slowly loosened and the pain alleviated. An animal trail winding up through the cliffs brought him to the footpath. After an hour of climbing, the sound of a woman's sweet singing mixed with sheep bleating carried on the wind. He paused.

It was servant Kate's voice. His father's lands were near.

He resumed his hike, following the sound. Some fifteen minutes later, he found her sitting on the main, low branch of an ancient olive tree. Sheep grazed in the surrounding fields. With her back turned to him, she finished her song, but the clinking of the knitting needles continued.

He stepped closer, leaned onto a dry stone wall. "Those are going to be a beautiful pair of stockings."

Twisting, she turned to him. In an instant, a wide smile spread on her face. "What brings you here, young Master Miles?"

Kate snapped her hands out of his and sprang to her feet. She stood aghast as the last image etched in her mind. She saw the girl's face every time she looked in a mirror.

"Kate." Miles stood, too. "Next time ask me to pause."

"She's me." She pushed the words out through her dry mouth. "Her voice sounded familiar. My great-great-grandmother—" Kate leveled her eyes with his. "—is me."

"No, Kate." Miles stepped closer to her. "She cannot be you. If anything, you'd be her." His thinned lips didn't match the caring in his dark eyes as he brushed her hair. "In appearance only, you have none of her memories."

Kate reached for a glass from the cupboard and filled the tumbler with water from the tap. "Is that why you sought me out?"

His answer came in the form of a nod. "And I believe that could explain why you heard me."

Her mind heavy, she returned to her seat. Though he had said so the first time he'd allowed her to see him, she had hard time believing their contact was possible due to the old grandma. After seeing her in a vision, this was the most plausible explanation so far. She shouldn't be surprised. All along, she suspected some connection, but couldn't put her finger on it. "It's possible."

"Do you want to continue with the vision or eat?"

"You must be hungry." She stood to get the dishes, but his hand wrapped around her arm.

"I'd rather we finish this vision first." He cocked his head. "It won't take much longer. What do you say?"

"Since you insist." Instinctively, she took a hold of his other hand and lowered to her seat.

"Remember to let me know if you want to stop." He sat, too. "Close your eyes," he said, closing his.

In an instant, the phantasm replaced her reality and she was transported to the olive orchard three hundred years ago.

The young woman, her great-great-grandma, had gotten to her feet and stepped to Miles. Deep creases replaced her smile. "Young master, have you fallen in the sea? Your clothes are crumpled and your hose ripped."

"Yes." He coughed. "I—I had an accident."

"Jesus and Mary, master. This is not good—in the middle of the winter. Do you want to catch your death?" Lightning flashed, filling the air with electricity. Soon rolling thunder ripped across the sky and muffled her words. First drops of rain sprinkled the ground.

Kate tucked the knitting under her arm. "The sheep." She winced. "I must get them in the pen."

With the skill of a shepherd girl, she herded the animals through a narrow entrance to a low stone building and closed the door when the last one passed through.

"I don't know what I'd do if I lost one or if they got sick and died." She shook her head. "I'd be blamed for the loss."

No doubt, his father would put the blame on her and

take the extra crops from her family until the loss of his livestock was repaid.

"Come, young master, I have a fire going in the shelter." She took a couple of steps toward the smaller stone structure. It had a low entrance and smoke billowed from its chimney.

He stood rooted. Afraid if he followed her, the demon would awaken and urge him to take her in a ruthless and savage way. Her scarf came loose and revealed the purple bruises caused by his hands. If he lived for an eternity, he'd never know how he snapped out the beast's clutch and stopped himself from strangling her two days ago. Even though he had caused her so much pain, she was always on his side.

"Please, young master. We'll both catch our deaths in this rain." Her cold fingers wrapped around his hand. "And you are already soaked and must be frozen to the bones."

Shivers ran through him. Strange, until she had spoken those words, he had felt no chills. Suddenly, he wished to warm up by the fire. Her face lit at his nod. Holding onto her hand, he let her lead him into the stark and tight interior.

A tiny fire flickered in the hearth, and steam rose from a cauldron hung over the flames. The smell of stew reminded him of his hunger.

"First we should remove these drenched clothes." Kate's fingers worked fast to undo buttons on his vest. "Where are your shoes?"

He reached for the loose end of the bodice lace on her peasant's dress. "Sea took them."

Without stopping, she proceeded to his shirt and trousers. "Don't you be thinking of it, master. We need to get you dry and warm. You don't want to catch pneumonia again." She took a wool blanket and wrapped his naked body. "There. I'll get you some food and you'll be as good as new."

After setting him with a hefty bowl of her hearty barley stew and a big slab of stale bread, she removed her wet clothes. Another bolt of lightning illuminated the interior and her glorious body. He was exhausted, but his hardness had different games in mind. Proving he was a man now, not a sickly, pale boy would require more than having his way with a servant girl.

Wrapped in a blanket of her own, she joined him on the dirt floor with food in her hand. They ate in silence. Unusual, as Kate liked to chat.

"The meal was exquisite." He placed his empty bowl next to hers. He spoke the truth. No banquet in the richest of parlors could compare to this. "I thank you."

She stopped, her spoon half way to her mouth, and pointed to a glass container with long, narrow neck encased in wickerwork. "There's wine in the demijohn. It will return the color to your cheeks."

Brushing a few wet strands from her cheek and neck, he whispered, "I know something we could do to redden yours."

The dish dropped from her hand before his lips pressed on hers. She returned his kiss with zeal. Her soft whimpers turned him harder than he'd ever been. He lowered her to the cold ground.

"Master," she whispered as he tugged on the blanket tucked tightly around her breasts, where he'd left his vicious bite marks.

Unprepared for the vision to take such unexpected twist, Kate squeezed his hands. "Can we, um, can we stop here?"

His finger tickled her palm. "Are you sure? This happened over three hundred years ago."

She opened her eyes. His handsome face had a puzzled expression. "What exactly do you want to show me, master?" she mocked him, with a twitch of her eyebrows.

"I understand your concern." He cleared his throat, shifting. "You see, I always considered her my friend and I thought the demon wanted her body, not me. The entity would cloud my mind and use me. It was like I stood there, cringing at my actions, yet unable to stop myself or do anything but what the beast wanted." He lowered his gaze and voice. "When hurting started, I fought the urges, begged her to run away. She wouldn't listen. Yet, despite all my efforts, the animal won each time. I could only stop when the beast was satisfied, but it pushed on for more blood, more pain."

Bile rose in her throat, she tried to shake off the uneasy feeling. "Yes, I get what you're trying to show me, but I don't think I'd like to see every detail. It's kind of creepy, like when you walk in on your parents."

His irresistible smile appeared. "I haven't had the unfortunate experience so I can't comment. But I suppose you're right." He winked. "We should stop here. Let's eat. You must be hungry by now. I am."

"Me too." She grabbed the plates and set them on the table. "Are the chopsticks in the bag?"

A knock on the door caused her to furrow her brow. Other than a custodian or a sales person, no one came to her door.

"Kate," Miller's voice came muffled from the other side. "Are you in there?"

She stepped to the door. "What do you want, Miller?"

"I wanted to get a head start on studying, but I can't figure something out. Can you open the door? So I don't have to yell through."

With a loud groan, she unlocked and opened the door only as far as the chain would allow.

"I told you to meet me tomorrow in the library."

Miller's eyes widened as Miles stepped behind her. "I see." He grinned, but disappointment replaced his initial expression of surprise. "You got yourself a visitor."

Silence followed. Miller glanced from Kate to Miles and back again. "All right then. I guess you'll help me with this tomorrow."

Miles grabbed the doorknob. "Yes, tomorrow."

"Wow, dude." Miller put his hands up, as if in self-defence. "Have yourself a great time. I'm leaving."

Miles slammed the door in his face before Miller could finish. Kate chuckled and returned to serving dinner. The smells wafting from the Kung Pao chicken had her mouth-watering. According to the logo on the bag, he got the food from an upscale restaurant. Did he cancel a hot date to dine with her in this dinky flat?

"How did you make yourself invisible to Potter?" She dismissed the notion of Miles on a date with some model and crumpled the paper bag.

"Same as I did with you." He placed his hands on her shoulders. His musky scent and husky voice surrounded her. "It's a simple trick of blocking one's mind."

"If it's so simple, can you teach me? I could use invisibility." Her stomach fluttered with his touch.

"No." He pulled her closer. "It can't be learned by mortals."

Her heart danced while his finger traced her jawline. His soft expression and a little smile set her body on fire. All he had to do was to lower his lips to hers. She surrendered to his caress and closed her eyes in anticipation. Instead, he kissed the top of her head and pulled back.

"The table looks good," he said, lowering to his seat.

"Thanks to your generosity. I'm afraid I have nothing to contribute to this fine fare." Kate joined him, her heart still drummed. This was insane. She shouldn't allow herself to fall for his aristocratic air. While her ancestor might have been an easy prey, she on the other hand knew better. "What do you want to do after we eat?"

Muscles on his jaw moved as he chewed slowly. "Your company is all I desire. However, you need to study, so I suppose I'll leave you to it. A deal is a deal." The tone of his voice indicated a hint of regret.

In an instant, her heart sank. She didn't want him to leave so soon. "I'm tutoring Miller tomorrow so I plan to study then." With chopsticks in her hand, she pointed to his Styrofoam cup. "How's your jasmine tea? I can warm it."

"It's just fine." He reached for her hand. "It's nice of you to help him."

"He needs all the help he can get." And she needed the money, but she chased the thought away. She was not greedy but, as a foreign student, her visa restricted her from finding employment and, in this society, one couldn't go far without cash. There, she did it again, justifying her actions to herself. Tutoring Miller wouldn't be stolen dough, but earned.

"If you want," Miles said, chewing, "we can finish the vision, but I'll fast forward over the scene you don't want to see." Another wink and a half smile flashed on his face and set her heart to a whole new race.

"I'd love to." She heard herself answer. So much for her promise to not to succumb to him. It was too late. He'd already gotten into her system. Her body seemed to have a mind of its own and no longer answered her commands. "Let me clear the table first."

She watched him, as his eyes roamed around her place and stopped at her daybed. He couldn't be serious. Just who did he take her for? By no means, would she let him use her for some frantic tumble as he had done to her great-great-grandma.

# Chapter 6

Miles's brow arched while he eyed the small bed tucked against the bedroom wall. His gaze turned to Kate then back to the bed. A nervous chuckle rolled out of her mouth. Damn it, why couldn't she hear his thoughts? Did she need to? The glint in his eyes spoke volumes. He wanted her. Truth be told, she wanted him too. The hurt of being used and discarded by the no-good two-timing prick was still too fresh. She must be strong and not let her desires take over her mind.

With a warm smile, he returned his gaze to her. "Mind if we sit on the floor? Don't take offense, but this plastic chair is getting uncomfortable."

He wiggled, causing the seat to rock, the legs clucked on the vinyl flooring of the kitchen.

"Oh." She chuckled in relief. His explanation was a reasonable one. "The floor must be uneven where you're sitting. I tried switching chairs and no matter which one I put there, they always wobble. I guess we can throw a few pillows down in front of the sofa."

Seated facing him, she shifted trying to get into a comfortable position. With his back leaning against the old recliner, he pulled her to him. "Sit in my lap."

She stiffened. Had she heard him right? "I'm fine here."

"I can see, you are not. Come." When she hesitated, he cocked his head. "Look, there is no need to fear me."

Her resistance loosened and she sat with her back resting on his powerful torso, while his arms closed around her. Pleasant vibes—the kind she had not felt in over a year—rushed to her core. Must be the way the cushion bunched up under her bum. Right, she could believe that little lie. The truth was, Miles's embrace caused her to react this way and she liked it. Suddenly the room turned too warm for her liking. There wasn't a need to fear him. Yet, she did.

He presented a whole different threat, the kind that made her open to temptation.

To hell with her upbringing. Why couldn't she have a causal relationship with a man? The societal pressure to wed the first man the girl dated was overrated. How else would they know if the guy was the one for them? No wonder many of her peers divorced a year or so after the wedding. Fear of social stigma and their parents' reprimand had forced couples to tie knots soon after they'd met, never giving the relationships half the time it needed to develop before rushing to the altar. Come to think of it, she was the only one in her classroom who continued her education.

Cold shivers raked her. She almost ended like many girls after graduating high school. Good thing her ex had never popped the big question. Back then, she would have jumped at the opportunity then, a year later, found herself divorced, most likely with a kid, and blamed for the failure of her marriage. For it was always the woman's fault.

"Comfy?" Miles whispered in her ear.

"Too comfy." She shifted, straightening her spine.

She paid attention to the elastic band holding her hair. Leaning against his chest, as amazing as it made her feel, was tempting.

"Last chance, do you want me to continue where we left off?" He pulled her back to him once her hands lowered to her lap. Well, she couldn't keep fixing her hair the whole time and sitting erect like that would cause her sore back.

She shook her head. The thought of him and her great-great-grandmother making love didn't sit well with her. And it could lead to something she'd regret later.

"All right." He pressed his chin on top of her head. "Let's see. Are your eyes closed? And no peeking."

"Um-hm." Could it be the warmth of his body, the food or his embrace, that caused her to melt into him? She no longer distinguished where the reality ended and the vision began.

෴

Miles had woken up with the first light and gently lowered Kate's head from his shoulder to sheep pelts beneath them. He felt invigorated. The demon inside had not stirred. Through the night, he had found intense pleasure in her. The beast had not used his mind and body to hurt her, or worse. Kate had treated him like the mother he never had. She had cured him of his illness, if only for a short while. It had to be her gentle nature, her slim build, and eagerness to please him that awakened the demonic urges. Damn it, if she would only run away when he'd started to manhandle her. Once his mind clouded, all he could do was obey the beast.

Her cries only provoked it to hit her harder, sink his teeth in her soft skin deeper. At the end of each beating, he'd thrust inside her like an animal in rutting season.

No, animals had more compassion. He was far worse.

Not long ago, he'd been disgusted over the wife beater his father had sentenced to rot in dungeons beneath the castle and his downtrodden spouse who had begged him not to send her husband there with the rats. Her man was not to blame, but the innkeeper and his crooked ways for getting the patrons inebriated.

Miles raked his gaze over the fading bruises of Kate's neck, shoulders, and arms. She too had tried to deny it was him who left his marks on her skin and blamed it on her tripping feet. He hated the vivid memory of his ill treatments of her, but it was her saving grace. If he wasn't aware of his actions, the guilt wouldn't eat him up like this. Although last night, he'd loved her sweet and gently, there would be a next time and the brute in him might succeed in commuting a torturous killing. She must go, she didn't deserve to be used and murdered. He'd see to fit her with a good man. And he knew the right one, but he must make haste if he was to catch his ship.

After scrambling into his trousers, he yanked his shirt from the clothesline above the smouldering fire. The sea salt hardened his clothes, making them rough against his skin, and they smelled of stale smoke. He tried to ignore the discomfort. He ducked and squeezed through the narrow doorway into the cold morning air. At least the weather changed overnight and weak sunshine appeared over the treetops.

He walked until he reached the top of the hill, which allowed him a perfect view of the small harbor. Leaning on the high wall of stacked stones held together by packed dirt, he rubbed his battered soles.

Master Rokov's tall masts with the sails neatly furled stood out among docked ships. Thanks to the storm, he hadn't sailed out with the first light. Miles's heart ached.

Though this was for the best, how would he carry on without his Kate?

෴

"I guess we'll leave it here." He pulled Kate to her feet with him. "It's getting late and you have to study."

Inhaling deeply, she opened her eyes and blinked as if she'd just woken from some sweet dream. A hint of anger mixed with her disappointment. "Ah, why stop now? I felt deep sadness in you at the sight of the tall ship docked in the small harbor. You married her off to this Master Rokov, but you didn't want to give her up. Am I right? That is where my last name comes from."

His piercing stare caused her to lower her gaze. "Save some fun for another day." With soft fingers, he cupped her chin and forced her to look at him. "Will tomorrow after your classes be too soon?"

She closed her eyes, surrendering to his feathery touch while butterflies stirred in her stomach. "Not soon enough."

Her husky whisper betrayed her attempt to stay composed. "This beast inside you, does it stir again? When you leave me so abruptly, I feel like you're doing it for my protection."

His stare deepened and he closed his eyes then gave a slight nod. "So far I'm able to control it, but promise me one thing. If I ever urge you to run away from me, you'll do it."

She exhaled a shaky breath. "Oh, God, Miles. I hope it'll never come to that. Where would I go? Or hide? When you turn into the beast or when the entity takes over, do your senses heighten?"

"Yes, they do. I can hear tiniest sounds and smell fear in my prey. My vision changes, I see in darkness. I hope you never discover any of my beastly ability. It's inhumane. That's why you must promise me. I cannot be in your company if you don't know what I'm capable of. If I don't visit for a while, it's because of the beast. I must conquer it before I put you in danger."

"I understand." She swallowed. "It'll be hard without you here, but I can bear it. How will you placate this beast?" Not with another unsuccessful suicide, she almost blurted, but thought better of it.

"I doubt the entity has the same grip on me as it did centuries ago, still I must be certain. There are no drugs or treatments for this, only love can cure me." He cast her a shy smile.

She loved him, but couldn't admit it to him. Maybe this speech was his way of getting into her pants, but so be it. Still, she couldn't bring herself to make the first move and plant a kiss on his lips. If his beast fully emerged, she'd try to help him overcome its urges. From a safe distance, and with a Taser in her hand.

She tapped her finger on her chin as realization dawned. "You could've stayed away from my great-great grandma and not hurt her like you did."

He lowered his gaze at his feet. Was he ashamed of his actions or her remark? "This is how I know the beast has no power over me. Each time I denied its urges, I somehow found Kate. That's how it started. Just an inno-cent chasing, cornering her, then I'd watch my hands squeezing her breast hard. She laughed at first, but when I carried it overboard, she'd cry out and pulled back. I'd grab her again and pinch her harder, next thing, I'd press my body on hers and my hands ripped the bodice of her dress."

"Her mother or your father never suspected what was going on between you two?" Kate crossed her arms over her chest. Should she pity him or blame him? His story about the beast seemed farfetched, a fabrication to excuse him for ill-treatment of her great-great grandma. Yet, deep down she sensed it was the truth.

The man standing before her wouldn't hurt anyone on his own accord.

"No, my father only cared that I stayed away from the Vitturi Castle and Kate was darn good at hiding her bruises and mending her clothes I tore from her body."

"Suddenly I have a whole new respect for her. Maybe that is what she's looking for, someone to understand what she's been through. Then her curse will be broken."

"Seems plausible. Now I should leave you to your studies." He raised his hand at her wide eyes and sharp gasp. "Don't fret. It's not because of the beast. I too have obligations. Thank you for the wonderful evening." Leaning toward her and wrapping his arms around her, he planted a kiss on her forehead.

Sad to see him go, she nodded as he pulled back. Did he hear the mad drumming of her heart? Or her crazy thoughts? "Good to know you're not being possessed at the moment."

He paused by the opened door and harrumphed. "Taser might work."

What? How could he know what she was thinking? She was beyond stunned.

"Don't forget the door." With a single nod, he stepped out and she locked up after him. He'd be back tomorrow. The power of wanting him near grew in her. Once again, she longed to be in his embrace. Did he know how much his company made her happy? Tomorrow she'd wake silent and resigned, and for the rest of the day she'd try hard to concentrate on anything other than him.

തരെ

Matthias clutched the steering wheel in his hands. With his head on the headrest, he listened to the fast clicking under the hood of his Lexus. The only light reaching inside the three-car garage was faint lamp on the side of the driveway.

For the past hour, he'd listened to the drone of the engine. He could've reflected on his life during his drive from Kate's place downtown Toronto to his home in the rural county. Yet he found the quiet garage the most soothing.

So far his plan had worked. He'd get the true story out and she'd record his words. Then he'd leave her as promised, but the memories he buried long ago had awakened something else inside him. A longing he wasn't aware he harbored.

Had he truly made love to Kate's great-great-grandmother inside the storm shelter? It seemed so. It was one and only time he had not acted on the urges from the beast. His mind was clear on that night. In the past, whenever the damn question surfaced, he'd dismissed the puzzlement. He'd had Emina then to make his life sweet and innocent and his personal demon purred with happiness until one day the entity ceased to exist. Or so he had thought.

'*You love me, master. I know you do.*' Kate's words from that night emerged in his mind. The words he had felt, but had been too afraid to hear.

'*Don't be daft. I cannot love a serf woman.*'

This was all a distant memory. What good would remembering those moments do? Denial and refusal to love a woman of common birth had made a fool of him. Things were different three centuries ago. No aristocrat had married a servant in his employ, but that hadn't stopped them from taking them to their beds.

He shook the flashback away, stepped out of the car,

and headed into the house. The house stood eerily quiet while the heavy furniture loomed in the darkness. After removing his coat and boots, he headed up the stairs. Stopping in front the double panes of his chamber, he turned his head at the faint blue luminous energy under the nursery's door. It couldn't be the babies' night light. The glow moved.

He stepped in front of the door to his left and halted with his hand on the knob. If he entered their room at this late hour, would they wake? How would he know? Since their birth, he could barely bring himself to look at them, let alone get to know them.

The boys had been discharged from the hospital only two weeks ago. It could be the children's nurse checking on them.

The luminescence intensified. The urge to investigate grew within him. Careful not to make any sound, he turned the knob and pushed the door open.

The three white cribs appeared blue, washed in the silver moonlight coming in from a large arched window.

A lullaby played, filling the room with soft tones. Matthias stepped to the babies' beds. Three boys born by medical miracles slept peacefully. The two little heads with puffs of black hair poked beneath their blankets.

The third boy, whose golden blond strands indicated he'd resemble his mother, sucked on his thumb eagerly.

Would he ever look at them without resentment? It wasn't their fault their mother died giving birth to them, yet the bitter truth hung heavy like a velvet curtain.

Cold air brushed Matthias's nape. '*You are here, at last, my love,*' a soft female voice asked in his head.

Tightness constricted his chest and his throat closed. His knuckles turned white as he clutched the crib's railing. All he could manage to whisper was, "Emina, my dove."

'*I'm here in spirit only. My body still lies where you left it.*'

Sharp pain stabbed his heart at the thought of his wife's body all alone in the dark soil on an island in the Adriatic Sea—a spot she'd adored. The surprise of finding Emina's spirit earthbound quickly left him. Though he had felt her presence in the hospital, she hadn't made her latency known, due to staff bustling around the neonatal unit. She had wanted to give him children and so she had, leaving him to carry on alone. No wonder her soul refused to cross until her loved ones were safe in doting arms.

'*This isn't how it's really meant to be,*' he replied in the same telepathic way they'd often shared while she was alive. '*You were supposed to be with us.*'

'*I am still here. I would not leave you. Not until you became the father I always wanted you to be.*'

What would he know of fatherhood? Nothing. His only role model, his father, had been distant, but that didn't excuse him from the job. No right reply to her plea came to his racing mind. It was too soon to bring Kate into his family. He must sort through his chaos first.

'*Don't blame our children. They are not the cause of my death.*'

His shoulders slumped. He relaxed his hold on the railing. Eleven months after Emina's death and his sons' birth, his grief hadn't abated. It never would.

The way her body, only moments ago so full of life, laid upon the surgical table, white and lifeless, haunted his dreams.

'*I don't blame them, but it is hard to look at them and not relive your last moments.*'

'*They need a mother and you promised to find love and happiness again. Don't disappoint me.*'

Guilt washed over him. She had extracted the promise from him, but he had no intention of keeping it. '*I can't replace you with another. Don't ask me to.*'

'*Kate will love you as I do, and she will love our children.*'

'*No, my dove. It's too much to ask of her. She must finish her schooling, go into the world, learn life's lessons. I cannot. It wouldn't be fair to burden her with my baggage and our children, and you must go into the light. You lingering in the world of living can't be good for you, or me.*'

'*I will not cross until I am sure of your happiness.*'

Emina's voice ceased and the blue light vanished.

"Master."

Matthias snapped his head toward the opened nursery door, housemaid stood on the threshold. Over a decade ago he'd given up insisting she called him Matthias. "Yes, Rosalia."

The stout woman tightened the belt of her housecoat and stepped forward. "They are angels, aren't they?"

"Yes, they are." Matthias straightened. "I hope I didn't wake you."

"No, master. I waited up for you." She crossed her wrists over her round midriff. "I meant to discuss a matter with you, but it's hard to catch you."

*Uh-oh.* From Rosalia's tone, he was up for another of her rants on how no good would come out of ignoring his babies. Of course, she had it right. His money could pay for the nurse but would never replace fatherly love.

"I know I haven't been around much lately." While everyone understood he was a busy surgeon, building his clinic, in fact, it was merely an excuse, and it ate at him. "What did you want to discuss?"

She studied him with her round eyes for a short moment. "At least you make a point now to come home at night. Six months ago, I feared you'd abandon your little ones. Now that it is certain the boys will live, perhaps they should be baptized properly, in the church. Mistress Emina prickled her fingers numerous times while learning to hand stich their baptismal outfits."

Matthias smiled. Rosalia kept him on his toes when it came to spiritual wellbeing. "You are right, of course. I trust you will see to it."

Her face lit up with his words and she straightened her back. Never before had she been afraid to ask him of anything, or to voice her displeasure. "Yes, master. I'll call our parish tomorrow. You may want to ask that nice couple up the road if they would stand as godparents."

He nodded with a smile. To call his minions *a nice couple* seemed natural to Rosalia, he found the analogy humorous. Fortuno and Adriana possessed mind-probing powers that would make mortals freeze with fear, but to their defense, they were *a nice couple*.

"You look tired, master. Get some rest." Rosalia's lips thinned. She waved her hand as she left for her room. "I wonder why am I saying this, when you never listen? You do what you want to do."

He closed the nursery door softly and headed to his chamber. Perhaps Rosalia was right. He'd been living on autopilot since Emina's demise and quiescence had not come easily to him. With the pain inside, every day had been a struggle.

He plopped on the big bed and hugged the pillow. Emina's flowery scent faded a little with each passing day, but he couldn't bear having the covering laundered.

How could he set her spirit at ease? What she had asked of him was not an option. But each time he looked at the young Kate, his chest tightened while his heart rejoiced. Could it be her ancestor wanted justice?

# Chapter 7

Kate's fingers were flying over the keyboard when Matthias entered her flat. The ticking of the keys ceased. She raised her head and pulled the lollypop out of her mouth, flashing her whites with her smile.

"Have I arrived too early?" With one hand on the door handle and the other removing his hat, he chased away the desire to rush to her. "Are you working on your school assignment?"

"No." She pulled the top of her computer down. "I was working on your story."

A jolt of joy filled him. The true events of his tale would see the light of the day, even if it was evening.

"Can I see it?"

"Not yet. When it's finished." Kate wrapped her hands protectively on her laptop. "I've got dinner on the go. Hope you like Italian."

"A takeout?" he said, kicking his boots off. "You didn't have to do that."

"I cooked." She cleared the table of papers. "A simple recipe that I'm sure will turn out right. All I need to do is stick a garlic loaf in the oven and drain the pasta." She paused. "I'm getting used to having to set two plates on the table." A hint of expectation laced her tone and flashed in her eyes.

Perhaps she hoped he would change his mind, once his story was done, and break the deal. If that was the case, she'd be disappointed. Hopefully, he wouldn't have to let her down too, but judging by the way her face lit up every time she saw him, her emotions were taking over. *Of course, they would, you idiot. Keep your hands to yourself and stop complimenting her with endearments.* He swallowed his breath before he spoke.

"It is nice to dine in company." He rubbed his palms together. "Can I help?" Though he never set a foot in the kitchen, maybe she'd have something for him to do.

Steam rose from the pot as she poured the water into the sink. "Almost done, but if you want, plates are in that cupboard and the cutlery in the top drawer." She nudged her head, shaking the last few noodles into the colander.

While he set the table, she danced in the small kitchen, stirred the tomato sauce in the pot on the stove, and checked on the garlic bread. He too was getting used to keeping her company. Once his story came to completion, he would keep his side of the bargain. It would be hard to part from her.

The promise to leave her alone was the one he intended to keep. No matter how many times he repeated it, it wasn't getting any easier.

"How did tutoring Miller go today?" he asked to stop the invading thoughts.

"Oh." She cut him a side glance, pulling the golden loaf out of the oven. The smell of garlic filled the air. "Would you believe it, he didn't do any work the whole semester, not even accessed the web? I don't know why that surprises me. All of his time went into playing sick pranks on me, drinking beer in the student hall, and video games. Honestly, I don't see how he'll get his grades up.

He'd need lots of help in all subjects, but it'll give me time to study, once he stops rambling."

Her ponytail shook as she sliced the bread. She paused and turned to him, waving the bread knife in her hand. "But he surprised me and apologized for his pranks. Said hotties like me are always mean to him, so he assumed if he's nasty to them first, they'd back off. Can you imagine? He confused me for a hottie."

"So he can be polite." Matthias smiled, taking his seat. "It's nice of you to help him. Just do your best and the rest is on him. If he truly wants to graduate, he'll warm up the chair and study."

"Being polite doesn't stick with him for long." With the noodles on the plates and bread served, she sat across from him. "He insulted me with the very next sentence calling my friend Andrew a *fruit cake*." She motioned with her hand. "Well, dig in and let me know how you like it."

Matthias stopped twirling spaghetti around his fork. Of course, if someone insulted her friends, Kate would take it as a personal offense. At the same time, she didn't realize what beauty she possessed. Not with the kind of attention she had gotten from her neighbors. He continued spinning the fork between his fingers while she grated a blanket of parmesan over her noodles.

She laughed, passing the block and the grater to him. "Want some?"

"No, thank you." He put up a hand. "To answer your question, I think Miller is right about you, but his remark about your friend and his conduct are not."

Her cheeks reddened. "You think I'm a hottie?"

"You don't?" Why was he asking her this when he knew the answer? Not a drop of makeup on her face and only a pair of faded jeans and a fitted baseball T-shirt for her attire.

Her simple tastes and low maintenance was attraction in itself, yet guys would pass her up for complicated drama queens.

Shrugging, she shook her head. "I never saw myself as one."

No, she wouldn't. She was a simple girl most guys wouldn't give a second glance, but modesty, once a virtue, had gone out the window while vanity stayed. He popped a forkful of pasta into his mouth.

Her eyes widened watching him eat. "How is it? Are the noodles al dente?"

"Um-hm." While nodding, he marvelled in her cooking. "This could measure up with a fine restaurant."

"I know you are not the King of England, but I never cooked for an aristocrat before so I'm glad you like it." She stuck a fork in the pile of pasta on her plate.

He rolled out a low chuckle. Just like her ancestor, she too fretted over small things to please him. Funny, Emina had never tiptoed around him. She'd let him starve for all she cared. What did he expect?

After all, his late wife was yet another highborn like him, used to others serving her. Not a woman who'd take on her wifely duties as far as cooking and cleaning went. "Aristocrats are a thing of a past, my dear."

Not two but three helpings later, he patted his bursting stomach. "Don't tell me there's dessert."

"There is. We'll leave the tiramisu for later." She stood to clear the table, but he grabbed the plates from her hands.

"I'll help with clean up," he said, shoving the dishes in the sink. "After all it's only fair. You cooked."

Her eyebrow arched. She doubted he'd do a good job, but he'd prove her wrong. "Let me do that—"

"No." Pushing on her shoulders, he forced her to sit. "You make yourself comfortable."

With her pursed lips, she cocked her head. "Since you insist."

Water ran over the sink's rim and splashed on the floor and he cursed. She snickered. A side glance confirmed her disapproving head shake.

She got to her feet and grabbed the mop from the broom closet. "Are you sure you don't want me to help?"

Pausing to rinse the soap off his hands, he turned his head to her. Time to man up and admit defeat. "I guess you can dry."

"You dry, I'll wash." Her plastic chair scraped the floor as she mopped the floor under the table. "Let me just do this before the water spreads."

He grabbed the dishtowel hanging from the oven's door. What the hell did he try to accomplish? His clumsiness only caused more work for her. "I'm afraid I'm not much use in the kitchen."

"There," she said, passing him a final plate. "It's the last piece. And you said you are of no use. So, can we continue with the story? I'm dying to find out what happened next."

Wiping the dish, he leaned toward her. "And I can't wait to tell you."

"I'm afraid the chair wouldn't be comfortable. Come here." He grabbed her wrist and nudged her to the floor in front of the bed. He was sure Kate's pride wouldn't let her accept if he got her a few decent pieces of furniture.

Surrounded with pillows, she propped her head on her elbow and extended the other hand to him. "Do we still need the physical contact?"

In an instant, he wrapped his fingers around hers. Goosebumps raced along her skin and she drew in a quivering breath. So much for his promise to keep his hands to himself.

"Squeeze my hand when the vision starts to play."

Brushing his thumb over her knuckles, he closed his eyes and reached into his memory.

എൗൟ

Sailors' shouts had replaced the silence of the early morning. Barefoot in crumpled clothes and his hair dishevelled, he approached Master Rokov's sailing ship anchored at the stone pier. The ship's ladder stood raised.

"Hello, sailor," Miles called to a young man in navy blue trousers and dingy white jacket.

The scornful look the youngster cast him confirmed his suspicion—for an aristocrat, his unkempt appearance was shocking.

"I'm seeking audience with your master." Miles struggled to maintain his authoritative demeanor. The sailor nodded and scurried to the deck. With his arms crossed tightly and hands rubbing his cold skin, Miles attempted to keep the early morning chill away. After several minutes, Master Rokov peeked over the starboard, his beret pulled low on his face.

"Young Conte Miles, what in the name of God happened to you?" Master Rokov turned to the side and barked, "Lower the sea ladder." He motioned with his hand for Miles to climb onboard. "Back to your work," Master Rokov ordered the men who paused scrubbing the deck to stare at Miles.

Miles followed the hunchbacked man. His wide dark coat cleverly hid his hump. He sat behind his white desk, which was adorned with gold trim, and pointed to a seat in front of him.

Miles settled on a firm cushion, but snakes stirred in his stomach.

"So what brings you here this early, young conte?" The man struggled to keep his left eye opened.

Miles tapped his fingers on the armrest and leveled his eyes with Master Rokov. "It is with great difficulty that I come before you, but—"

Master Rokov put his hand up. "Say no more."

Papers on his desk rustled as he stood and walked to the small window. With one arm behind his back, he stared out for a few moments. "I may not have lots of experience in the matters of the heart, but even I can see by your sorry state it is woman trouble that brings you here."

A huge relief flooded Miles. Master Rokov opened the difficult topic. "Yes, you guessed right."

The master turned to him. "Who is she?"

His dry tongue stuck to the roof of Miles's mouth as he tried to swallow. "Servant girl, Kate."

"Hmmm." Master Rokov returned to his seat. "She's a real beauty, that one. I cannot deny, she caught my eye. Oh, what a mistress she'd make, had she not been born a serf."

More relief flooded Miles, his suspicions proved right when he had caught Master Rokov gazing at Kate. "I can free her."

The man in dark coat shot him a stern glance. "Why?"

Damn, Master Rokov suddenly turned the conversation difficult. There was no need to keep beating around the bush.

"Will you wed her?" Miles blurted.

Eyebrows of the man across the desk drew closer. After an immeasurable amount of time his face relaxed. "She's with your bairn?"

"No." Miles shook his head. "I can assure you. All of the children she gives you will be from your loins."

Master Rokov's left eye blinked incessantly. "But she's no longer a virgin, is she?"

A heavy weight pressed on Miles's chest. "No," he

said through his tight throat, but despite his racing mind, he couldn't come up with anything else to say.

Master Rokov fell silent. He drummed his fingers on the desktop. Impatience got the best of Miles and he scanned the pictures of ships on the walls to focus his thoughts.

"God knows—" Master Rokov broke his silence and shifted, shaking his stubby finger. "It is time for me to take a wife. When polio left me disfigured, my future seemed grim. And though I'm no longer a sickly young-ster, I know very well no lady of status would want me unless she's fallen from the grace." He stood and reached out his hand. "Today is your lucky day."

Miles got to his feet, his spirits low. Although he had hoped for this outcome, deep down he wanted her to stay. Slowly, he wrapped his fingers around the extended hand, giving it a firm shake. "You won't regret this. When are you sailing out?"

"Look at the sky tonight and follow the proverb. Red sky at night—sailors' delight."

"Red sky in the morning—sailors' warning." Some-how Miles hoped for the latter, but the sooner Kate left, the sooner he'd get to mourn the loss. Tomorrow she'd be miles away. Crushing pain pressed on his chest.

Master Rokov tapped his arm. "Have the girl here by the first light."

"I will." Miles opened the door to step out. One more night before he sent her away for good, her new life would start, and he—he would stay here and wait for Do-brila. Tomorrow, Kate would discover the future he'd planned out for her. How would she take the news?

"Young Conte Miles?"

He halted with the questioning voice of Master Ro-kov. "Yes?"

Master Rokov clasped his fingers, giving him a suspicious glance. "I believe your father is in agreement with this?"

Miles arched an eyebrow. A minor detail he had overlooked. Kate and her family belonged to his father, but he had a plan how to deceive him. "Of course."

 భాఎ

"Stop right here." Kate's hiss and yank of her hand out of his brought the vision to a halt.

She towered over him when he opened his eyes. Puzzlement replaced his easy feeling as he rose to his feet.

"You disgraced her, used her whenever it pleased you, then you married her off to a cripple. Why?" Two deep creases appeared on her forehead as her eyebrows drew closer.

"Kate," he said, taking a step forward. "Yes, my hands beat her, after my lips kissed her, but I had no power over my body's actions. Violence escalated each time. For weeks, the beast ordered me to kill her in a most savage way, disembowel her. I fought the fiend, but I could feel the drive for blood grow within me. The entity wanted to turn me into a monster. It was the best I could do for her. Master Rokov was a good man. He loved her. Not an aristocrat, but a rich merchant. His family owned lands."

Taking a long step backward, she widened the distance between them. "Oh, he owned lands. That makes all the difference. He was a hunchback."

"A childhood disease disfigured his face and body, but he was born healthy and able bodied." Matthias refused to believe Kate could be so superficial. But he had to admit the sight of Master Rokov wasn't for the faint at heart.

"He was like Quasimodo." Her voice shook.

Her remark filled Matthias with anger. With a swift move, he flattened her back against the wall and caged her in his arms. "Never forget where you came from. The Quasimodo, as you called him, was your great-great-grandfather."

Tears glistened in her fear-filled eyes. "No wond—" She swallowed hard. "It's no wonder Kate's soul is unsettled. Three centuries ago, it all went wrong. She had high hopes, and with you, she believed her life was worth living. I understand her curse now. She must've been crushed when you told her."

Seeing Kate disturbed like this, broke his heart and he mellowed. He had torn her ancestor's hope apart and turned her dream to shame. "Yes, she was. Let's leave that for the next time."

"I fear—" Her eyes traveled around the room, settling on his face. Her sobs stabbed his conscience and he pulled her to him. "She'll come for me and drag me to the abyss where her soul resides."

His hand inched behind her head and the other around her waist. He tightened his embrace. "She won't. I won't let her."

Her body jerked with sobs, but she wrapped her arms around him and pressed her face to his chest. "You can't be with me all the time."

*But I want to.* He placed a kiss on her head. "No I can't." He rocked from side to side. "I too sense that Kate may be up to something, but I have a different feeling. A good one. She's not on a quest to kill you."

She sniffed, stopped crying, and tilted her head toward his face. "You think?"

"I do." He brushed his finger over her lips. So full, soft, and inviting. *Yank her hair, let me hear her cry in pain.* His fist tightened, grabbing her mane as the beast's inhumane voice echoed through his mind. He must be imagining things.

Lowering his head, he caressed her rosy buds with his lips. A tentative kiss confirmed she wanted this as much as he. She tightened her hold and he deepened his kiss. Sucking on her lower lip, he forced her mouth open. Her warm tongue met his in a slow motion at first then her rhythm intensified, rushing blood to his groin. *Bite her, let me taste her blood.* There was that demon's voice again. Why was beast stirring up? He must stop before things heated up.

Pinned against the wall by his torso, she broke the kiss and pulled her head back. "You should go," she whispered. Her hot breath tickled his neck.

Thank God, she was sending him away. He sucked in the unbearable desire to spread her lithe body under him. He must never allow his cravings to turn into actions. The woman in his arms was not the same Kate he'd used centuries ago, and his love for Emina still burned in him, never to be replaced by another. This Kate deserved better than him.

# Chapter 8

The interior of Matthias's car had cooled off some time ago, and the air nipped at his fingertips and earlobes. Lost deep in thoughts, he stared through the glass at the large snowflakes covering the windshield.

For over two weeks he'd stayed away from Kate, the beast had not surfaced. Hopefully, it wouldn't show its ugly presence ever again. Destiny seemed to steer him to her. After three blissful centuries he had spent with Emina, Kate found her way back to him—in the body of her great-great-granddaughter. Could his and her souls be two halves of the one? The twin flames maybe? The theory had some merit, though the article he'd read in the medical journal seemed quick to dismiss it as some bombastic nonsense. What would those talking heads know? All their framed diplomas and credentials could not explain matters of the heart. Time presented no barrier when two souls must find one another to be complete.

No, he must not think of Kate in such a way. He'd be the wrong man for her. She had agreed to write down his story and that was where her role would end. No matter how much it would hurt to let her go, he couldn't stop the unavoidable. His love for Emina still burned strong, and

Kate would only be someone he'd use as a distraction for a short time. It wouldn't be fair to her. She had her whole life ahead of her.

The sooner he told his story, the sooner he would get rid of beast inside him for good, and part with Kate. He already dreaded the day, but he needed time to grieve, to heal from Emina's death. God he missed her. His demon quieted every time he spoke her name.

Matthias stepped out of the car. The fresh snow crunched under his boots on his way to Kate's apartment. Shivers ran down his spine, but not from the cold. Today he would tell her of the last day he'd seen her great-great-grandma. A flight of cement stairs stood between him and her basement flat. He pushed his feet down the familiar steps and paused in front of her door, took a deep breath and turned the knob.

Kate sat on the sofa, her attention at the screen of her small television set, the sound of the pipe organ blared inside the tiny unit.

He waved his hand in front of her unblinking eyes. "Kate?"

Glued to the television commercial of "The Phantom of the Opera," she swatted his hand away. Perhaps it would do them both good to spend an evening out, forget about his biography for one night.

The advertisement ended, and she snapped her glance at him. "Hi, Miles, sorry for slapping your hand, you can talk now."

"Goodness, girl." He didn't mean to scold her, but anyone could've walked in, she wouldn't notice. Good thing those two pranksters one floor above didn't get any dumb ideas to entertain themselves by playing their sick jokes. "You should lock the door. What if Miller or Mason came in?"

"Mason moved out and Miller better not get any ideas or I'll stop tutoring him." She unfurled her long legs clad in yoga pants and reached for the remote on the side table to lower the volume on the TV.

Matthias removed his coat, contemplating a question. Invading her mind and influencing her to write his story had been easier than asking her out on a date. Would she say no? Where did people go for an evening out these days? The last time he'd taken Emina out for a night on the town had been...he couldn't remember. They'd lived their lives separate from ordinary people, and he liked it that way. Why did things have to change?

*Chillax, man, it's not a date.* He simply wanted to take her out. Chillax? He'd reprimanded the two young medical residents for using the slang with the patient, yet the same word popped in his mind now. The ways of new generations were rubbing off on him. One must keep up with the times.

"I've been thinking," he said, stepping toward Kate. "You like The Phantom. Would you like to see it?"

"Oh, I would," she gasped. "What I wouldn't give to see it onstage."

"I'd love to take you. Unfortunately, we're some seven years late to catch the performance in the Pantages Theater in Toronto. I think the curtain lowered on that stage for the last time in October of 1999." He shrugged one shoulder, flashing a lopsided grin. "However, there's this new movie production, I hear it's quite something. Would you like to see it—with me?"

She nodded, a smile lighting her emerald green eyes. "It would be my pleasure."

In the next second her happy expression vanished, sending dread through him. "Something wrong?"

She shook her head and waved her hand as if to dismiss some silly thought. "No, it's nothing. I was just thinking what to wear, but I'll find something."

"Nothing too extravagant, we are just going to see a movie." He pulled the chair out then decided against sitting on the plastic patio seat. Instead, he opted for the floor in front of her rickety sofa.

She sprang to her feet. "Here you take the sofa. I don't mind these chairs."

He took her hand and gave it a tiny squeeze, her dainty fingers wrapping around his. "How about you join me down here?"

"I guess that works too," she said, lowering to the floor. "Are we going to continue where we left off?"

"Yes. Have you eaten? I don't want you to put food off on my account."

"Yes. You?" She was about to stand up. "I can whip up something for you."

He had to chuckle at her enthusiasm. Just like her ancestor who had mothered him. He'd enjoyed her care, knowing it gave her a great pleasure. Besides, no one else could have laundered his shirts the way he demanded. The aristocracy had turned into a bunch of spoiled weaklings. The nobles had become dependent on the working class, and ultimately the ruling class brought on their own destruction.

Who would've thought they had descended from mighty warriors, knights, and kings who led wars, conquered territories and nations? Generations before him had been tutored in swordsmanship, yet never got to hone their skills on the battlefields. Instead, common men bled on the front lines. Hell, the closest he'd come to any battle was a tavern brawl.

"So, can I warm you up a plate of spaghetti?" Kate's voice yanked him back to present.

He tapped the carpeted floor. "I may get hungry later."

"Are you planning to make this session long?" She

kicked off her fuzzy slippers and sat cross-legged in front of him.

"I don't know how long it'll take, but I want to show you every detail. That day was hard for me and Kate. It's not something I'll forget—or forgive myself for."

"I was thinking about my reaction to your decision and I—" She pressed her lips into a thin, tight line. "I owe you an apology. If you hadn't cared about my great-great-grandma, you wouldn't have bothered to secure her future. You did the best you could, and I overreacted. You must think I'm really sappy."

"Not at all. You're taking this entire thing pretty well. I was prepared for your initial shocked reaction." Matthias rubbed her bare arms. Her smooth skin against his palms caused a pleasant shiver to rush to his groin. At the urge to pinch her hard and bruise her flawless skin, he pulled his hands away. He suppressed the thought, shutting the beast down. This was insanity and torture. Her soft smile melted the ice in his chest, but knotted another guilty string. The time would come when he must part from her. She should know he would bring her nothing but heartache. He couldn't go through the same pain of losing her all over again.

"So, shall we continue then? I can't wait to see how the rest of the story plays out." She reached toward him. "I'm sure you must be dying to tell me the rest."

*Not really.* But he couldn't escape this. He wanted his story told, every detail of it. She lowered her lids and her lashes splayed, almost reaching her high cheekbones.

He closed his eyes too and let the memories unfold. Kate's breathing slowed, indicating she was entering his vision.

"Tell me what you are seeing. I need to know we both see the same."

"I see the courtyard of your castle. By the stretched

shadows, I'd say it's late afternoon, there's no one about. Wait! I'm wrong. There's my great-great-grandma entering the storage room through the heavy double door. She's got a demijohn in her hands."

"Correct. She was sent to fill it up with vinegar from the barrel. I followed her in." He reclined against the sofa and lowered Kate's and his hands to his lap.

"That's why I smelled vinegar that day. I wasn't suffering heat stroke." Amazement colored her voice.

"Now let the rest play on its own." He tightened the hold on her hands, pulling her deeper into the vision.

"Okay," she whispered and silence fell upon them.

இஇஇ

Kate hadn't heard him when he closed and bolted the heavy door. She crouched in front of the large barrel and hummed, tilting the demijohn, not wasting a single drop of the sharp-smelling vinegar that poured fast into the wicker-encased bottle.

Matthias approached her with slow steps, stopping behind her. She snapped her head in his direction, but didn't cease filling the bottle.

"Young master, I didn't hear you come in."

"It's all right, Kate." He waved his hand to dismiss her from failing to bow to him and forced a grin, faking enthusiasm. "I bring good tidings."

Her forehead wrinkled. She suspected something already. Her silence unnerved him deeper.

He gulped, drew in a long breath. She'd take the news easier if he put her family before her. "I freed your family—and you."

She corked the bottle and straightened, lines deepened on her forehead. "Why would you do such a thing? Did my father beg this of you? My brother wants to go into the military, and I know they won't allow serfs to join, but—"

He touched his fingers to her fast moving lips, and she fell quiet. "No, no one asked. Doesn't this make you happy?"

She pushed the strands of her sandy hair under the headscarf then shook her head slowly. "I don't believe this just came about. There's a price to pay, always is."

Damn it, he should've known she was smart. "Well, yes there is a price, but it's a nice one."

"What must I do?" Her voice was barely a whisper, her eyes big and round.

He scratched his chin and gave a nervous chuckle. "Marry a wonderful man."

Her mouth hung open. "No," she gasped, dropping the demijohn from her hands. "Something tells me that man is not you."

"Kate, he's a very rich man and he—"

"I don't care about another man. I love you."

He clenched his fist, his nails dug into his palms. "Forget me. It's for your own good. I almost choked you to death two weeks ago. Why did you stop fighting me?"

Deep crease formed between her eyebrows and her lips thinned. She lowered her head at the terracotta floor, chocking a sob. "You're my master. If you wanted to kill me, so be it."

"Look at me, Kate," he demanded. She slowly raised her head half way and stared at him from under her eyebrows. "You'll be a mistress, and you're perfect to lead the household. Master Rokov loves you. I know he'll make you happy."

She snapped to full attention. "Master Rokov? The crippled man?"

"He's disfigured, not crippled." Miles struggled not to let his anger boil to the surface. Kate wasn't superficial. She could see the beauty in people beneath the physical appearance.

"It doesn't matter who you'll marry me off to, he's not you." In a swift movement, she wrapped her arms around him and pressed her head to his chest. "Don't give me away, master. I'll do anything you want."

His gut clenched with her actions and the despair reflected in her voice. Damn it, he'd expected she'd be difficult and he anticipated some of her reactions, but he was not prepared for such deep grief.

"Kate," he seethed, peeling her away from him. His fingers dug into her shoulders, he gave her a shove, but swallowed the anger down and loosened his hold on her. "Listen to me. I can never be yours. I'm using you for my pleasure."

She wiped tears on the wide sleeves of her peasant shirt. "I'll take you any way I can. Just don't send me away. Who'll care for you?"

He released a breath of vexation. Kate would forgo the freedom of her family and settle for a few crumbs of his brutal attention if and when the beast inside him demanded.

She must be far away from him before the demon possessed his body again and forced him to hurt her—or worse, kill her.

"Please don't make this harder than it already is. I caught my father eying you. It's only a matter of time before he forces himself on you. This is your way out."

Kate nodded, wiping away a never-ending stream of tears. "His lustful glances did not escape me. Gave me cold shivers. So did the stories I heard."

"You must leave. Now, go home and pack. You father is to deliver you to Master Rokov's ship by first light." His throat closed in and he barely uttered the last few words.

She wrung her fingers. "What will my parents think of this?"

"They are happy for you. Your brother can now have his military career."

She spun away from him and sniffed. "Will you visit me?"

"No." He leaned against the large barrel. "It's best we sever all connections."

Sobs choked her voice, her shoulders jerked with her spasmodic breaths. "I can't bear to part from you."

It was killing him too, not that he would show or admit it, but this was the only way. He took hold of her shoulders and forced her to face him. "I'm still your master until you're delivered to your future husband. Promise me that you'll let Master Rokov love you, and that you'll be his dutiful wife in every sense. This is my last order."

She pressed her lips tight, making them turn white, and stifled another sob.

"Promise me, Kate." He put emphasis on her name, hoping he'd sound authoritative, but she remained silent. "Kate, I need to hear it from you."

"I promise," she whispered.

"Say it like you mean it."

She angled her head up and locked her gaze with his. "I promise."

"Better." He wanted to pull her to him, embrace her one last time, tell her what she meant to him, but it would make things worse for both of them. So he flashed a half smile and nodded. "Now go. You must be ready before dawn."

Disbelief still lingered in her red and puffy eyes when she slowly stepped away from him. Her unblinking stare pierced his very soul, but he couldn't give in. Thankfully, she scooped the demijohn off the floor, and rushed out the door.

The rough wall of the wine cellar scraped his knuckles at the contact with his fist. Not caring for his already bloodied hand, he threw another punch and another until pain ripped through his arm. He grabbed onto the rusty bars of the high window and stretched his neck to see out the dinghy glass pane above the door, he stared after Kate. Her thick braid bounced on her back with her hurried steps, and then she rounded the corner and disappeared. He drew in a long breath and let it out slowly. The tightness in his chest remained. The fact he was giving her to a good man who'd love and provide for her didn't ease his anguish. She'd be another man's wife and this would be the last time he got to see her.

ဇၢဇ

The connection between them ended, vision ceased. Silence loomed over them and Kate's grip loosened, her hands slipped out of his. Her sob broke the quiet and made him open his eyes. One lonely tear escaped and raced down her face. His heart ached as he relived the hurt he inflicted on her great-great-grandmother over three centuries ago. He scooped her in his arms.

"It hurts to breathe," she wheezed, clutching her chest.

"Take full breaths, fill your lungs, and slowly exhale." He ran his hand on her back until her breathing resumed its steady rhythm. "These are not your emotions. You're reliving hers through me."

"I felt her sorrow and betrayal." Kate's melodious voice returned. "She didn't see the deal you struck with Master Rokov the same way as you."

"No, she didn't," he murmured, pressing his chin on top of Kate's head.

Had he been that daft to think his Kate would be

happy about the so-called freedom he bestowed on her and her family?

She must've agreed mostly to please him, and her folks, and to escape his father. The man would've no doubt force himself on her at the first opportunity.

"How did you convince your father to free them?" Kate's tears ceased, but the redness in her eyes and puffiness around them remained.

"There was no convincing him. I fooled him." Matthias stretched out his legs. "His scribe was efficient and kept a scroll or two ready. Sort of like a template. One was for freeing serfs. All I had to do was get him to sign, and put his seal on it. Obtaining his signature was easy. I slipped the scroll under my diploma he'd been pestering me to see. The university required his signature and seal on a letter that came with my credentials. When he pressed the hot wax of his seal on it, it transferred to the scroll." Mathias couldn't stop a chuckle. "He never did find out that the diploma was counterfeit."

Kate sat up straight. "Really? Your diploma was fake?"

"My father thought I was studying commerce as he wanted. Once I arrived in Venice, I changed the program and enrolled in medicine. He would have had a fit if he'd found out. Fortunately, there were artists who could produce remarkable replicas of any diplomas, for a good price, but it was worth it."

"Oh, so you were a defiant one," Kate said, reaching for the tissue on the table. "Why did you choose medicine?"

"To keep the beast's urge for blood in control and at the same time to help heal and ease human suffering."

He gauged Kate's reaction. Admitting the drive for blood, even if he hadn't consumed it, could scare her from hearing more of his story.

She played with her hair, deep creases on her forehead. "What happened to her family?"

"Nothing much changed for them. They stayed and worked the patch of land their simple house was on, only now they owned it. Her brother's military career was short lived. He was killed during his first battle. I don't know if his sister ever found out."

Kate wiped her nose then shook her head. "How unfortunate. I don't think she could handle more sorrow if she knew."

He squeezed her shoulder and sighed. "You may be right."

She reclined against the couch. He would prefer she leaned against him, but on the other hand, it was better she kept her distance. The beast seemed to stir with her closeness.

"Would your dad really have forced himself on her?"

"Hmm," he said on a half chuckle. "As I said, the man would be in prison had he lived in today's world. Back then, he exercised his rights. I don't want to talk about him, though. There's a little bit more of my memory. Would you care to see it?"

"Will it be as sad as this last one?" Her face crumpled as if she was about to start crying again. "It's like watching a tear jerker movie. I don't think I cried this much since I watched 'Gone with the Wind'."

"The rest is not sad. Actually, you should find this one fascinating."

"Since you put it that way, how can I refuse?"

He reached for her hands, his heart rejoicing. She would love this part. "Great. Close your eyes then."

For a few moments, all he heard was Kate's steady breathing.

Then she spoke. "I see it. I'm back in the courtyard of your castle, only this time, all I smell are roses.

There's the bush against the stone wall. They are beautiful, red in full bloom."

"They were my mother's favorite. What else do you see?"

"Stone steps leading to the heavy double door you stepped through in the earlier vision."

"Yes, the wine cellar." She was in the same vision as he, now was the time to show her the rest.

He had pulled the door open and there she sat, on top of the steps. Hadn't he told her to go home and pack? Wait, something was different about her. She was younger, a child almost. Her hair was tied in a high ponytail, her clothes—God almighty! She was naked, save for a few scraps. Could her breeches get any shorter? The threads hung loose from the frail hem, as if she put shears to her leggings. Her long, tanned legs were bare for all to see. Her shirt, if one could call it such, sleeveless, backless even, held by two thin straps tied around her neck, depicted a pony. Whoever put animals on their attire and with glittering mane of all things?

"Oh my God!" Kate screeched, but didn't pull her hands out of his. "I remember this encounter. That's me."

"That is you. The last time I saw your great-great-grandmother was the first time I saw you."

"Wicked." Her voice showed her fascination. "It's some kind of an omen."

"Something or someone tried to tell me something," he said. Maybe they were destined for one another, and nothing he did would keep them apart.

"Now I know why you scrutinized me as if I came from some other world. In your eyes, I did. To me, you didn't appear out of place. I thought you pulled your clothes from your grandpa's chest for the local festivity. I figured the weakness that poured over me as a sign of heat or sunstroke."

"How do you explain the rose I gave you?" He snickered at her last comment, remembering the old clothes stored together with mothballs in squeaky chests with rusted hinges and used on occasions, such as festivity, to resurrect the old traditions and attract visitors.

Her long gaze and soft smile settled on him. If she was trying to play cool and not show how much she wanted him, her pretending failed. "My memory has faded a little since then, but I clearly remember you picking the flower and offering it to me. My mom is adamant that I picked it myself. She said it was as good thing the custodian didn't catch me."

His heart sank at the mention of the home he grew up in. It had been decades since he'd last touched its stone walls. The once mighty castle, closed for the family affairs, was now open for everyone to roam about for the price of the admission. At least the money generated was used to preserve the building and grounds, and employed a few people.

"So that's it. You sent my great-great grandma on her merry way, you were free to pour your efforts in getting together with Dobrila, and the rest, as they say, is history." Though her tone didn't match her expression, her words stung his core. It sure sounded wrong now that she put it in that perspective.

"Come on, Kate. You know how the rest of the story played out."

"The times were different and you did the best you could, and I'm glad to have the opportunity to thank you in person." Her eyebrows twitched. "From what I could gather, Kate was unhappy, but secure, and she gave her husband four sons."

"You don't need to thank me for securing her future. Thank you for filling me in on her. I often wondered if she kept her promise." Though he was glad his Kate obeyed him to the end, a tinge of jealousy stung him. Another man had lived to have children with her. At least it was a good man who otherwise would not have his family.

Clinking of plates brought him back to Kate. She was dishing out food. "You sure you don't want anything to eat?"

"No, thanks though. I should leave you to get your studying and rest. What day is the best for you to see the movie?"

She played with her hair. A sure sign something about his invitation made her nervous. "Let's go this weekend."

He rose to his feet and stepped to the coat closet. Should he ask her what was making her unsure about going out with him? No, she might change her mind, better to just reassure her. "You'll see, getting out for one night will do us both good. Take a break from the story."

"Yes." She sighed. "I have a feeling the story will shift from here."

"It will. With your great-great-grandma gone and Dobrila returned from Vienna, things were different." He scrambled into his coat. "Leave it for some other night."

The longing in her eyes begged him to stay and spend the night with her. For a split second, he considered the possibility. The demonic growl filled his head and shattered the fantasy. *'Make her squirm under you, beg you to stop, cry you're hurting her—'*

*'Shut up, beast! Go away.'*

Kate's loud yet steady breaths pulled him out of fiend's control. The voice ceased and his shoulders relaxed.

Everything he'd worked so hard for would go terribly wrong if he succumbed to his desire for her. She was a friend, and he couldn't hurt her in any way.

A peck on her cheek and a quick hug would have to do.

"Sweet dreams," he whispered and stepped out of her basement apartment.

# Chapter 9

The locker door provided a perfect divider between Kate and Andrew. Rugged edges cut into her gripping fingers. She let go of the cold metal pane. How long before he noticed her jittery state? Just as Miles predicted, the rumors about her and coach what's-his-name had ceased, but a whole new vexation brewed in her. She had no one to blame but herself.

Why had she agreed so eagerly to go see a movie with Miles? He must think of her as some lonely, pathetic girl, waiting for someone to ask her out. There was still time to cancel the whole thing. And then what, sit alone at home and watch some mindless TV program? At least that was familiar, comfortable, and safe. Oh God, she was desolate and sad.

A small group of Asian girls giggled on their way to the classroom, talking rapidly in their language. No wonder she felt left out. All other students belonged to some clique.

She rummaged through her school bag, looking for a textbook for her first class. The contents of her backpack spilled on the floor.

"Crap." She shoved the bag inside her locker and

crouched to scoop her pencils before the hallway got too crowded.

Andrew closed his locker and bent to help her gather her stuff. "What got you all in knot this morning?"

She drew in a slow, long calming breath. "It's—nothing."

"Got to be something." He extended his hand to her, her lucky pen between his fingers.

"Thanks." She reached for the multi-colored pen, but he pulled his hand back.

"Not so fast. Speak up or I keep this." He teased her by jiggling the pen in front of her nose. His mocking grin annoyed her further.

She swayed her hand in an attempt to grab her favorite writing item from him, but he was faster.

"Uh-uh. No you don't." He pocketed the pen. "What's bugging you?"

"Fine, I can live without the stupid pen." She hugged her books and turned away from him.

"Oh, yeah? We'll see about that when you get your first B."

His words stopped her mid-step. Damn it, he was right. Ever since she found that pen, she had kept straight A's—okay one, maybe three B+'s—and taking notes during the class seemed easier with it. Oh what the hell, she could share her annoyance.

"Well, I agreed to go out to see a movie over the weekend." The words left her tongue so fast she barely registered what she said out loud.

Andrew frowned, then shook his head, the so-what written on his face. "There's got to be more to that."

"A friend of mine invited me. He said it's only a movie, but I still want to look nice..." She cleared her throat. Confessing made it real, maybe that explained her reluctance to talk about it. "For him."

"He?" Andrew gasped. "Is it a date?"

"Not technically, I wouldn't call it a date." She shook her head, staring at him for any signs of disbelief.

"Really?" He changed his dubious look to a grin. "Say no more. You're in luck."

An uneasy feeling forced her to flash a tight-lipped smile. "What do you mean?"

He opened his arms wide as if to hug her. "I thought you'd never ask."

"What am I asking?" She slapped her hand on her thigh.

Andrew returned her pen and held her elbow, directing her down the hallway to their classroom. "What you need for your 'technically not a date' is a makeover, and I'll get you an appointment at the Tresses salon."

"The one where it's virtually impossible to get an appointment for months?" *Could he actually get me in there? But I couldn't, it would be way over my budget.* If he had a connection to get her in, it would be embarrassing to decline. She'd have to, no matter how badly she wanted to have this done.

"The very same. I'll call my friend Raul, and he'll take great care of you." He pulled the cell out of his pocket and scrolled through his contacts. "Since you'll need 'the works' I better make sure he clears his schedule."

"Pfft." She jabbed her elbow in his ribs. He'd see who would need *the works*. "Don't think I'm ungrateful. I really am grateful, and I'd love to have 'the works,' but I can't afford it. I can't even afford a new pair of socks, so no need to call your friend."

"Don't you worry about that now, I'll handle it. And as for a new outfit, we'll go shopping. I'll find you something sexy." He pulled her in a tight hug. "This is going to be so fun. I've been dying to doll you all up. That *friend* of yours will be knocking down your door for a second date."

"I told you already, it's not a real date, and you shouldn't go through all that trouble." Though Andrew's enthusiasm was catching, she wasn't at all sure she wanted to be his pet project and let him "doll her up" as he put it.

"No trouble at all and you're not backing out of this." He put one finger up and cocked an eyebrow. "I know what you're thinking, but you're going through this, even if you cancel your date."

"It's not a date," she hissed, to prevent from shouting. Experience told her she could keep saying that, but in Andrew's mind she was going out on a date, and it was pointless to deny.

"Ah, you'll see a whole new you." He scooped her tresses on the top of her head. "There's a pretty face behind that curtain of hair. A touch of make-up, a nice outfit, and voila, you'll have a brand new look."

She heaved a sigh. Well, she may as well go for it. What did she have to lose, other than to feel awkward and out of place so Miles would never ask her out again. "Okay." She pointed a warning finger. "Just this once, and if you go overboard with the makeup, I'm washing it all off."

Her hair slid back to her shoulders as he offered his hand.

"Deal." Andrew already had his phone plastered to his ear. He lowered his cell and nodded at her. "How's nine o'clock sound?"

Nine seemed a bit early to get all done up for an evening outing. Would her hairdo hold up? If it went flat by the time Miles arrived at least she'd have an excuse for combing out the style and doing it the way she always wore her hair. "Nine would be perfect."

He returned the phone to his ear. "We'll be there."

She waited for him to end the call. "You don't trust me, do you? You don't need to be there. I know how to find the salon."

"I want to be there," he said, taking the seat next to her. "But you're right, I don't trust you. Knowing you, you'll change your mind come morning."

"No, I won't," she whispered when the professor entered the classroom. Her lucky pen clicked at the press of her thumb, and she made a note to set her alarm for the weekend beautifying torture. Why the heck not? It would be fun.

'*Fun?*' Her dad's growl and scowl surfaced. School was to study hard and graduate in time, not to have fun or waste her money frivolously. God, the man never had a moment of fun in his life.

ℰ∽ℰ∽

Kate took two long steps backward, and banged at the open bathroom door. From this distance her face appeared normal in the mirror. Only her lips glittered in the light. Still, this was too much paint. Her eyelids stuck together every time she blinked. Specks of shiny spray shimmered in her twisted bun. This new and improved appearance reminded her of those cupcakes topped with whipped cream and sparkles. Miles liked her natural look. Why go out of her way to impress him? She just might regret this.

"Oh the hell with it." She squared her shoulders, grabbed the tissue and wrapped the soft paper around her index finger, then moved to the mirror. So much for psyching herself up before Miles arrived.

Raul had warned her eye makeup wouldn't come off with a tissue, still she leaned over the sink to wipe off the mascara. The doorbell blasted through the apartment. Her knee hit the cabinet door when she jumped.

Shoot, Miles arrived early. She rubbed her knee and tossed the crumpled tissue in the trash bin. It was too late to salvage her face now. At the front door she clutched the knob, took in a deep breath and prayed he would like her new look.

The doorbell rang again, two short rings this time.

She peeped through the hole to make sure it was Miles and not Miller asking for help with a math question. The overhead light reflected on Miles's jet-black hair. Her heart fluttered, and her stomach flipped. What would he think? Only one way to find out.

She pulled the door open and held her breath. He froze—his finger about to press the doorbell again. His gaze raked from her face to her toes. Her cheeks heated. Just what she needed—more blush. He didn't like it, his silence and rigid posture indicated as much.

She wrinkled her nose. "Tacky, I know. I was about to wipe this glitter off when you rang the bell. Give me a second to finish the job."

He grabbed her wrist. "No, don't." His voice emerged husky. He must have noticed, as he cleared his throat. "Sorry for my initial shock. When you said you were going to get your hair done, I…well…you know."

"No, I don't know." She shrugged. What was he trying to say? And more importantly, who was he seeing, her or her great-great-grandma?

"Forgive me, I haven't seen you with your hair up before and for a moment there I thought you were—" He shook his head. "I couldn't believe my eyes."

Um-hum, she had guessed right. At the same time, her insides twisted. After three centuries, he was still searching for the old life. Perhaps he was lonely, looking for familiar ground. Immortality was nothing to be desired. Standing by as all family and friends died, times changed, yet he kept going. How easy would it be to adapt?

She cast the thought away. Tonight was meant for the two of them to enjoy time together and, for a moment, forget about the past.

"In that case, I shall keep it." She spun around. Her flared skirt swirled with her movement. "What do you think of my outfit?"

An honest smile lit his face then his gaze lingered on her hips. "It becomes you. It's the first time I've seen you in a skirt."

It was the first time he'd seen her wearing anything other than faded jeans, track pants, or a hoodie. His black suit was a bit out of character. She had gotten used to seeing him in designer jeans and shirts. He was taking her to the movies. Had he changed his mind and decided to take her to a black tie cocktail party?

"I can't take all the credit for it. My friend and his boyfriend took me on a shopping spree," she said as she twirled once more. "You should've seen the scraps of fabric they call evening dresses." The thought of wearing only a patch of material out on the town made her burst with laughter. "Not only would there be not much left to imagination, but I'd freeze to death if I wore it."

Miles's deep laughter filled the small apartment. "I agree with the freezing part. Still, I'd love to see you wearing such a dress. I'm glad you listened to your friend if, only partly."

God, not him too. She'd heard from her personal shopping aids all about how conservative she was. "It's not a practical outfit. Where would I wear something like that?" She stepped to her closet and pulled the door open. "Anyhow, I'm glad I listened to Andrew. He made a joke, about almost wishing he was straight so he'd ask me out. Then Raul asked him on a date. You should've seen Andrew's face. He was stunned. They make such a cute couple."

"There, you see? You make good things happen." Like a real gentleman, he took the coat from her hands and held it open for her arms to slide through the sleeves.

She zipped the coat, but had no comment. If she made good things happen, how come nothing good had happened to her? How forgetful of her, of course. What would she call today's pampering and great lunch with two of her friends? Yes, Raul was a new friend. She'd connected with him in an instant.

"I made a reservation at a posh little restaurant. Are you up for a light dinner after the movie?" Miles asked, stepping out of the apartment.

"It'll be my pleasure." She locked the door and climbed the basement narrow flight of stairs behind him. Butterflies stirred in her stomach with anticipation. At least their evening wouldn't end with the movie. He had thought of her, he must've, or he wouldn't have made the reservation.

"Kate! Wait!" Math textbook in his hand, Miller ran down the stairs, skipped two last steps and jumped in front of her. His eyes widened as he emitted a low whistle. "Wow! You look amazing."

He scowled at Miles, his glance darting between her and her date. "Is this a bad time to ask you something?"

She plastered on a fake grin. "Unfortunately, yes. Feel free to email me or leave it for our Monday tutoring session. Your make up test is not until Wednesday. You've got time."

"Come, Kate. We'll be late." Miles extended his hand to her and held the main entrance door open.

She took his offered hand and flashed a sorry smile at Miller. "I'm sure you'll figure it out on your own."

His face soured. He turned and took the steps up toward his apartment door.

In the parking lot, Miles pointed at the black sedan. "This is our ride. It has heated seats."

Two sharp beeps pierced the silence, followed by a flash of headlights. He opened the passenger door, and she slid onto the seat. After closing her door, he walked around the hood to the driver's side. Two loud thumps rattled her. A rush of cold air wrapped around her ankles when he slid in behind the wheel. "Sorry if I startled you. I kicked the tires to get the dirty snow and ice off."

She glided her hand over the soft leather interior, thanking God Miles had not mentioned the awkward interaction with Miller. "I could get used to this."

He chuckled and started the engine. "Oh, before I forget. I've got something for you."

She took the wrapped gift he handed to her. "What is it?"

"You'll never know unless you open it."

Pink paper crinkled under her ripping fingers and a CD revealed the masked man embracing a woman. She gasped. "You got me the Phantom soundtrack."

"Knowing how much you love the music, how could I resist? I suppose I should have asked if you had a CD player before I got you the disc." He smiled at her astonished look.

"Thank you. I play CDs on my laptop." She turned the case over to read the list of songs. He was taking her to see the movie, so listening to the disc on their way may be too much. Not everyone could handle loads of Phantom music as her.

"Miller seems a tad too eager to learn," Miles said as he pulled out of the parking spot.

"At least he got his grades up, so I must be doing something right." This day seemed full of surprises with gifts and special treatments. Should the sceptic in her awaken? She was not used to all this kindness.

"Of course you're doing a great job." In the dark interior of the car, dashboard lights reflected blue on his dark coat. His fingers wrapped around the steering wheel. If only he'd take those leather gloves off and hold her hand.

She ran out of things to say. Her mind was a jumbled mess. All they ever talked about was his story and now she wanted to ask a slew of questions, but couldn't single one out. The monotone drone of the engine stretched the uncomfortable silence. *God, are we close to the movie theater?* If he didn't say something soon, she'd start rambling.

He signalled and changed lanes, then took the highway exit. Where was he taking her?

"Another surprise. We're going to see the movie at the Met Opera theater. Hope you don't mind going downtown tonight. It's the next best thing to seeing it onstage."

"Are you kidding me?" Her jaw dropped. She'd give anything to watch the live performance directly from the Metropolitan Opera on high definition screen.

"Would I do such thing?" Miles flashed a lopsided grin. He reached out and took her hand, placed a soft kiss on her knuckles, then lowered their joined hands in his lap.

Heat pooled in her core with his small gesture. Of course, he wasn't kidding. How had she deserved all this attention today? Perhaps luck smiled down on her. She relaxed against the firm seat. Knowing good fortune would not stay for long, she decided to enjoy every little bit Lady Luck was willing to offer.

"Good thing I've got tickets. If this traffic doesn't let up we may miss the opening." He put on a signal and changed lanes.

She glanced at the clock on the dashboard. The neon blue numbers displayed 6:40. Would this special theater run coming attractions before the live performance? "I don't want to miss a thing."

"No worries, I know a shortcut. Hang on! The road is bumpy through the back roads." He wrapped his fingers around steering wheel.

She grabbed onto the handle above the window and swayed with the car while he swirled around the slow moving vehicles. Her head almost hit the low ceiling as he zipped over the potholes. A few drivers laid on their horns while a couple didn't hesitate to give them the middle finger.

"Sorry about that." He shrugged and a sheepish smile appeared on his face.

"Just get us there in one piece." The seatbelt dug into her shoulder, but her efforts to loosen it up proved useless. His foot must be on the brake. If the drivers shouted profanities at her, she'd reciprocate the same, but Miles only waved his hand.

"Look at that," he said, skidding into the parking lot of the movie theater. "We have five minutes to spare. Want anything from the snack bar?"

"No, thank you." Good thing her coat provided some cushion for the tight seatbelt. At last, she was able to unbuckle and rubbed the sore spot on her shoulder.

He cupped her cheek and brought her gaze to his mesmerizing blue eyes. "I promise to drive more carefully on our way back."

God, could he get any more gorgeous? She pulled her bottom lip between her teeth and sucked in a breath. Yeah, she was looking forward to the opera, but the slow drive back home got her stomach in knots. Would this night end in a sensual kiss or perhaps something more? She tried to imagine what making love to him might be like, and the thought sent strong vibrations to her midriff. She pulled away and bent to grab her purse from the floor. In truth, she was hiding her face. No doubt he noticed the lust in her eyes. How stupid of her to let her desire for him get the best of her.

ເວເວ

The car engine purred, idling in front of Kate's apartment building. She focused on the warm air pouring from the vents and the dim illumination of the dashboard lights. The Phantom's smooth voice filled the silence. Miles had kept his promise and drove in the slow lane on their way back. He hadn't as much as blinked at all the cars passing him on the road.

"The opera was truly amazing and so was the dinner. I'm glad we shared the chef's sample platter, but you shouldn't have ordered that cheese cake." Kate lowered the volume of the music, but pressed the up arrow with the beginning of the next song. "This one's my favorite. Well, they all are. I get goose bumps all over when the orchestra joins in with Christine. What would it be like to stand on the stage at the end of the show and take in the standing ovation?"

"Thrilling, I'm sure." He shifted in his seat. "What's a life without a little cheese cake? Une cuisine céleste has the best cheese cake in the world. I love that little restaurant. I get to practice my French there, but our waiter spoke Québécois." He licked his lips as if reliving the taste of the smooth desert. "Anyway, I enjoyed watching you watch the opera. I saw your eyes tear up a couple of times?"

Oh no, he'd noticed. It was hard not to let tears spill out. She smiled and shrugged, tapping her chest. "What can I say? The scene where Christine parts with Phantom got me right here, but what kind of life could he offer her deep down in the vaults?" Her voice trailed off. Miles couldn't offer her much of life either, that had to be the logic behind his determination to leave her at the end of the story, not just his pinky promise.

"Very admirable ability when you can let your feelings out." That tiny devilish smile still lingered on his lips.

Her heart raced, taking her on a journey to a sweet intoxication. She was dying for his kiss. "Is that why you took my hand right at the beginning?"

"Not the only reason. I guess I'm used to us holding hands." He gave her hand a soft squeeze.

A whimper escaped her, his answer leaving her bereft of words. The soundtrack ended and the world stopped. The anticipation of his lips on hers hung in the air and pulled her closer to him.

He leaned toward her. An eloquent silence filled the car while he touched his lips to hers. The softness of his kiss raced shivers down her spine. His mouth teased and prodded her to open while wild flames of desire licked her insides. A deep moan slipped out of him when their tongues met in a ravenous kiss, his mouth exploring and dominating all at once. Heaviness pressed on her breasts, and her core ignited. What if he asked to take this to the bedroom?

He cupped her face in his hands, broke the kiss, and pressed his forehead to hers. "No, Kate. No. We can't—I can't."

The fantasy shattered and coldness engulfed her. She licked her lips, her mouth dry. "Why not?"

"I lost her, Kate. I lost my wife less than a year ago and without her…" He gulped. His warm breath tickled her skin. "I'm lost too."

Her heart clenched. She wrapped her arms around

him and pulled him close. The pain was all too fresh for him, but she had to ask. "Was your wife Dobrila?"

Stupid question, she realized. Who else could have been? He couldn't mourn anyone like this.

He pulled away from her and sank into the backrest of the seat. His nod was barely noticeable, but confirmed her answer. By the deep crease between his eyebrows, she suspected he had more to tell but couldn't quite get the words out. Not wanting to pry, she chose her next question carefully.

"The legend goes she committed suicide after her father killed you." Curiosity stirred in her. She wouldn't get a wink of sleep if she didn't learn everything about this newly discovered bit.

"She did." His voice cracked and he cleared his throat, then he drew in a long breath. "I'll leave that for the next time."

"When will that be?" Her throat tightened with his strangled tone.

"I must work over the holidays, but I'll keep in touch."

In an instant her eyes misted, she swallowed. "You mean I won't see you for a long while?"

"Kate, I'm in the process of opening my clinic and still working at the hospital. Besides, a few days apart will do us both good." He opened the car door. "Come, I'll walk you to your apartment door."

She sat stunned, unable to move. A terrible heaviness pressed on her chest. He wanted some time apart from her. But of course, why was she surprised? Hadn't every guy dumped her on the first date or shortly after? *Expect nothing and you shall not be disappointed.*

Strange, every time she repeated her mantra she felt better. Not this time. She expected something—Miles's attention, friendship and love, things she would not get.

Time to start believing in her phrase again.

The passenger door opened and his hand wrapped around hers. Cold air rushed to her feet and crept up her legs, until it stung her face. It helped her to blink away the tears brewing in her eyes.

"Come now. It's not the end of the world. I'll call you every day." His tone changed for soft one and he brushed his knuckle on her cheek. Still, she wasn't persuaded.

Her feet, heavy as lead, carried her to the front door, then down the cold cement steps to her apartment.

"I'll be looking forward to your phone calls then." She swallowed a sob and nodded. This couldn't be goodbye. He hadn't finished telling his story.

"I'm sorry you're feeling like this. It's my fault. I never should've led you on to think we could be more than friends." His apologetic tone touched her heart. Friendship had been in the deal since the beginning, but now she was ready for more.

"It's not your fault." She stepped inside the foyer, but didn't face him. Good thing he couldn't see her heaving chest underneath her winter coat. Her closing throat hurt, but she forced the lump down so she could talk. "I never expected anything more than friendship."

"Please, Kate, look at me." The pleading in his whisper turned her around. The grief on his face churned her stomach. "I'll see you again very soon. We had many days apart before. Why are you taking this so hard?"

"You're right." She smiled to show him she understood, but her quiet tone told a different truth. "I'm sorry, I got used to you being here. Time apart will be good for me, too."

"There, we are square then. Right?" The funny frown on his face eased her pain a notch and even incited an unexpected chuckle.

"Of course, we're square." Still, she couldn't guarantee she wouldn't break into tears once he was gone from her doorstep.

"In that case, I will leave you to peaceful rest. Promise you won't cry after I leave." He stood frozen, not moving.

Sure she couldn't keep the promise, at first she frowned, but nodded all the same. "Are you planning to spend the night there?"

Steely sheen glossed his crystal blue eyes. "No, close the door so I can leave."

"I don't want to close it in your face."

He slowly turned on his heels then headed for the stairs.

She shut the door and pressed her eye to the peephole. He paused at the bottom of the stairs, and, for a few seconds, gazed over his shoulder at her door. Would he change his mind and try to find solace for his pain in the pleasures of her body? Would he barge into her apartment? Take her in his arms and plop her on the bed? Then make mad love to her?

He continued up the steps and disappeared from view. Of course, he wouldn't. The sorrow ripped through her body anew with his departure. Another night on her own, she'd spend between cold sheets in her empty bed.

She turned on the television and cranked up the volume to muffle her sobs. Obviously, he had failed to see how much she wanted him, needed him. Did she have to spell it out for him?

He wouldn't have to work hard to get her. Then again, she'd feared getting all dolled up would produce the opposite results.

How awful of her to lust for him. The poor man had lost his wife less than a year ago. He was still mourning her and here she expected him to jump in bed with her.

'*He's stubborn, I should know, but don't give up on him. He'll be yours.*'

Kate snapped her attention to the television. Had the woman's voice been part of the program? No only men were on the old black and white movie playing across the screen. She had thought the television was set on French channel when she first turned it on. Cold air wrapped around her and she shivered. Her eyes widened as the temperature plummeted. Fuzziness filled her head. With her last bit of energy, she pulled the blankets over her and drifted off to sleep.

# Chapter 10

The light in the garage had gone out, leaving Mathias in the darkness of his car. The kiss he'd shared with Kate replayed in his head and needles prickled his stomach. He had said he wouldn't kiss her anymore and there he'd gone and done it again. Not wise to cross the line of friendship. God almighty, what had possessed him? Ah, her plump lips and the closeness of her body. The perfume, her silky hair brushing his hand, all of her was there for taking, and he wanted to taste her. Instead, like some coward he'd scurried away from her. It had taken a tremendous will power he didn't know he had not to succumb to his desire.

Not a manly move, but a century from today would be too soon to jump into a new relationship. The guilt of Emina's death would forever keep him from dreaming of finding love again. The beast however, had stood quiet, most likely waited in anticipation for him to claim Kate then, when he couldn't stop, the thing would cloud his mind and use his body to hurt her. He must learn how to bear a lonely life. As Kate had said, what kind of life could he give her? Of course, she'd referred to Phantom and Christine, but Kate might as well have spoken of him and her. Yes, he could provide for her, but not give her his heart, and love without heart just wasn't love.

A corner of clear plastic case sticking out of the pink wrapping on the passenger seat caught his eye. Kate had the CD in her hand when she left the car. She'd put the soundtrack in her purse. How had the case found its way back to the car? Perhaps she left it behind to make sure he would return it. No, she wouldn't do such a deceitful thing. She had promised she believed him when he'd said he would see her again. He placed the CD inside the glove compartment.

He opened the door and set one foot on the concrete. Emina's ethereal whisper stopped him from exiting his car.

'*The CD is a guarantee you'll pay Kate a visit.*'

His heart ceased for a few beats, pain stabbed at his chest. "Emina, my dove. You must not interfere."

'*You promised me, Matthias.*' Scolding in her tone made her voice louder.

He sank against the backrest. How could he keep his vow when he spent every moment thinking of what life might've been had she lived? "That is one promise that will have to go unfulfilled. I can never love another."

'*I will not cross over until you fulfill my dying wish. And there's a matter of karmic debt you created during your time with servant Kate. It must be repaid with this Kate. The imbalance in your life goes back over three centuries.*'

He raked his fingers through his hair. Karmic debt, the concept of compensating for the ill treatment of an essence during its past life had to be repaid to the reincarnated soul was not new. Emina was right. Her wish was selfless. She had thought of him and their children, wanting him to find someone who'd love them and who they'd love in return, and reclaim the balance in his life.

'*Open your heart and you'll see there's room for love. Kate is not just another woman. She loves you to a fault.*'

"This Kate is not the same woman I love—" He clamped his mouth shut before his tongue could complete the word. Preposterous to think he had loved a servant. "You saw me kiss her in the car?" Blood rushed to his head. What would she think of him?

'*You should be ashamed for allowing your stubbornness to get the best of you. Why are you turning your back on her, on love?*' Her whisper faded, and he strained to hear the last few words.

"I'm not stubborn. It's a sense of propriety. Stay with me, love. Let me explain. Don't leave." Desperation edged his voice and closed his throat. '*With you gone, I fear the beast is stirring inside me,*' he confessed, despite his qualms. By not admitting the fact he hung onto a false hope that he imagined the urges and the voice every time he succumbed to desire for Kate.

Warmth spread over his chest. Emina's whisper echoed in his mind. '*The beast is part of you, has been for centuries. Without it, you wouldn't be where you are today. Once you allow yourself to love Kate, the entity residing in you will be placated.*'

Her voice faded. He waited. Had she gone or chosen to give him her famous silent treatment? How he missed her getting miffed at him when he did something not to her liking. And he had wronged two women tonight, a new record for him.

No point freezing in this cold garage. He eased out from the car then crept inside the foyer. The house was dark, but babies kept all hours and there was no guarantee he wouldn't bump into Rosalia or a nurse rocking one or all three to sleep.

He tiptoed to the foot of the stairs, unzipping his

coat. The table lamp in the den clicked on, its dim light cast long shadow over the hallway.

"This is not good, master, you are gone all days. Don't you love your sons?" Rosalia's scolding stopped him at the first stair. How long had she sat there brooding and preparing her speech?

He'd now beat his own record. In no time at all, he'd ticked off yet another woman. Tonight was not his night. He straightened and faced her. One of his babies eagerly sucked his thumb during slumber. "Of course, I love them. It's just that I'm reminded of their mother each time I look at them." That line should put a stop to her questioning, but to be safe, he changed the subject. "I hope I didn't wake you up, Rosalia."

"Good thing you did or I'd get a hell of a cramp sleeping in the chair. The nurse had to go home, her husband's sick. She'll be back in the morning." She clumsily got up from the recliner, yet expertly enough not to wake the child. "Poor Teo, he refuses to be comforted, having a hard time."

Matthias nodded. "He's missing his mother. They all do." Knowing Rosalia, she'd rant on about him having to do the job of both parents. Before she could open her mouth to speak her mind, he continued. "You should not get him used to falling asleep like this. He must learn to sleep in his bed."

"Ah, master, all you know about raising children is from those books of yours." She slouched past him and up the stairs, giving him one of her disapproving looks, coupled with a head-shake and tsk of her tongue. "At least I hope you're looking for a good woman who'll love you and these angels. I'm getting too old for this, you know. I've raised my fair share of younger siblings and cousins."

She grumbled on her way up. Stairs creaked under

her weight, and she disappeared behind the nursery doors.

Inside his study, he headed straight for the liquor cabinet. It'd been decades since last he'd had a strong drink, but tonight's developments called for a double shot of neat single malt. Glass clinked as he rummaged through the buffet. At the back of the compartment, the golden label on the bottle came to focus. Emina had gifted him on their trip to Scotland, the eighteen-year-old Bunnahabhain from Islay. He'd never cracked open the bottle—it had been sitting in that cabinet for another eighteen years. The amber liquid filled the bottom of the snifter as he poured. He brought the glass to his nose and took a whiff. He was no connoisseur, but the scotch had a perfect balance of smoke and peat at a level of impact agreeable to his nose. He took a sip and welcomed the initial burn in his chest. The hints of subtle smoke, brine, malt sweetness, fruit, and nuttiness bloomed on his palate. The enticingly rich flavors lingered in his mouth and demanded another taste.

He lowered to the sofa, leather creaking. He sipped his scotch in silence. Experience had taught him getting inebriated made things worse. The beast seemed to love his drunken state. He stared at the tantalizing liquor in the bottle and smacked his lips. Instead of draining the golden liquid, he corked the bottle and returned it to the cabinet. Why give Rosalia more reasons to badger him? And she would if she found him passed out drunk in the morning.

The grandfather's clock struck two. It was too late to call Kate. Funny, he missed her already. He got used to her company. She cheered up his gloomy days, and he wanted to have her during his lonely nights. His bed was empty, but he shouldn't allow his soul to turn the same. Emina wanted him to find love again, not to be alone. It was a hard decision to make, and harder to keep his desires in check. No woman would take on a job of raising three babies. Though he would trust Kate with his kids, he couldn't burden her with his problems. She had her life to live, mistakes to make and learn from them, and he shouldn't interfere.

What the hell, one more drink wouldn't hurt him or wake up the beast inside him. He reached for the bottle and poured half the shot this time, to be safe. He returned to the sofa, twirling the snifter nestled between his fingers. The swirling golden liquid awakened a deeply buried memory...

༺༻

His father's chamber had reeked of liquor and something else. Blood permeated the putrid, heavy air. Step by slow step, his feet carried him inside the large room. The woman Father brought home as his new wife and her wretched daughter feasted on the master's veins. Miles's breath hitched. His stepsister tore her fangs from his father's flesh and glared at him at the foot of the bed, drops of thick crimson racing down her chin. Her demonic, blood-laced eyes sent ice through him.

Run! An urgent female voice rang in his head. He forced his frozen legs into action and bolted out of the bedroom. He ran into his room. His heart pounded in his ears. Her blood stained hand grabbed the door before he could slam it shut. Scrawny as he was, he pushed his body against the door, to no avail. The bitch was strong and pushed the door off its hinges, sending him to his rump.

He crawled backward on his behind. Her sinister laughter rang in his ears, curdling his blood. His back hit the wall. Her fangs elongated as she neared him. Fear rendered him frozen. The bite to his neck came fast and paralyzed him. Darkness closed in on him. The world was slipping away. He was dying.

Bright light erupted in the room. The vampire girl burst into flames. A female's form emerged from the blinding illumination and held his half dead body, humming to him until he took his last breath.

For days or weeks, perhaps, he had drifted in and out of consciousness. Servants whispered while bustling around his bed, changed sheets and sponged sweat off his body. Then he heard her song and forced his shaky legs to take him to the window. A young peasant girl sat on the stone steps of the storage house, rocking a rag doll in her arms. At a man's harsh call, she ceased her song and snapped her head in his direction. He called her Kate and told her to quit daydreaming and help unload their cart.

⌀ↄ⌀ↄ

Matthias smiled. His stare still on the swirling liquid in the snifter. So long ago, her song had lured him out of bed. Their friendship bloomed over time. The beastly presence in him had not awakened until the day he caved in to his desire for her, and her willingness to please him confirmed she wanted him too. She pulled him from the brink of the death, eased his loneliness and pain over his and Emina's forced separation. Life had its strange ways, presenting him with a chance to love her as he should've loved her centuries ago.

⌀ↄ⌀ↄ

Kate clamped a pencil between her teeth, while her fingers flew over the keyboard. The click clicks loud in the quiet library, like a mouse scurrying along the walls looking for crumbs. Music from her headphones replaced the college library hush. Miles's story was coming together. The songs from The Phantom would motivate her to type faster. Strange, the CD was missing. Positive she had dropped the case in her purse before she stepped out of Miles's car, she'd torn her bag to shreds looking for it. Should she call him? No, she couldn't admit she already lost his gift.

He had kept his promise and called her once, excusing his lack of attention to the busy ER. It was for the best. Once her head had cooled off, she was glad he hadn't taken advantage of her needy state. The three weeks of winter holidays proved too short for her embarrassment to subside. Would she ever stop blushing at the memory of her stupid actions?

An email notification broke her reverie. She double clicked the blue bubble and Dyane's message popped on the screen. It read *card 1 Lovers*. Okay, that card had appeared with every read so far. *Card 2 The Devil*, nothing new with that one either. She wouldn't have what her heart wanted the most. *Card 3 The Emperor, elusive success. Card 4 The Sun, happiness.*

*God, Dyane, I hope you're right.*

*Card 5 The Moon, deceitful people around you.* The gossipy girls would love to see her crash and burn. *Card 6 Judgement, an opportunity will present itself and must not be ignored.*

Kate closed the email as a thick hand grabbed the backrest and pulled out the chair next to her from under the table.

Miller dropped his large frame onto the plastic seat. His lips moved. The idiot failed to notice the wire connecting her ear buds to her laptop. She plucked the phones out. "Did you say something?"

"I said, do we have another essay due? I hate those assignments."

He leaned toward her computer, eager to sneak a peek.

"You can relax. I'm working on a project." She pushed him away, then saved and closed the page, before he could glimpse the screen.

"Oh, yeah? What kind of project?" He sat straight and pulled on her computer, but she was faster and grabbed the frame before he could turn the laptop toward him. Instead, he took out a book from his torn bag. "Hey who's the dude I saw you with the other night?"

"A friend." She gave a nonchalant shrug of one shoulder, but inside, her panic started to brew. Miller would have more questions. Would he see on her face she had more to tell than she was letting out?

He quirked his eyebrows then a dumb grin appeared on his face. "With benefits?"

"None of your damn business, Miller." She squirmed in her chair, lowering her gaze to the open book. Sooner or later, the big mouth would talk and this little tidbit would spread like a wildfire. Why couldn't people worry about their own lives? "Have you figured out the math problem?"

"I see. The guy gave it to you good. Didn't he? So, are you g-spot or clit kind of girl?" He elbowed her arm. "Ah, like you'd know what I'm talking about. Anyway, thank God you got laid. The whole campus mistook you for one of them."

"One of what?" She struggled to keep her tone calm and play dumb. Hanging out with Andrew earned her a lesbian title, but she let them think what they wanted. Life was too short to argue and prove them wrong. "Half the campus mistook *you* for a jock."

The table creaked when he leaned on his arms then pressed his thumb into his chin. "Trust me. You're not like that floozy Amanda and her minions. Every guy here would give his left nut to be with you, but you like that f—"

She shoved her hand in front of his face and bit down on her anger. *God give me the strength to deal with this dumbass.* "Don't you dare say the 'F' word."

"Imagine everyone's faces when I tell them you've got a boyfriend. They'll all be like 'but I thought she's queer.'" He jerked his head to his left at the table where Andrew sat alone. "You won't have to hang out with that sorry ass."

Why was Andrew afraid to join her just because a campus jerk sat with her? She pulled a chair out, ignoring Miller's appalled expression. "Andrew, come sit with us."

"You want that fag to sit here? At this table? With us?" He pointed his meaty finger at the tabletop.

She groaned. No point wasting her time on changing him. "Yes, Miller. I looked at that math problem and couldn't figure it out. Andrew is the only one in here who can help you. So stop insulting my friend and open your book."

In slow motion, Andrew stood up, gathered his stuff, then approached with even slower steps. "Are you sure you want me to sit with you? I mean, you're tutoring now."

"We need your help." She pointed at the chair she'd pulled out for him. Miller scooted away from Andrew and closer to her. "You're safe, Miller. Andrew's got a boyfriend and besides, you're not his type."

A lopsided grin appeared on Miller's reddened face, but his shoulders lowered. "He's not mine, either."

"Now that's settled, let's move on to our problem at hand." She flipped a math textbook at Andrew. "Can you help with this one?"

He glanced at the open pages. "The professor said

not to worry about it. It's advanced math and he won't put it on the exam."

"Ah, problem solved." Miller leaned back and cradled his head in his laced fingers. "I spent the whole damn weekend shitting over nothing."

"Don't you want to know?" Kate scowled. "I mean, you spent so much time on it, you may as well get the result."

"Why bother?" Miller closed his book and shoved the loose papers in his bag. "Now our little friend can go to his boyfriend and you to yours." Surprisingly, he faced Andrew. "You should see the guy Kate's dating. Now that's one fine dude. Even I'd go out with him. On a date, that is."

"Really?" Andrew winked at her. "Maybe I should check him out."

Heat seared her cheeks. Gay or straight, it took exactly two minutes with Miller for Andrew to turn into one of the guys. "Both of you stop. I'm not dating anyone."

"Oh, no?" Miller raised an eyebrow. "I saw you sucking his lips in his car and then he walked you to your apartment door."

A knot tightened her stomach, but she flashed a slow smile at him. Damn Miller and his snooping. "Then you also saw him leaving a few minutes later."

Miller snickered. "Yeah, the guy's fast. Must've had some serious hair-trigger."

"Oh, shut up," she hissed and sprang to her feet, shutting her book with a loud thud. "I've had enough of this."

Andrew placed his hand on her elbow. "Come on, Kate. Miller's a jerk, but there's no shame for being in love."

She swallowed her anger. It was good to have a friend on her side.

"Stop calling me a jerk, you queer," Miller seethed.

"At least I'm not ashamed to admit what I am." Andrew pushed his index finger to his chest.

Kate chewed on her lower lip, pondering Andrew's words before Miller interrupted. She widened her eyes. "You think I'm in love?"

"It's showing on your face. You daydream of him all the time. Every empty space of your notepad has Miles written in little hearts, so cute." Andrew traced heart in the air.

"It's useless, though." She hung her head, her shoulders slumped. The tormenting thought forced her to heave. If she didn't speak out she'd burst. "He loved me three centuries ago in the body of my great-great-grandmother."

Silence fell over the table. Miller's mouth hung open. He turned to Andrew, his eyebrows drawing together. "Is she for real?"

Andrew placed his hand on her forehead. "You're not burning up, so I can't say you're delirious with fever."

She swiped his hand away. "I'm not sick. Forget what I said. I blurted out something I shouldn't have."

"Well, I'd love to stay and chat about this in detail. But I'm late for beer fest at the pub." Miller drew his wallet out of the back pocket of his jeans. He angled his head at Kate. "Hey, you should check it out. They have a wet T-shirt contest every Wednesday. With your tatas, no girl stands a chance." He withdrew a ten-dollar bill and tossed the crisp note on the table. "It wasn't a full hour of tutoring, but you can keep the change." He scurried out of the library, meandering through scattered chairs and tables.

Andrew pointed his chin at Miller. "He'll make a wonderful teacher someday."

"So wonderful, it's scary." She snorted. Miller's re-mark about her 'tatas' infuriated her, but she clamped her mouth and let him slide this time. Since her body finally decided to develop, she'd heard all kind of jokes about her chest. "His father has connections. He'll find a cushy job for his son. What are you going to do after gradua-tion?"

Andrew shrugged. "There's still a big stigma about gay teachers working with young students. I guess I'll continue school."

"Your sexual orientation has no bearing on your job performance." Anger boiled in her. Society and their skewed perception could go to hell. Andrew would never harm a child and he'd care and inspire his pupils to learn, makings of an exceptional teacher.

"With all the cuts to social programs, school boards won't be hiring. Raul offered me a job. I'll take what I can." He glanced away as if ashamed he would think of abandoning the teaching profession. "What about you?"

"I'll have to find any job and start paying off my loan." Her chest tightened, she blinked the stinging tears away. Too often she pushed the desire down to return home and said it didn't matter, but it did. She couldn't go back and burden her mother with her financial struggles. Chances of finding a teaching position were slimmer, if not impossible, in Croatia.

"Let's not worry about the future. It'll work out one way or the other." Andrew's cheerful voice returned. "Tell me about this guy you're seeing. You said he's quite older than you, but I figured some ten plus years."

"It's nothing. Really." She closed her notebook and clicked on her email icon. "I hoped you'd at least try to understand, but how could you? I don't understand it my-self."

He placed his hand on her shoulder. "Maybe you

shouldn't see him anymore. He could be some nut case. Try to persuade you to do God knows what."

She tore her glance from his hand and stared into his chocolate-colored eyes. "Do I tell you who to see?"

"No, you are the only one here who understands me. But you can't compare me being a gay to that man who claims he's been alive for three centuries. Or does he think he's reincarnated after three hundred years? I think that's more plausible. You know I love you. As a friend, of course, and I'd hate to see you hurt." Concern reflected in his eyes and his tone softened.

"The only thing he persuaded me to do was to write down his tragic love story. Once he's done with the tale, he'll leave me alone, and I won't see him anymore." Her throat closed in and cut her voice. The last few words came out as a squeal. Miles wanted nothing more than friendship. The hell with friendship, she wanted him to love her like a man.

Andrew let out a long breath and flung his arms. "I know how it feels, you must do what the heart wants or you won't be happy. When I decided to tell my parents I'm gay, well…" He swallowed. "My mother understood, but Dad blamed her. Blamed her for mothering me too much—one must be tough with boys. He couldn't take it and left us."

"Oh, Andrew." She gave his arm a sympathetic rub. "I hope you don't blame yourself for it."

"I did at first." He shook his head. "Not anymore. I'm happy now with Raul. He's a great lover, very attentive." A dreamy smile lingered on his lips, as if he was remembering a passionate night in his lover's embrace.

She winced, staring at him, her mouth hanging open. "You slept with him already?"

"I've known him for years, been there when he went through bad break ups, betrayal, and hurt. We're past the 'get to know each other' stage." His forehead wrinkled and he chewed on his nail, but sparkles appeared in his eyes. This must be the first time she had seen him this relaxed and happy. "Plus, we had to get the need out of our systems, but making love only fed my fire. He's picking me up after classes tonight. I'm sure his hot car will provoke some gossip around campus."

"I'm happy for you." She pulled the coat from the back of the chair. Yep, Raul and his flamboyant ways would stir jealousy and hurtful comments. It may steer the attention from her, but she wouldn't want Andrew under scrutiny.

"But?" He cocked his head.

"There's no buts." Though her tone was a bit snappy, she tried to mask it with an awkward smile.

"There's more. Something's bugging you again."

"Maybe." She shrugged one shoulder.

His lips thinned into a white line. He wouldn't drop the issue.

"Possibly." At his unyielding stare, she threw her hands up in the air. "Okay, yes my heart wants him, but I'll never have what it wants. He is mourning the death of his wife and I know how much they loved each other. You have no idea what they had to endure and overcome to be together. Getting over her death will take a long time. He will forever keep her safely tucked in his heart." She shook her head. "Seldom had a woman had such husband. I doubt he would love anyone else."

"Don't say that. You don't know what the future holds for you."

"Something tells me not to set my hopes high." A tiny light kindled as she was reminded of the female's voice asking her not to give up on Miles. She extinguished it fast. *Expect nothing and you shall not be disappointed.* "It's best not to dwell on this."

"You'll let me read the story when it's done? I'm very intrigued."

"Sure, you can be my first reader if the narrator gives me the permission to share it." After all, it wasn't her story, but Miles's, and she only served as a means to write it down.

She scrolled through her email, stopped and opened Miles's message. Her insides fluttered.

"Good news, I hope." Andrew's voice drifted to her. She was already in her fantasy world with Miles.

"Yes, he wants to get together this weekend." The keys clicked under her fingers. *I can't wait to see you,* she replied, closed the program, then logged off. After placing her laptop inside the bag, she swung her canvas tote over her shoulder and headed for the exit.

Andrew trailed behind her. "Look, I trust your judgment and if you're comfortable with this guy then, by all means, listen to his story and write it down."

The tale was coming to an end, and she must start to prepare her heart to say goodbye to him. The pain sliced her chest at the mere thought.

Tomorrow, she would call her mom and find out more about Great-Great-Grandma. Life must not have been easy for her after her master gave her away to another man. It could be Miles's story, but fear of her ancestor's curse no longer pressed heavily on her mind. Had her unsettled spirit finally found peace?

# Chapter 11

Matthias's boots sploshed through the slush on his way across the parking lot of Kate's building. He was looking forward to seeing her. Three weeks apart had gone by too slow, but he had to make sure the monster inside him had stopped stirring. The story could have wakened the beast. Or karmic debt as Emina had claimed. Or Kate's resemblance to her great-great-grandma, but whatever the cause, he would not let the fiend have this woman, not his Kate.

"Well, hello there, handsome." A sugar-laced female voice stopped him in his tracks. A young woman flicked the cigarette into the puddle and propped her chunky hands on her wide hips. She flipped her long, straight hair, blowing the smoke between her thin lips, smothered in pale pink lipstick they resembled two rain warms. "You the guy who's been hanging around that foreign student? What's her name? Katya or something? "

"I am. What business is that of yours?" He resumed his hurried steps, but she trailed after him.

"Why would you want to be with that frump girl? She must be boring as hell. Why not spend some time with a fab girl like me?"

Before he could reach for the main door handle, she rounded him, blocked his way, and shoved her rather large cleavage in his face. Her fake smile exposed her uneven, coffee-and-tobacco-stained teeth.

"I'd rather spend some time in the company of a frump girl than a tramp."

For a moment, he entertained an idea to satiate his demon's demands with this woman, but the evil spirit residing within him did not want her. Lucky for her. If it did, he could be charged with an assault—or worse, a murder. He couldn't have that on his conscience, or his record.

She gripped his forearm and he frowned at the chipped nail polish on her yellowed fingers. "Come on up. My friend let me use his place for a few hours. We'll have a grand time."

Had he heard her right? Since Emina's death, gorgeous women had offered to ease his pain and loneliness, but none had been this forthcoming or this unattractive.

He probed into her mind and planted a subliminal message. '*Show less skin, guys will like you more.*' If she ever got the meaning and how long the effect would last, he couldn't tell.

She winced, as if jolted with a cattle prod, and stepped aside, unblocking the entrance. "Oh, yeah? No one turns Amanda down. You'll regret this."

"There's a first time for everything." He winked, but judging by her downturned lips, she didn't take the rejection well. Perhaps he should warn Kate. This girl could retaliate, making Kate a target of her ill temper.

No, in her last semester of school, Kate didn't need the added worry. It would be him who'd keep a closer attention to any suspicious activity around her.

On swift feet, he closed the distance from the front entrance to Kate's apartment door. He knocked. To enter without being invited after three weeks of separation seemed impolite.

The door swung open, and she greeted him with her warm grin. He stood rooted, unsure if she'd be scared if he scooped her in his arms.

She took a step toward him. "I missed you."

He couldn't control his need for her and wrapped her in his embrace. The three weeks apart only increased his desire. "I missed you, too."

He wanted to stay like this forever, holding her pressed to him. Perhaps it was good that she made the first move, pulled away from him, closed the door, then extracted the hanger from the coat closet and handed him the plastic frame.

He rubbed his hands to warm them up, then pulled out the Phantom CD case from his leather coat pocket. "Before we start, have you been looking for this?"

Her mouth dropped open. "I tore my place apart searching for your gift. I thought I lost it and you had it the whole time?"

"I found it on the seat when I got home. Must've fallen out of your purse. Sorry, I meant to tell you, but I forgot." He handed the case to her, glad she didn't question why he didn't mention earlier that he had the sound-track he'd gifted her. "So, are you ready for me to continue on with the story?"

"Can't wait." She pointed at the cozy corner on the floor in front of her bed. "I redecorated. Do you like it?"

The bubble gum pink coverings and oversized buttons broke the glum of the dark place. He gave Kate the once over. She too wore a bright red top and her old sweatpants, but with a flowery trim. Definitely not a frump girl. Unassuming, quiet, the kind most men wouldn't give a second glance, but those who did were in for a rare treat.

"Yes, the fluffy pillows add a nice touch. Did you make them?"

"Um-hum, Andrew gave me a bagful of fabrics and ribbons. His mom's abandoned project. So I got creative." She swept her arms as if she was on a TV commercial, displaying the hottest products.

"You've been busy." His guilt over letting her spend the holidays alone eased. She had not wasted the time apart as he'd pictured her, sulking and waiting for his call.

"Let's start then." She ushered him toward the nest of cushions.

"You're really anxious," he said, laughing. "Okay, I can't wait to try out this new and improved space for our séances."

A shy smile lingered on her lips while she stared at him getting comfy on the floor.

He settled and opened his arms to her. "It's perfect."

She rushed to him. He wrapped her up and pulled her to the protective wall of his chest. With his chin pressed at the top of her head, he rocked from side to side. She felt so good, so right. If only he could keep her in the nook forever.

'*What stops you?*' Emina's whisper echoed in his mind.

Was she here or did he imagine her? He cleared his throat and squirmed.

"I just got off the phone with my mom." Kate sat up straight. The little smirk on her face said she had more to tell. He arched an inquisitive eyebrow. "She didn't want to talk about Great-Great-Grandma Kate, but I made her. As I figured, Kate was consumed with sadness for the rest of her life, despite all the riches." She tucked lose strands of her hair behind her ear, a grin lighting her face. "Mom had some great news to pass on. My little cousin is

starting to regain feeling in her legs, the doctors are opti-
mistic she may recover fully. I may be wrong, but I'm
feeling the old curse losing its power. Still, it feels like
there's something more Great-Great-Grandma wants before it is completely broken."

"She wants closure." An urge to beg forgiveness
from her ancestor overwhelmed him. He wrapped his arm
around her shoulders and cupped her chin between his
fingers of his free hand, tilting her head toward his face.
"I know you're not her, but this is the closest I'll come to
her, so please don't think me strange if I ask forgiveness
from you in lieu of your great-great-grandma. Will you
forgive me?"

Kate's chest and shoulders rose and fell with her
snickering. "I think she forgave you long ago."

"No, say it as if you are her. I need to hear it."

She gulped. "I—I." Her breath hitched. "I feel silly. I
can't."

"Try again. Please. Imagine you're her."

She shut her eyes and bit her lips. In the next instant,
she locked her gaze with his. Her mesmerizing emerald
eyes held him captive, and, for a moment, he believed he
was transported three centuries back.

"I forgive you, master," she whispered.

Stunned, he tightened his hold on her. "What did you
call me?"

She pulled back. "I called you Miles."

"No, I'm positive you said master."

She snorted and dismissed his claim, lightly slapping
his upper arm. "I would never call you master."

"I heard you say master." He relaxed his shoulders. It
could've been a slip of her tongue or trick of his mind.
"Thank you for this. Guilt, for the lack of better word, has
been sitting on my conscience for too long and I needed
to apologize. I feel freed, absolved of a crime. She

touched my soul, taught me love, and I—" He swallowed audibly. "Well, I—I feel my shame inside me. I didn't deserve her."

"What crime? She couldn't break free from the pain of never seeing you again." Kate clasped his hand. "Well, now that you settled the wrong doing of your past, can we get to the story?"

"Oh, of course. I'll let you get comfy and then we can start."

"I'm ready." She closed her eyes again, never letting go of his hand. "You may begin at any time."

"All right." He closed his eyes, and let the ancient memories unwind. "Can you see it yet?"

"Yes, the dark corridor of your castle. I don't think I've seen it from inside yet. I can't make out shapes. Was it always this glum?" Kate's soft voice transported him deeper into the memory.

"I remember my birthplace as dismal. After my mother's death, servants whispered the place was not the same. Heavy curtains covered the windows. The sun hit the walls in thin lines through the slits of hanging fabrics."

"There's a woman hidden under the curtain. Do you see her?"

"Yes, she's Dobrila's governess. She was the liaison between us, brought the messages back and forth. Now let the vision play out. No more talking."

"Okay," Kate whispered.

*e∽e∽*

"Young master Miles." The instant the woman had called him, joy swirled through him. She'd have a letter from Dobrila.

He scanned the hallways. Not a soul around.

"Has anyone seen you?"

"I was careful, as always." She pulled a thick envelope from under her apron. "Young countess sends this and her love."

"Thank you." He pulled on the drawstring of his coin purse tied to his belt and plucked out a golden ducat.

She stared at his offered gift, but didn't take it. "Thank you, but it's too much."

"You deserve it, risking your life coming here. Take it." He jerked his hand. The poor woman had most likely never seen a golden coin, much less held one in her hand.

Her shaky fingers scooped the coin from his palm. "She'll wait for you. Tonight."

With a curt nod, he dismissed her. She bowed and left. He stared after her until she rounded the corner on quick and quiet feet.

Safe in the sanctuary of his chamber, he sat on the canopy bed and opened the envelope. The first sheet was an invitation to a masquerade. How clever of Dobrila. Disguised, he could enter her father's castle and dance with her. Right under her parents' noses.

He pulled another piece of paper from behind it with Dobrila's elegant writing. His lips stretched into a full-blown grin as he read the note. She would dress in a teal blue gown with matching Venetian mask.

The soft featherbed sank under him. He sighed and pressed the scented note to his nose, then to his chest. He couldn't wait until tonight. Their love had withstood a year of separation imposed on them by their parents.

"Miles!"

Father's shout shattered his tranquil moment, and Miles jumped to his feet. The chamber's heavy double door flew open, hitting the wall and shaking the solid wood furniture.

Miles shoved Dobrila's envelope under the pillows

just as his father barged through the door. The old man had entered his quarters on a few occasions, all of them bad. The fact he flew into the room couldn't be good. Miles assumed a relaxed pose, despite his rigid spine. "Yes, Father?"

Father halted in front of him, mopping sweat off his round face with a lacy kerchief. "The young countess is back from her schooling in Vienna and rumor has it she's putting up a masked ball."

Miles frowned and shrugged, faking indifference. "So? What do you expect me to do about it?"

"Don't play dumb, boy. I trust you wouldn't go anywhere near the Vitturi castle." Father waved his thick finger in front of Miles's face, then filled his chest with air in some feeble attempt to appear taller.

Miles could hardly control his anger. Damn it, he should be free to love and marry whom he loved. The hell with the family feud. Why couldn't they settle the age-old dispute over feudal rights? He couldn't care less about any of that.

The whole world was changing, except for this corner, stuck in the middle ages.

"Father, this is the Renaissance. We've lived in this era for some time now. Isn't it time we caught up with the rest of the world?"

"Don't you lecture me about all that nonsense from the western world." He pointed at the window, as if trying to prove his theory. "Such radical ideas give those unruly peasants the notion that they can control us, the aristocracy. Over my dead body. But that is not why I'm here." Father changed his voice to impose his authority. "Listen well, boy. The deal is that you stay away from Vitturis. If you get caught sniffling around the countess again, I'll send you into military service in Venice."

Miles thrust his arms out in frustration. "I'm a count

too. Do you see any other countesses around for me to marry?"

"You are not count until I'm dead. We'll find you a suitable wife, if that's what you want." Father turned to leave the room, but glanced over his shoulder. "Sometimes, you get handed a queen of hearts, but it's queen of diamonds that you need. Same rank, wrong suit. Just stay away from this countess."

"I don't want just any wife," Miles shouted after him, but the old count didn't spare him another moment of his time.

Like hell, he'd stay away from Dobrila. Miles yanked open the armoire, the heavy doors squeaking on their hinges. In haste, he rummaged through his clothes until he found what he was looking for. The black leather eye mask, wide brimmed hat, and silk blouse. He tied the strings behind his head, pulled the headgear low and scrambled into his shirt.

Darkness engulfed the town and cooled off the sun-bleached stones heated by summer's sun. With each brisk stride he got closer to Dobrila. The supper hour kept the people around their tables, leaving the narrow, cobble-stone paved streets empty.

He halted in front of the long bridge, noting the increased guards. Guests poured at the main entrance. Checking his hat sat low enough over his forehead, he made his way toward the heavy wood door.

A guard scrutinized him through narrowed eyes, but jerked his head when Miles waved the invitation in his face. He followed the crowd through the courtyard, surrounded by the three tiers of hanging balconies, then up the marble steps to the ballroom.

The orchestra, consisting of a lute, a trumpet, cymbals, and a tambourine, opened up the first dance with a popular Galliard. He scanned the room and spotted Dobrila stepping up on the marbled dance area. In a quick move, he took the spot facing her, making sure when the dance started, he would be partnered with her. Their hands met as the two lines of dancers moved to the middle of the floor.

Her chocolate brown eyes shone behind the turquoise mask, while her mocha hair bounced on her shoulders in sugar coated ringlets. With their palms pressed together, they spun.

"Meet me after this dance," she whispered, pressing the palm of her other hand to his.

He nodded so slightly, paying attention to watchful eyes. The usual bodyguards were posted around the room. The same ones who had beaten him on several occasions.

The dance partners changed around the circle. Absent minded, he performed the steps, keeping his eyes to Dobrila until she made her way back to him. Too bad the more intimate version of Galliard, Lavolta, was considered inappropriate in this court. He would lift Dobrila so high she would screech.

The music ended and so did the dance with him kneeling in front of his lady. She granted him her hand for a kiss. The scent of her flowery perfume registered in his brain as her branding. Young, vibrant, full of life and all his. Only if their families would give them their blessings.

In a whirl of turquoise sea, Dobrila greeted the guests on her way out of the ballroom. After a few moments, he too slipped out though a different door. He took off his shoes to prevent the soles from clicking on the marble floors and ran to the garden where she waited. Out of breath, he arrived to the secluded and now overgrown patch.

She sat by the fish pond, dipping her hand in the still

water. She was like a breath of fresh air, music of angels, the light of a sun.

"My Dove," he whispered, not wanting to disturb her tranquil moment.

Her breath hitched, and in the next instant, she flew to his arms, then pulled down on his eye mask.

"Oh, how I missed you." She managed to say before his mouth devoured hers.

He pulled her to him, holding tight, not letting her go and ended the kiss with a nibble to her lower lip. "These months apart almost killed me."

She took a hold of his wrists and pulled back. The glee in her face faded. "Is it true, Miles? Is it true you loved a peasant woman while I was gone?"

His chest tightened. He couldn't lie to her, yet the truth would hurt her. She would not understand the bestial urges for Kate. "No, dove. They feed you lies. It wasn't love I felt for her. I used her for my pleasure. Do not fret, I only love you and her future is secured."

That same sparkle returned to her eyes and she wrapped her arms around his neck. "Someday you'll show me the same kind of love."

If she referred to him making love to her, he would prefer if he didn't have to wait for someday. He dipped his face to the cleavage revealed under the sheer fabric of her low cut bodice. Her soft moans with each kiss he placed as he trailed his lips toward the swell of her breast were his undoing. In two steps, he backed her against the rough wall and lifted her, pressing his body against her softness. The velvet of her gown swished as she wrapped her legs around his hips.

Their mouths met in a feverish demand. Her fingers worked fast, undoing the tiny clasps of his blouse. She slid her hands inside and caressed his bare chest, rushing blood to his groin.

Had she read some inappropriate literature while away? She was never this brazen.

"Make love to me, Miles. Like you did to your peasant woman." Her voice was hoarse. She cradled his head and kissed his neck. Her eyes smoldered in intensity he'd had not seen previously.

Before she could say another word, he wrapped his fingers around her nape and pulled her to him, meeting half-way in an exquisite, hungry kiss. Her need fueled his hunger and he allowed his tongue to delve deep in her mouth. He wasn't gentle anymore. His hand glided along her thigh, stopping when he sensed the silk ribbon securing her hose to her skin. What color was it? Soft pink, he imagined.

Men's shouts reached him from afar. Dobrila gasped and froze. Fear replaced the lust in her eyes. "Run, Miles. They'll kill you."

"I'm not running like some thief." He clasped her wrists. "Unless you are coming with me."

"I cannot. You know I can't disappoint my parents." She swallowed hard. "I'll beg my father. He'll come around, you'll see."

"Dobrila, you're not asking him to buy you another porcelain doll. He'll never give us his blessings."

"There he is!" Count Vitturi pointed at them. "Dobrila, step away from him."

She lowered her head and obeyed her father, clasping her hands in front.

"You whore! You've brought nothing but shame on our family, sneaking with this low life under our watchful eye. Had we not arrived in time, God knows how far this would have gone." He seethed, "You're to spend your days under strict house supervision." Turning on his heels, he faced Miles. "And for you, I was clear when I said to stay away from my daughter."

Miles gave a courteous nod. "With all due respect—"

"Do not speak of what you know nothing at all," the count roared, his thin face turning red. "If you respected me, you would not show your face here." He grabbed Dobrila's elbow and yanked her toward the door. "Gentlemen, he's all yours," he said, pushing Dobrila toward the garden's exit.

"Please, Father, don't let them hurt him." Her voice on the verge of tears, she turned her head in his direction, but followed her parent with fast and unsteady steps.

"He asked for it." Conte Vitturi's sneered words drifted to him, and he caught a glimpse of him manhandling Dobrila down the corridor.

The three stout men circled him, two rolling up their sleeves while the third one punched the palm of his hand.

He laughed and proceeded to roll up his sleeves. "Let's see what you've got, gentlemen."

⌒⌒⌒

Matthias coughed, indicating the story had ended for today. Kate blinked and gave him a dubious look, but sat straight all the same. "You sure you want to end here?"

"Yeah, the rest isn't pretty. Besides, I took too much of your time already. I'm sure you're busy with finals."

"Busy is an understatement," she mumbled. "So did the 'gents' beat you up?"

A chuckle of amusement escaped him. "If you must know, I showed them what I could do when provoked, but as I said it wasn't pretty. They never spoke of it, you know, their pride hurt more than swollen lips, black eyes, and bruises. The three burly men got beat up by me, a kid."

He disengaged from Kate's hold, slowly got to his feet, and stared at her as a smile danced on her lips. Better he left now, before he succumbed to his wont and re-gretted his rash actions. He headed for the coat closet. "I'll let you study, don't stay up too long. You'll need adequate sleep to retain the knowledge."

She scrambled to her feet and followed him, her stare focused to the floor. "After this story, I'm not sure I can study."

"You must." He brushed her cheek. "Or I'll keep away until graduation."

She snapped her glance at him. "I'll do my best then. When will we continue?"

"How's your schedule next week?"

"Oh…" She blew her breath out, fluttering the loose strands of her hair. "Doesn't look good. Or the week after that. More assignments are piling up each day. Study and study some more."

"Keep plowing at it. When you graduate, it won't feel like it was hard." He laughed, remembering his uni-versity days. So long ago and yet he recalled each lesson, exam, prank pulled by students—those were the days. "I'll check in with you in a few days and we'll decide then. How does that sound?"

"Great." She awarded him with her winning smile.

"Okay, hit the books then." He leaned in and pecked her cheek, taking in her scent. All she had to do was to ask him to stay. But she didn't.

"Bye, drive safe." She held his hand in hers, not let-ting go. His feet refused to leave her apartment. Yet he stepped over the threshold and she closed the door behind him.

On his way to the car, a distinct feeling someone was watching him pressed on his mind. Slipping behind the wheel, he glanced at the second story window, just above Kate's apartment. The woman who'd intercepted him on his way in stood on the other side of the glass and blew him a kiss. She then pointed her two fingers at her eyes then at him.

She was watching him all right, and he would make sure to keep a watchful eye on her.

# Chapter 12

The phone's shrill ring pierced Kate's sleep. Her head still swam while she tapped her hand in search of the blaring device. Her fingertips brushed the handheld piece under the sofa. She hit the talk button and the noise ceased. Thank God.

She kicked off the covers and rolled over enough to press the phone to her ear.

"Hallo," she croaked, blinking and trying to get her bearings. Where had she fallen asleep? On the floor, on top of the cushions she'd sewn for her and Mile's séances. Yes, they smelled of him, but there had to be some other reason why she wound up in the living room in the middle of the night.

"Are you planning to come to school today? I hope you're not sick." Andrew's worried tone blasted though the phone.

"Shit!" She jolted to a sitting position and glanced at the digital clock on the stove. Green numbers flashed 10:29. Double shit! "I slept in."

"At least you're fine. No worries. You didn't miss anything. The test got postponed until next Tuesday. The teacher's sick."

She staggered onto her feet. "I want to go to the English class." A long yawn broke her words. "I think the teacher said we'll go over the final."

"I can take notes and one extra handout for you. Take the day off. You worked hard all these years, never missing a class."

By all means, she deserved a break. Still, guilt plagued her and so did the concern in Andrew's voice. "Thanks, but I'll come to class."

"No, go back to bed. I think I know why you slept in." He dropped his voice to a whisper. "Your pupil and neighbor won't stop bragging about him and Amanda last night."

"That was her with him?" Kate rubbed her sore eye that wouldn't stop tearing. What had possessed the college's most popular girl to jump in bed with that low life, Miller? It could be he was the only guy she had not slept with yet. After all, she wouldn't leave any man behind, if she'd thought they were halfway decent.

"Did they keep you up?" Andrew's mocking tone irked her.

"Keep me up? I'm surprised the dead haven't risen. Must've been well after midnight by the time I fell asleep, only to be awakened again by her screeching like a hell cat, bed creaking and thumping against the wall."

"Shoot, not something I'd like to listen to while trying to catch some shut eye. Apparently she's climbed on the good ol' Miller express many times." Andrew's snort blared in her ear.

Kate fluffed up the pillow Miles had leaned against last night and caught a whiff of his cologne. Why couldn't it have been him who kept her up all night long? "How many times did Miller say she took the ride?"

"Oh, last I heard six times, but the number keeps going up."

"Right." Her voice dripped with sarcasm. "Had he forgotten my apartment is under his? It was more like three times and the last time it sounded as if she'd had all the fun."

"Um-hum. I thought so."

"What possessed her to stoop so low?"

"Well, according to Miller, she bumped into your friend in the parking lot and...well...offered him her..." Andrew cleared his throat. "...services. But he declined and when she got upstairs, she jumped Miller and couldn't get enough of him."

"What?" Kate gasped. This bit of info chased away the last trace of sleep and she stopped her hand from rubbing the tired and sore eye. "Why would she—How did she know Miles?"

"Miller told her, sort of to defend you. Amanda called you lesbo. She's cunning, that much is clear, but my guess, she's just jealous that a good looking guy would hang out with you." Loud voices drowned Andrews's words. "Look, if you're planning to come to class, I'll meet you at the cafeteria."

"I'll hop in the shower, then I'll head to the campus." She ended the call and stretched her arms over her head while another yawn pushed a long moan out of her mouth. The hell with Amanda and her insatiable desire for men. For once, a guy had not taken her up on her offer. Perhaps Miles's refusal would show her she wasn't all that bootylicious after all. But could Amada handle a rejection? Well, Kate would find out the moment she stepped into the classroom, if she stayed clear of Amanda long enough to reach the room on the second floor of the D wing.

She flipped on the bathroom light and headed toward the shower curtain with its pink sea shells. The bright colors of tropical fish on her toothbrush holder and matching trash bin never failed to cheer her up. The oil beads inside the round dish on the bath filled the small room with sea breeze scent. A year since she'd purchased those pricy scented balls, and they still held their fragrance. Few things in life were worth splurging on, and the way her bathroom transformed her to the beach where warm breeze and sun caressed her face, was invaluable. She could never bring herself to drop one of those beads in her bath water.

She cranked the shower dial as high as it would go and took her time stripping. "Fast" and "hot water" didn't go together in her basement apartment. What a dump.

Her phone rang. She flipped the towel over her shoulder and pressed the phone to her ear. Assuming Andrew got impatient waiting for her to show her face in the cafeteria, she blasted. "I said I want to shower first."

"Okay!" Miles's sexy voice filled her ear. "Now I'll spend the rest of the day fantasying about you under the steamy water."

A short chuckle shook her, but heat rushed to her cheeks. "I thought it was Andrew. He's got some gossip he wants to share with me."

"Gossip? Since when are you interested in rumors?" Miles's voice changed to high pitched and surprised.

"I'm not, but—" A nagging deep down told her not to mention his encounter with Amanda.

"Listen, I'm taking a few minutes' break. I thought I'd leave you a message on your answering machine, but to my pleasant surprise, I caught you at home." His voice changed again. "You're not sick, are you?"

"No, I slept in. Hit the snooze button and woke up two hours later," she lied, hoping he wouldn't catch the tremble in her voice. Though her excuse was the truth, she had heard the alarm go off, but couldn't keep her eyes open for longer than a few seconds.

"Hate when that happens." He seemed to dismiss her predicament. "I won't keep you then. Would you be up for getting together this Saturday?"

"Sure." She couldn't suppress a smile. "Are we continuing with the story?"

"And to share a nice meal. I don't want you to think I'm using you only as my writer."

"I would never think that." Her heart sank. The story couldn't be so close to the end yet. Maybe she should stall for more time. "You don't have to rush it. I mean, there's time."

"Don't worry. Lots of story left to be told." A female voice cut through the background, probably through the hospital's PA. "I'm being paged, have to go. See you on Saturday then. Would around six in the evening be good?"

Kate couldn't distinguish the name of the announced doctor, but she could swear it wasn't Rušinić. "Yes, doctor, um, what did she call you? Something like Zrin."

"You must be hearing things again. Got to go. Bye." His abrupt end of the call had her raising her eyebrows, but maybe he was right and she'd heard it wrong.

The splash of running water had her rushing to the bathroom. She'd forgotten about her shower and now steam filled the small space. After adjusting the water temperature, she stripped off her panties and bra and stepped under the spray. Despite the contact with warm water on her bare shoulders, she shivered. Amanda's unavoidable scolding caused a tremor. The slithering woman had had plenty of time to stew and build up her venom. She took pride in splitting couples up, so no girl stood a chance if the boyfriend caught her eye. Only Miles wasn't a boy. This time she'd face the ultimate challenge, one she couldn't hope to win. Neither would she accept defeat.

Why hadn't he mentioned anything to Kate? Maybe he wanted to spare her worrying. She lathered up her hair and tilted her head back under the warm water. An image of his face replaced the fear of Amanda's fury. His lustful gaze roamed over her naked, wet body. Would he only fantasize about her in the shower or could he see her across the distance? He was capable of many mind-blowing things. Maybe he really was watching her.

That was another crazy idea. If he was somehow present, he'd be a perfect gentleman as always, not invade on her privacy like some Peeping Tom. Still, the idea he might be looking in on her made her hurry up with her shower. She turned off the water, reached for her towel and wrapped her nakedness. How silly of her. Miles wasn't here, though she wished he was. His devouring stare, the one she'd imagined, sent pleasant, vibrating heat through her core and forced her to press her hand to her lower abdomen. For a split second, she wished she could be brazen like Amanda, to get Miles into bed under any circumstance and not think of complications of their actions later.

Why did sex have to complicate everything? She missed the closeness of lovemaking. Maybe she should try—crazy! Why stoop so low? He would refuse and think less of her. She worked a comb through her wet tresses. There was no time for foolish notions about him. It would never happen. No point losing her head and getting all worked up with fuzzy feelings.

She dressed in haste, shoved her books into the backpack and left the apartment. The bus pulled up around the corner, and she yanked the monthly pass from her coat pocket. She rushed up two steps, flashed her pass at the driver, and settled into a window seat. A few stops later, the university building appeared, filling her with dread. The best way to deal with Amanda's bitterness would be to ignore her, because there was no point in trying to prove to the class bully whether or not there was something going on between Kate and Miles. Besides, since when did she owe any explanation to anyone?

The bus pulled up to the curb and she lined up at the exit door. The door flung open and wayfarers poured out of the vehicle.

With both hands pressing on the horizontal bar of the main entrance, she swallowed her breath at the sight of Amanda and her cronies leaving the cafeteria with extra-large paper cups, munching on danishes. They were a strange sight to behold, all three of them dressed in bell-bottom pants and bulky turtlenecks, not showing an inch of bare skin. Must be a new fad in one of those magazines Amanda hid inside the textbooks and flipped through during classes. Kate flattened against the wall. If luck was with her today, the lockers would hide her. She wasn't ready to face the spiteful wench and her tag-alongs.

Thankfully, the trio seemed more immersed in their treats than who was around. Once her adversaries ambled away, Kate rushed to the cafeteria. Andrew tapped the stir stick against the tabletop then straightened in his chair.

"Finally." He slid the second cup toward her. "It's lukewarm by now."

"Just the way I like it." She popped the slit on the lid and took a sip. The bitter coffee filled her mouth and coated her throat. "It's fine, I haven't had my cup yet and by now I'll take it frozen." She sipped again. "So, what have you discovered?"

He scowled, tilting his head. "Nothing that I haven't already told you. I'm afraid Amanda's bent on humiliating you. She's been making distasteful jokes about you all morning."

Kate placed her hand on his jittery one. "Don't worry. I know how to handle her once and for all."

"I do hope so. In that case, we have five minutes to make it to class." He got to his feet, slung his backpack over his shoulder and picked up his coffee cup.

"Okay, let's sink her." Kate grabbed her stuff too and followed Andrew out of the cafeteria.

A few people she met in the hallways gave her puzzling glances. Some hid their snickers behind their hands, while others nodded their heads and said a friendly hi.

Silence engulfed the classroom on her way to her desk. Heads moved closer together and voices dropped to whispers. She plopped on the chair and proceeded to take her book out of the bag. The stench of stale cigarettes alerted her of Amanda's approach.

"So, have you bored that fine man to death yet?" Amanda's snarl reached her and her platform heels entered Kate's vision.

Though her heart pounded, she ignored the menacing classmate, keeping her focus on her things.

"Look at me, rock bottom, or whatever your name is." More anger resonated in Amanda's tone.

Kate got to her feet and pursed her lips, staring her down. "You should mind your own business and stay out of mine."

"Oh yeah? I'll do just that, once I find out what you have that I don't." Amanda leaned forward, her expression as if she was about to vomit. "That man's got some serious cash. I can tell. Not like these losers here. I'll be damned if I let you enjoy it."

"From what I heard, in the absence of my friend, even Miller was good enough for you. Whatever happened to the coach what's his name? You claimed he was your man." By now, Kate's heart threatened to burst out of her chest. The students in the classroom uttered a long, collective ooh, turning to Miller. He grinned and pounded his meaty chest.

Amanda's face reddened, most likely not from embarrassment. She shrugged. "I'm sick of coach's smelly truck. Bet screwing in the back of your friend's car is hell of a lot better. And Miller's a moron, I wouldn't do him again."

*Good to know I'll get some sleep tonight.*

"I bet you won't find out if my friend's car seats are comfortable," Kate spat. "Back off and leave me and my friends alone, or this won't end well for you."

"You've got nothing on me," Amanda pointed at Kate then spun away.

For a second, Kate clamped her teeth, but anger burned through her nostrils. Her enemy was backing off and she should let go too, but she just couldn't. "Now that you mention it, I think I do."

Amanda halted on her way to her seat and snapped her head in Kate's direction. "What?"

"I saw you with crib notes during many tests."

An insecure laugh crossed Amanda's lips. "What crib notes, you liar?"

"Don't play dumb. You know I saw you. Or have you forgotten how you pleaded with me not to tell?" Until now Kate had kept quiet, but it was a fact she'd planned to use against Amanda if need arose.

"I saw you with crib notes too." A student seated behind Kate chimed in, his thick East Indian accent.

Amanda glared at him. "As if none of you never cheated on a test."

Guilt stabbed Kate's conscience. Not that anyone could prove an invisible man had helped her during the exam, and if she admitted no one would believe her, but she had technically cheated once. Better to steer clear from this topic before she lost her bravado. "I'll keep quiet if you stop intimidating teachers and students."

Amanda glared and pursed her lips.

"Stop putting in complaints if you flunk a test. It's not the teacher's fault. Don't harass and make fun of students you don't like." Kate glanced at the teacher, who'd entered the classroom, but she remained standing. Sitting down would indicate defeat.

"Cut it out and take your seats. That goes for you too, Miss Fournier." The teacher's tone was uncompromising.

Amanda huffed, scowling at Kate, but took her seat all the same, a promise of future retribution in her narrowing gaze. Kate drew in a long breath then let it out slowly. Andrew pushed a piece of paper under her nose.

*Good job handling the wicked witch,* the note read. She smiled, but her gut feeling wouldn't let her enjoy this victory. Amanda was not likely to give up once she dug her claws in deep enough.

# Chapter 13

The vacuum cleaner drowned out the music coming from Kate's old boom box. Immersed in her thoughts, she pushed the appliance over the worn - out carpet. It had taken three steam-cleaning treatments to remove the stench of stale cigarettes from the broadloom. However, there was nothing she could do to revive the dull beige color. Lucky for her, the superintendent had the carpet steam vac and was more than willing to lend it to her. The super's eagerness probably had something to do with the fact that it was his duty to keep the place spotless between the tenants. Pity, she learned of this only in recent months. It would've saved her fortune on cleaning supplies and not to mention the time and effort she put into getting the flat up to her standard of cleanliness.

The weekend couldn't have come fast enough, no matter how busy she kept. The saying about time passing slowly to those who wait showed its true meaning. For the rest of the week, Amanda and her cronies had sent hateful glares Kate's way. At least they kept their distance. Rumors the three of them had spread failed to hurt her. Their venomous tongues could lash, but she ignored the lies. They would stop once they figured out she wasn't flinching and their distasteful jokes got old. Kate shook her head, if Amanda and her friends put this much effort into school work instead of wasting their energy on gossip, they'd be scholars.

She shut off the vacuum and retracted the cord then glanced over the apartment. Not a single thing seemed out of place. The doorbell rang in a series of long buzzes indicating a person lacking patience was on the other side. Lost in her thoughts and the drowning hum of the vacuum, she must have missed the doorbell earlier.

A peek through the peephole confirmed Miles waited on the other side. She pulled the door open, greeted him with a grin she couldn't suppress. In an instant Amanda and her evil plotting was forgotten.

He stepped inside the foyer and closed the door. "Sorry if I annoyed you with the ringing. The vacuum stopped so I leaned on the bell before you turned it on again."

"It's a noisy bugger," she said, storing the appliance inside the broom closet. "But it does the job and it came with the apartment."

"I'm not keeping you from house chores, am I?" His eyebrows rose and he gave her a puppy-pleading look.

"No, I'm almost done," she lied. Even with her long to-do list, she couldn't turn him away after such a display. "It's been a crazy busy week and I didn't have time for any tidying. Plus with the weather finally turning warm, it's hard to stay indoors and do house work. This dank weather forced me to do all the chores I've been putting off for far too long."

"Well, in that case, I hope you're ready to continue our story." He brushed his index finger down her cheek.

His touch caused a pleasant shudder straight to her core. If he hinted to spend this rainy day in his embrace, she'd put all her plans aside. Alas, he didn't. All he wanted was to carry on with his life tale. "You mean your story."

"By now I prefer to think of it as ours. After all, you spent many hours reliving this with me, then you wrote the story down. Hope you can see it the same way—it's your story too." He leaned and placed a soft kiss to her cheek.

"Now that you put it in perspective, you're right." She pointed at the cups on the cardboard tray in his hand, hoping he didn't see her pucker her lips and close her eyes in anticipation of his kiss. How stupid to think he'd kiss her like a lover not a mere friend. "What you got there?"

"Neither of us are drinkers, so I brought us large coffees." He placed the holder with two paper cups on the table and removed his shoes. "It would be a shame if I dirtied your clean floors."

She nodded, scrutinizing his footwear by the front door. Though his loafers appeared brand new, the grooves of rubber soles were caked in mud. She joined him on the floor. He handed her one cup. She wrapped her hands around the warm beverage. He sipped his coffee, tapping the floor with his free hand for her to sit closer.

She scooted on her behind along the carpet, stopping by his side. His hands wrapped around the paper cup and she abandoned the hope he'd pull her in his embrace she'd craved so much. It was better to focus on the story and forget the giddy girly thoughts. "Did the burly guys bother you after Dobrila's father ordered them to beat you up in the garden?"

He nodded, took another sip, then wrapped his arm around her shoulders and pulled her to him. She breathed in his musky male scent. He knew just what she needed.

"They tried, but shortly after the garden incident, I was sent to Doge's military service in Venice."

"Your father came true on his threat." Her heart sank to her stomach. The few tender moments he got to spend with Dobrila only meant more separation. Their parents must've believed the distance would do its thing and the two lovers would forget each other. But their parents didn't plan on time apart to make love between their children stronger.

"Most of his threats were empty and I didn't fear them, but this time he acted on the advice of his magistrate. Dreadful man," Miles mumbled, dropping his glance to the cup in his hand, then shook his head as if trying to dislodge a painful memory.

"Let's continue with the story, then." Not wanting to cause him more grief, though the way history recorded the unfortunate love, the sorrow was guaranteed. She placed the cup on the floor and reached out to him.

He lowered his beverage at his side and took her offered hands. "At least my family and Dobrila's agreed on one thing, to keep us apart."

"Seems they would stop at nothing to put distance between you two. What happened to Dobrila?" The sting of tears in her eyes came unexpectedly. Kate dabbed her eyes on her sleeves before the tears spilled out.

She was the biggest sucker for tragic love stories, and to see them play out before her eyes, turned up the dial on her emotions.

"Dobrila was under strict house supervision. Not allowed to leave the palace unchaperoned. It was a hard, miserable time for both of us." He squeezed her hand. "No more talking, let the vision take over from here."

"Sure," she whispered. Images invaded her mind.

∽∾∽

Dank soldiers' barracks sat in rows in the deep mud. A heavy downpour pounded on the thin roof, while rusty buckets, placed over the stuffy room caught leaks. The small fire in the corner smoky stove had died hours ago and a chill crept through the cracks in the walls.

He sat on his bunk. For the fifth time he read over Dobrila's aunt's letter brought to him by a soldier, hoping on this occasion the words would somehow change. The old Countess Demetrija had her doubts regarding the nature and righteousness of such a marriage. Papers rustled as he dropped them to his lap. No, Conte Vitturi wouldn't go this far to stop their love. He wouldn't force Dobrila into a marriage with such an old man, be that man of noble birth or not. Of course, he would—anything so Miles and his family wouldn't win the century-old feud.

He let his gaze trail over the barrack. How many months had he wasted here? He lost track, every day was the same. Men in poor state, sick, tired, and hungry occupied their free hours by playing cards, smoking or just sleeping. Night after night, he fall asleep, staring at the Dobrila's image his mind conjured up in the tarnished window pane. Enough was enough, he'd get out of here first chance he got and stop the imposed marriage.

The opportunity presented itself a few days later. His orders were to take the correspondence to the troops stationed a day's horseback ride away. He didn't care to stop, only hurled the bag over his head at the gate and spurred the horse on into a full gallop, ignoring the shouting voices behind him.

He had to keep going. Dobrila would be wed in four days and he faced two leagues of hard riding. By the end of the second day, he traded the exhausted military horse for a strong mule. At least the animal was eager to carry him on his journey. He rode day and night, staying off main paths, avoiding direct routes for fear of getting spot-

ted. After all, now he was a deserter. His life had turned
into one dark nightmare.

The dawn of the wedding day found him a few miles
away from his village, but the mule had taken its last
step. After emitting a loud neigh, the animal collapsed on
its side, gulping air. He pulled the dagger from the saddle
and left the hinny lying on the road. He continued on hurried feet, pushing his stiff and sore body. Seemed the
beast residing in him decided to retreat and let him deal
with this predicament on his own.

The church bells rang over the village, announcing a
joyous occasion from the belfries. The first few dwellings
had banners on the house Vitturi and some other man or
house he didn't recognize. Most likely, the one of his beloved Dobrila's soon to be husband. Not likely to happen
while his heart still beat.

People clad in their Sunday's best rushed to the village square in front of the church. He followed them,
keeping his distance. No one paid any heed to an unkempt hobo, for that was how he must've appeared. Four
days growth of beard itched and dirt caked in every
crease of his body mixed with his sweat. There'd be time
to wash and shave later, now a more pressing matter required his attention.

The village square spread in front of him, decorated
in lavish décor, promising an elegant wedding venue. His
heart clenched. This should've been for him and Dobrila.
Tables laden with platters of food and sweets, and many
casks lined the stone walls assuring wine would be
poured freely, attracted peasants and pocket pickers to the
square. In the corner, three pigs rotated slowly over the
open fire, grease dripped and sizzled on the red embers.
Suckling pig—he'd love to sink his teeth into tender
meat. Despite his growling stomach and dry throat he carried on toward the makeshift pulpit in deep shade of foli-

age canopy where Dobrila stood in her white gown. The puffiness around her eyes confirmed she had spent the night before her wedding in tears. The man by her side attempted to take her hand, but she jerked her arm away from him, then slapped the bouquet of white roses at his shoulder.

No, not white roses, Miles always envisioned she would hold a bucket of crimson roses at *their* wedding. Flowers in their full bloom picked from the bush his mother had adored during her short life in Rušinić castle.

The priest carried on with his muttering, reading passages about sacred marriage duties and love from the Holy Bible. What would he know about committing to a woman?

Soon, the man of the cloth leaned forward and changed his intonation, asking the Dobrila's would-be wedded the dreadful question—if he would take this woman to be his lawful wife.

Before the elderly man could answer, Miles broke into a run and reached the altar. "No! He cannot wed her. She loves me."

All action halted, a collective gasp came from the crowd and heads turned to the unfolding drama, but he grabbed Dobrila by her waist and pulled her to him. Terror on her frozen face alerted him of impeding danger.

"No, Miles. This will make things much harder for us," she whispered, but he couldn't care anymore. Why couldn't their families see the war they wagged on each other would destroy them and there'd be no winners, only losers?

"Who the hell are you?" The bridegroom's long face contorted, and he turned his head to Dobrila's father. "I don't need this humiliation. The deal is off," he yelled, ripping off the white ribbon tied around his arm identifying him as a groom, then hurried away from the altar.

The priest's mouth hung open and his hand hovered over the open Bible held by an altar boy. "Sacrilege!"

"Don't worry, Father. I'm sure Conte Vitturi already paid you well for your service." Miles turned Dobrila away from the altar, but men in her father's employ surrounded them.

Two bulldogs tore Dobrila away from Miles. Her father, his face red in rage, stepped to her and slapped her across her cheek. "I've had enough of this shame. Take her."

"Do not touch her," Miles growled, jerking against the restraining hands, and imagining Conte Vitturi's skull cracking under his. Someday he would have the pleasure of inflicting the pain on the despicable man.

He faced Miles and smirked. "Don't think I wasn't counting on you showing up here. This time I'll make sure you two never see each other again."

"Where are you taking her?" Miles glared at the spiteful man in front of him. Dobrila struggled against the grip of the two men who dragged her toward the coach. The rage inside Miles reached over boil point, erasing his exhaustion. Still, he couldn't break the constraints of the three brawny ruffians Conte Vitturi employed.

"None of your business." Conte Vitturi spat and glanced at his men. "This time I want him dead. Do not fail me." He left the scene to follow his hysterical daughter. Miles had to hand it to her, she gave those browbeaters a hell of a time, kicking their shins and biting their wrists. If only she'd be brave enough to slam their groins.

He wrestled free from his captors, rushed toward the carriage where the cretins shoved Dobrila. The reins cracked the mules and the closed, black coach took off before he could reach it. His sore legs wouldn't listen. The crowd on the village square parted to let the carriage through. It sped and disappeared from his view.

"We can't kill you here in front all these people, but we'll find you." A brute he had not seen before in Dobrila's father employment brandished his knife, making a throat slashing gesture.

Miles gave an exhausted chuckle. *Fool beyond compare.* "I'd like to see you try."

The same brute halted, turned around and approached with slow steps. "You're getting too cocky for your own good, you shrimp."

Miles scratched his cheek. By now, his body stench must've attracted flies. "And you may want to ask the previous guards about a kid beating them to a pulp. I may appear scrawny to you, but trust me, you don't want to find out how strong I can be."

The man snorted, contemptuous smile stretched his thick lips. "Right."

Miles thrust his hand against the chest of the man standing mere inches in front of him. The wall of muscles stumbled backward, flapping his arms in a feeble attempt to regain his balance. Despite his efforts, his backside hit the stone paved ground and he emitted a deep growl. Miles spat and left for his castle. He'd listen to his father's sermon on how his rash actions brought such shame on both families today and then find a bath. At least he'd achieved his goal and stopped the wedding. Knowing Dobrila, she'd find a way to get word to him. Then he'd find her and take her away once and for all. Someplace no one knew them, where they could love each other without fear of getting caught.

సౚస

Kate sat in silence for a while. Miles's story was as recorded in history, only seeing it before her eyes had a whole new impact on her. He was right, though. It was her story, too, and not because of his involvement with her great-great-grandmother prior to Dobrila's return from Vienna. She lived every moment of Miles's troubling journey together with him.

She glanced at him. He sat next to her, stroking his chin and staring straight ahead, barely blinking. Then he slowly closed his eyes, letting out a long sigh. His rage had caroused through her when Dobrila's father struck her. She wished she could crawl into the story, slap the conte's long cheek, and shout at him. Poor Dobrila always so quiet and obedient would never disappoint her father, let alone hit him back.

The dusk slowly settled and extinguished little light coming into the apartment from the high basement windows. Kate pulled on the string hanging from the lamppost.

"Wow," she croaked, blinking until her eyes adjusted to the light. "I've got a sense of triumph and a growing determination for the two of you to find a way to be together."

"I hoped you'd get that from today's session." He drew in a loud breath as if to release tightness in his chest. "After this there was nothing but heartache for us."

"No, it can't be. The legend says your parents reconciled and they agreed for the two of you to marry." She clamped her mouth shut. How could she blurt out something like that? That harmony was short lived.

"It's quite all right. No need for you to feel ashamed of the comment you made." He stroked her arm. "This all happened so long ago."

She picked her coffee cup off the floor, cold by now. Damn it, he always seemed to know what she'd thought. "Perhaps you'd like to stay for a dinner."

"How about I treat you to dinner? I spotted a posh little French restaurant on the corner." He arched, pressing his fists into the small of his back. "Ugh, sitting on the floor is hard. Let's eat now. I'm getting hungry."

"That's newly open. Looks pricey." She glanced at the laundry basket. Her best pair of jeans was in there, waiting to be washed, but she couldn't pass up on this offer. "Can I quickly throw a load in the washer and change? And do something with my hair?"

"Of course." He got to his feet, shook his legs loose, then pulled her up. Her knees buckled, and she leaned against his chest. He wrapped his arm around her shoulders and pressed a kiss to her temple. "Our time together means a lot to me."

"Means the world to me too," she whispered, tilting her head toward him, hoping he would press his sensual lips to hers. Safe in his embrace, there was nothing more she could ask for in her life. She loved him just like her ancestor. Unlike her old great-great- grandma, if they couldn't be together, she wouldn't let that send her to madness.

His eyes narrowed but instead of a kiss, he brought his forehead to hers. "Go do your laundry."

# Chapter 14

The red sun dipped behind the tall maples by the time Miles swung the car into the visitor's spot at Kate's apartment building. His leather coat creaked against the car seat when he turned to her. Butterflies fluttered inside Kate, making her skin tingle. During dinner he had seemed distant and reserved. Maybe he would end this evening with one of his toe curling kisses, but if she was reading his signals right, this date would follow a different route.

His eyes crinkled at the corners. In the fading light they appeared dark as midnight, bearing intensity in their depths and making her shiver. The smile on his face widened, showcasing a set of perfect white teeth. How she loved his seductive appearance. She drew in a sharp breath.

No woman could resist his charms. No wonder Amanda desired him.

Kate swallowed against her dry throat. "That was a wonderful early dinner. The restaurant's name Soufflé suggested French, but I never expected it to be Greek."

Two irresistible dimples formed on his cheeks. "Up until the late '70s, French was the most taught language in Greek schools. It's no wonder that many French words made it into Greek."

"Really? I had no idea." Wow, the extent of Miles's knowledge never ceased to amaze. Of course, his long existence provided him with opportunity to experience many of the world events firsthand.

"No, I prefer keeping a low profile and stayed away from the history turning points. Most things I've learned from books." He shrugged one shoulder as if to say "sorry to disappoint you."

She cocked her head, frowning. "How do you always know what I'm thinking?"

"I can read you." That same seductive smile lingered on his lips. Why wouldn't he kiss her already?

"Am I that obvious?" One of the reasons her ex-boyfriend had dumped her so callously was because he never knew what she was thinking. He'd said her quiet irritated him. Sometimes words were not necessary and silence spoke volumes. Despite her efforts, the two of them had nothing in common to talk about.

"Sometimes. Other times, I just guess."

Miles's soft voice pulled her from entering a dangerous path of painful memory. She'd promised she wouldn't wallow in self-pity over the no good two-timing buffoon who wanted nothing from her but sex. What stung the most was the fact she'd fallen for the jackass. She was old enough to know better, yet she'd caved in to his persuasions, and once he got what he wanted his interest in her dwindled.

"Oh." She wanted to say more, but Miles's answer left her bereft of words. Yet, he hadn't seemed to guess what had bothered her during the dinner, or perhaps she'd hid her annoyance well. She'd tried to discuss Amanda and her rudeness, but somehow couldn't find the opportunity to bring the issue into the conversation. Besides, that stupid girl wasn't worth wasting a single moment of her cherished time with Miles.

Judging by his distance, perhaps she was wasting his time now. She grabbed the door knob. "I think I'll make it an early night."

"You sit tight. I need to check something first." He pulled the keys out of the ignition and opened the driver's door.

"What do you need to check?" Perplexed with this sudden turn, she opened the passenger's door and put one foot out.

"I want to make sure the coast is clear. No one's waiting in the dark for you." He threw his replay over his shoulder before exiting the vehicle and shutting the door.

She paused and got out of the car. *Jeez, the doctor lacks tact when it came to breaking bad news.* At least her date wouldn't end here kissless and on the parking lot. She skirted around the hood. "Potter's gone and Miller's not a threat any more. I'm not some damsel in distress who needs a big guy to save her."

He took her hand in his, sending pleasant warmth along her skin. But it was his stern expression that delivered cold shivers up her spine. "I insist. Not because I think of you as some helpless damsel, but due to a danger I sense."

Her legs stiffened and knees locked. Ice laced her skin, extinguishing the heat flames. "What danger?"

"I wasn't going to bring it up, but…" He shrugged. "One of the girls from your school is bent on harming you. And she doesn't work alone."

"If you are talking about Amanda, I've heard and I handled her." At least she thought she did, but one couldn't be too sure when it came to Amanda. The girl seemed always on the manhunt and she had no trouble trading them for a "better model," as she'd put it. Little did she know, money only impressed lazy girls. If a woman worked hard, a wealthy man was a bonus, not a ladder to upgrade.

"No, she won't stop and you know it." He pointed at the building entrance. "Let's go inside. I want to make sure the air is clear."

Oh God! Where would this animosity end? First she had to put up with Miller and Potter and their sick pranks, now Amanda wanted to sink her claws into her skin. Kate's heart squeezed and tightened in her chest. The hurried feet and snickering she'd heard after she got out of the laundry room crossed her mind. At the time, she believed it to be nothing. Students in her classroom often whispered and snickered behind her and she never paid any heed to them. Miles's concern, however well intended, made her lose her nerve. What kind of surprise waited for her?

He held the door open and stuck his head in, reaching for the light switch.

"You should've told me about Amanda's brazen interception in the parking lot." Aside from the echo of the slamming door, the staircase seemed normal from where Kate stood, but she trusted his intuition.

"Yes, now I see it wasn't a wise decision to keep quiet about her, but at the time I underestimated her. Plus, I didn't want you to worry, especially during your finals." He turned to her and took her hand. "Everything seems fine, but let's keep our eyes and ears open."

"Maybe you're exaggerating. I mean, she is unpredictable, but I doubt she'd resort to violence." Kate's own words failed to calm her. Amanda might not get physical, but she would make complaints to student committees and bodies until she got what she wanted. That was how she rolled.

Kate followed him down the stairs. Nothing was out

of place and no one waited in the shadows. The tension between her eyebrows eased. "See? There's no danger."

"I must be sure." He turned toward the laundry room door. "Who has access to these facilities?"

"Every tenant has. Why?" From her purse, she removed the pendant holding her key ring and selected the one for her apartment.

Miles twisted the knob. "Can you unlock this door first?"

"Sure, my clothes are still in the washer. Since we're going in I may as well transfer them into the dryer." She slid the key inside the hole and pushed the door open.

Miles placed a hand on her shoulder, stopping her. "Let me go in first."

She propped the door open with her foot, while he scanned the room then turned to her, nudging his head for her to enter.

"You really are taking this a tad too far." She tried to lighten up his serious mood with some joke, but his stern expression remained.

She scanned the narrow room housing two appliances and a long table in the middle. Her laundry basket was on the linoleum floor next to the washer. Except for the drone of the dryer, everything appeared the same as she'd left it. "Didn't I tell you there's nothing here?"

He stared at the dryer. His shoulders did not relax. "When did you put the clothes in the dryer?"

"I didn't. My stuff is still in the washer. Someone must've come after me to do their laundry." She halted, her hand on the lid. If someone had found her stuff inside the washer, they'd empty it into the basket. No one would volunteer to put her clothes inside the dryer and insert coins required to operate the appliance.

A quick inspection of the washer confirmed her fear. It was empty. Her heart beat in her ears, while she placed her hand on the dryer's door. Again, Miles's hand landed on hers, stopping her before she could open the appliance.

Holding onto her hand, he pulled her closer to him and yanked the door open. Her clothes spilled out, but it was the state of them that had her gasp in shock.

"Oh! God! Who would do this? All of my clothes are ruined." She dropped to her knees and shifted through her shredded laundry. All her best pieces were ripped to rags.

A slightly wrinkled sheet of paper fell out of the pile, judging by its coolness, it must've been placed into the dryer minutes ago. He crouched in front of her while she read the typed message.

*The same thing will happen to your face if you don't show up and clear the lies you spread about me cheating on tests. The university is re-examining all my records. After all my hard work, I will not lose getting my degree this close to graduation. 9 a.m. sharp tomorrow, Student affair's office. Be there!*

She didn't need to look for the signature of the person who'd left her the threat. Miles took the paper from her hand. Miller must've given Amanda the key to the laundry room. The disgusting woman was watching her and knew she'd started a load of clothes before leaving for dinner with Miles.

"What am I going to do? If I go and say that I lied about Amanda using crib notes during tests, it'll look bad for me. If I tell the truth, she'll never leave me alone and God knows how far she'll carry this revenge." Kate buried her face in her hands. There was no way of winning this.

Miles wrapped his arm around her shoulders. The warmth and closeness of his body instilled her with calm. "You'll know when you get there. Your heart is never wrong. Listen to what it's telling you and you'll be safe."

"You think?" Following her heart so far had led her to choices she regretted. If she could rewind the past and make better decisions, her life would be better today. She tossed the shredded shirt on the pile and wiped a tear. "I could take her handiwork and her threat to the police and put in a restraining order."

"You could, but a piece of paper won't protect you. I'll stay with you tonight."

What? He couldn't read her signals for a kiss and now he wanted to stay with her the whole night? Yet, the thought of being alone tonight filled her with wretched misery. "You—you don't have to do that."

"I must. You're visibly upset and shaken. Don't worry about your clothes. I'll give you money, and you can go on a shopping spree." He squeezed her arm, pulling her closer to him. "Let's go into your apartment."

"You don't need to give me any cash. It's just one load of clothes. I have more." Worn out, stained, or shrunk rags for the most part, but she'd survive. Accepting money from him filled her with embarrassment. She scooped her ruined clothes into the basket and got to her feet. Amanda's plan had backfired if she'd planned to keep Miles away from her. Now, he was spending the night in her apartment. Not that any sexual activity would happen between them, but knowing she'd won this little battle made her insides flutter. A few less shirts were worth it.

Miles held the laundry door open and took the basket from her hands. "It's no trouble at all. I'm responsible for this mess. Please accept my offer. It'll make me feel better."

In a few steps, she crossed the hallway. She pulled the keys out of her pocket and unlocked the door to her apartment. It would be a travesty to pass on his gift, and how could she refuse after his begging tone? Heaving loudly, she pushed the door open and pinned him with the sharpest glare she could manage. "Okay, but only because it'll make you feel better."

His soft chuckle followed her into the foyer of her unit. She headed for the cabinet under the sink. How would this night play out? As much as she wanted him, due to Mother Nature's unexpected visit, she was not in position for anything physical. He lowered to the couch, stretched his long legs out and propped his back with a cushion. Judging by his relaxed pose, she didn't need to sweat if he'd be in the mood. She slouched to grab the garbage bag from the box.

"I'll take a couch." His voice reached her and she almost bumped her head on the piping.

She straightened and faced him. Okay, despite her indisposed condition, she had hoped they'd share her bed, however small, but clearly he had a different game on his mind. "Are you sure? It's lumpy. It's better to sleep on the floor cushions."

"Don't worry about me." He dismissed her with a wave of his hand. "I'm used to sleeping on all kind of beds. There's not much choice in hospitals and night shifts can be exhausting."

His words extinguished the last kindle of her hope. Shoving the ripped clothes into the garbage bag gave her an excuse to not to maintain eye contact. "I'll get you some bedding in a moment."

*God, can he hear disappointment in my voice?* It was her raging hormones. Damn that time of the month. Her face heated, and she hid behind the linen closet door, shifting through the sheets she could put on the couch. Once her heart rate returned to normal, she emerged, holding the double-sized set.

"Let me pull the sofa bed out. The couch is small for you to stretch."

"No rush." He patted the couch cushion next to him. "It's barely seven in the evening."

"Oh." How stupid of her. So focused on getting him into bed, she'd completely lost her mind. "Sorry, felt like it's later than it is."

"If you're tired, feel free to turn in for the night, but I was hoping you'd stay up with me." A slow smile bloomed on his face and melted any doubt. No matter how tired she might be, she would stay up with him.

"Of course." She shuddered. How on earth to occupy him and get her mind out of the gutter? In her past, she never spent the whole day, and a night, with a man. *God, he must think me pathetic.* "Do you want to watch TV or we can put a movie on?"

"Come here." He tapped the empty couch next to him.

In a few slow steps, she approached him and lowered to the couch. Left bereft of words, she fiddled with her fingers.

He wrapped his arm around her shoulders, bringing her closer to him. His features softened for the first time since they'd returned from the restaurant, and so did his voice. "I don't think you're pathetic. I was clear when I said it's not an appropriate time to start a new relationship. Sometime in the future we'll have the rest of our lives together. I gave you my pinky promise. And I'm a man of my word. I'll find you."

Her chest squeezed. He would keep his word he'd given her in the beginning and disappear from her life once he was done telling his story.

A deal was a deal, only now she wished she'd made a different arrangement.

He eased back into the couch cushions. "Continuing with our story will help you forget your anxiety over to-morrow's ordeal. However, the part I wanted to show you is a bit racy. Given your state of mind at the moment, I'm not sure how you'd take it."

Racy? She'd play dumb to his last comment because she must hear this. "What do you mean? I can take it just fine, I'll have you know."

"Are you sure?" He squeezed her hand as if in some reassuring gesture. "I can read you. I hope this won't come as a great disappointment, but what you desire will not happen yet."

"I don't desire anything." She faked a hurt tone, but when his eyebrow arched, she can under his inquisitive gaze. "Okay, I admit. A girl could hope, right? After all, you did kiss me before. Then you said it was a mistake."

He wrapped his fingers around hers. Warmth seeped from his skin and traveled up her arm, easing her awkwardness. "I'm sorry if I misled you. I shouldn't. It was my weakness. I won't let that happen again."

Oh no! He wouldn't kiss her at all. Never? She'd never feel his luscious lips? How she longed for her body to tremble against his firm form in anticipation. Stupid, developing feelings for him beyond friendship was not a good idea. She cleared her throat. "What did you mean by us getting together in the future?"

"Exactly that." He brushed hair off her forehead. "When the time for us comes, we will be together. Now is not the time and we should not force it." He shook his head. "I wouldn't be any good for you. I need to mourn her until sorrow no longer resides in my heart."

"Of course." How selfish of her. He was still not over the death of his wife and here she—oh God. Despite her tightening throat, her womb tingled. "So you don't love me now?"

"Kate," he whispered and closed his eyes. His shoulders rose and fell with his long breath. When he opened his eyes, longing reflected in those deep, blue orbs. "Of course, I love you. It's just…I'm not free to show you how much I love you." After an audible gulp he continued. "It's not proper. I hope you understand."

"I do understand." The ending of Phantom of the Opera replayed in her head. Despite the heroine's love for the masked man, he granted her the freedom to leave, and she left him in the vaults of the opera house. Miles could offer her little happiness and likely didn't want to compromise their future by rushing into an unstable relationship.

The old saying if you love someone, set them free, bounced in her mind.

"When is this future going to happen?" She blinked tears away while a shower of sadness poured over her. His sigh conveyed his desire. He wanted her. Maybe as much, or more, than she desired him.

His voice remained a bit shaky, despite his throat clearing. The two irresistible dimples appeared on his cheeks and melted her heart. "Sooner than you think. Right now, I want you to go out in the world and experience life, make mistakes and learn from them. Challenge yourself and grow as a person. I'll be here, waiting."

"Why can't I do all this with you?" The tears she'd been fighting spilled free, the test of curbing her thoughts and desires too much to take.

"Life with me will not be fun. Too often sadness pulls me under and suffocates all life in me." The softness of his thumb brushed tears off her cheek. "Let's go on with the story. Maybe you'll find the answers you're looking for in this vision."

"Yeah," she whispered, nodding and swiping her fingers under her eyes, then wiping her hands on her jeans. She braced for this *racy* part. After all, the events unfolded in this order and skipping or changing them would not do.

"Before we start, I need to excuse myself." He got to his feet, stepping toward the bathroom.

The box of tampons she'd left on the sink counter plunged to her mind. Her eyes widened and she let out a loud gasp. She sprang up and grabbed his arm, stopping him from entering the bathroom. His bicep muscle flexed under his shirt sleeve.

"Let me get in there first," she said.

A quiet laugh resonated from him and he lowered his chin while a playful glint sparkled in his eyes. "Go put your lady's unmentionables away before I can see them."

*Damn, how does he know what I'm thinking about?* This was beyond him reading her, or guessing. He must've heard her thoughts, no other explanation.

The weight of his gaze pressed on her as she crossed the room. He might say he didn't want her, that the time wasn't right, but the desire in his eyes told her otherwise. The talk about their future seemed plausible. He would wait for her, and she'd hold him to that promise.

# Chapter 15

Miles stepped into the small room, closed the door, flipped the switch on the wall, and sat on the toilet cover. Kate needed a few minutes to regain her composure. So did he. How had he managed not to scoop her in his arms and take her straight to bed?

He leaned against the cool water tank. It had to have been Emina's doe like face flickering in his mind that helped him turn Kate down. He scrubbed his hand over his face. God! Would he ever get over her death? To stop loving her wasn't in the realm of possibility. Not after three hundred years and everything they'd endured. The euphoric bliss replaced the hardships of their mortal days. Only their forevermore had not lasted, and death never should've ripped them apart. This should've been the happiest time of their lives, raising their little family as Emina longed for. Instead…

Kate had spent enough time alone. By now she must be feeling better. He punched his thigh and got to his feet. After splashing cool water over his face in the small sink, he pulled a towel with a dolphin from the rack. The whole room was done in sea motifs. A sea breeze fragrance even perfumed the air. Poor girl missed her home.

He opened the door and strode to the couch, gauging Kate to determine if she was more composed by now. She sat cross-legged on the floor. Her scowl was directed at his hands as he was wiping every finger on her white hand towel. "A professional hazard." He shrugged. "To a surgeon, washing hands is a full time job in itself."

The terry cloth draped over the chair backrest, he joined her on the floor. "Well now, we're both feeling good. Right?"

She gave him a curt nod and a half smile. "Have you felt your demon stirring lately?"

"A time or two, but as I said, the beast doesn't have the same grip over me as it once did. However, there's always the possibility." Wrapping her in his embrace, he gave her a slight squeeze.

Losing the monster's all-consuming hold had proven to be both the blessing and the curse. Ever since his bodily fluids returned, Emina would stop at nothing to give him children. Guilt was his. She wouldn't have disobeyed him had he not forbid her to risk her life with experimental pregnancy method. The drugs she'd taken were meant for mortal women, no one could have predicted the medicine would have poisonous effect on an immortal female. Babies were trapped inside their dying mother. There was no time to think. The gruesome picture of Emina's butchered abdomen would stay burned in his memory for an eternity. Kate's hand squeezing his shoulder yanked him away from the mournful state he was entering. "I'm glad you understand I didn't reject your love, only asked for some time to mourn. Let's put that issue to rest. Onto our story now."

The redness in her cheeks and eyes had receded. He was right, a short break gave her the opportunity to cool off her head, regain her composure and she seemed collected.

He extended his hand to her. A moment of awkward silence passed, she stared at the floor not accepting his offered hand. The words he'd uttered before he'd taken bathroom break, bounced in his head. Kate had fallen prey to her emotions and it was his fault. It hadn't been a year since he'd lost his wife and here he became close to Kate when he had promised he'd keep her at arm's length.

She expelled a tight breath, accepting his extended hand and closed her eyes.

"Wait, you're not going to ask me a slew of questions before we begin?" He liked her easygoing mood. At the end of the day, she was still his best friend.

She laughed, meeting his gaze. "Like what?"

He let go of her and scratched his jaw. Pondering her question, he flipped his hand palm up. "Like where was Dobrila sent after I crashed her wedding? Or how did my father handle the embarrassment I brought on the family name yet again?"

"Oh—h—h, that. From what I read, she was sent to a convent of St. Nicolas in Trogir and you were imprisoned in the monastery on Visovac." She arched an eyebrow, folding her legs under her.

"Correct." He nodded.

"But how did you restore the connection so far apart and under constant supervision?"

"Aha! A question." He raised his index finger. "I knew you'd eventually ask. Well, Dobrila's old nanny came through. Her nephew supplied monks with provisions. Every couple of weeks, he would arrive in his small boat to the tiny island in the middle of the lake. There'd be a basket of food for me with a letter or a note tucked under the pie. Monks never inspected the delivery."

She scooped her hazel-colored hair in a bun. "I often

wondered what it must've been like for you living there amongst monks. Did they try to get you to ordain?"

"Oh, they tried." He paused, and his gaze drifted toward the floor. He uttered a soft humph in a memory. "One brother in particular was quite persuasive, kept saying I would find inner peace if I opened my heart to God." After another short pause, he shook his head. "It didn't work."

"I can see it didn't. So, how did you slip out of the monastery? I thought the monks watched you day and night."

He allowed a slow smile on his face. "Dobrila had a plan to escape on the night of high prayer when all nuns are preoccupied with their pious obligations. The nephew hid me under some sacks in his delivery boat and rowed away from the island. I kept to myself, never joining monks in their prayers, so naturally no one went looking for me. They just assumed I was reading in my room or somewhere in the garden."

"Yes, but—"

"Uh-uh, no more questions." He pressed his index finger to her lips. "Let the images take over and you'll get your answers."

He reclaimed her hands and she closed her eyes. For a moment, he concentrated on her breathing. It wasn't long before the crunching of hurried feet on the gravel road replaced the sound of her steady breaths. Worn out black leather riding boots appeared behind his closed eyes. He was rushing to rendezvous with Dobrila.

"You are exhausted, your legs ache, but you keep pressing up the steep and narrow path. Last night's thunderstorm forced you to take shelter. You lost time, and you are worried about her. The last redness of the dipping sun left the sky dusky. Soon the darkness would engulf you. On this desolate mountain, road robbers and ruffians are a common occurrence. If something happened to Do-brila you would never forgive yourself for agreeing with her to run away."

The squeeze of her hands on his confirmed she was seeing his vision, and he slipped deeper into the séance, pulling her into the moment with him.

ᴄ⁄ᴐᴄ⁄ᴐ

He peered into the receding daylight. The boulder at the end of the dirt road stood devoid of any sign of life. His heart sank into his stomach. Dobrila had not made it to their meeting place. What would he do now? Wait for her, as he had done for years. She would make it...unless she wandered off when she couldn't find him. Where would she have gone?

Coldness of the rock pressed through his sweat soaked shirt. Soon, the night would turn cold and his drenched skin would cool off fast. After he took care of unbearable thirst, he must find a shelter for the night. He tilted his water skin, but only a dribble reached his parched mouth. Damn, he should have listened to the young man who'd snuck him from the island and taken two of the offered skins, but with all the food the boy stuffed in Miles's pockets, he believed another provision would slow him down.

The darkness fully descended on the earth. He must've fallen asleep, for the click of a metal pierced thorough his haze. When he opened his eyes, he was staring down the barrel of a flint pistol in a dirty hand. Slowly, he trailed his gaze up the tattered shirtsleeve and torn neckline to a face overgrown by a dark, thick beard. The man grinned, flashing a golden tooth.

Six more men stood behind him. It didn't take a genius to realize he was ambushed by highway robbers.

He'd welcome it if they found a way to kill him, to end his misery once and for all. He raised his hand in a surrender gesture. "If you find anything of worthwhile on me, take it."

The same man crouching in front of him put the pistol down and offered him his hand. "We're not here to kill or rob you."

"We're not?" One of his fellows spat on the ground. "How are we to collect the rest of the prize on his head?"

"The prize?" Miles frowned. What else could God want of him? He had nothing else to offer.

"Shut your mouth, you idiot." The gang's leader barked at the questioning man. He jiggled the coin purse fastened to his waist. "We already collected the prize, only Conte Vitturi doesn't know. Or perhaps by now he should."

"So, he hired you to kill me. I'm glad you helped yourself with the full reward. He will not pay you when you finish the job. One question, how would he know you'd find me?" Miles accepted the offered ruffian's hand and let him pull him up to his feet.

The ruffian didn't answer. Instead, he flashed another grin and tapped Miles on his shoulder. Perplexed, Miles scanned over the unkempt group of men. "What made you change your mind?"

"Not what, but who." The gang leader waived his hand over his head.

Small and fast steps approached. Dobrila's dirt coated yet sweet face emerged from the crowd of bearded men. Her blotchy eyes widened. "Miles," she exclaimed, grinning. She flew to his embrace and he pressed her to his chest.

"Oh, my love. I lost all hope. The nuns at the convent of St. Nicolas said you ordained. When I couldn't find you, I almost believed that." She rained kisses over his face. "I was desperate. These men found me roaming the mountain road and offered to help. I was sceptical, but what else could I do?"

He could barely part his lips from hers to utter a few words. "I am sorry, my dove, I'm sorry I was late to meet you. I'm not a monk. I can assure you of that. Everything will be fine now."

"Ah, a young love. Always gets me right here." The gang leader tapped his fingers at the left side of his chest, his face crumpled.

Who would've thought? A romantic ruffian. He wouldn't start crying, would he? Miles pulled Dobrila closer to him. That she'd led these men to him meant her father knew of her escape.

The man raised both arms over his head and whistled. "Time to return to our village." He faced Miles and Dobrila. "You're coming with us. There's a cottage you can stay in for a night or for life. We don't care, everyone's welcome to our lot."

Miles tipped his chin at Dobrila in his arms. "What do you say? Shall we live free as peasants in their village?"

She gave him a soft smile, her gaze following the man leaving them to the darkness. "It'll have to do for tonight. You wouldn't seriously think about spending your life with them. Life is easy picking for them, robbing law abiding folks."

"I would. Our social status, the wealth, the pompous families, nothing matters, if I cannot love you." He turned in the direction the men had gone and followed them down the same road.

"But, Miles, truly. The education we received means nothing to you?" She wrapped her arm around his waist, and gathered the long skirt of her torn dress in her free hand.

"No, without you the world around me would change." He pressed a kiss to her head. Perhaps she would see his reasoning and abandon her rich life.

They walked in silence the rest of the way, following their captors turned rescuers. The cluster of stone built huts with thatched roofs appeared in the valley. They descended a steep hill and were greeted by women and children who met them at the village. Two young women rushed to the leader's arms, their loosely laced bodices revealing the bouncy swells of their breasts. He wrapped them in his embrace and spun, then crushed his lips to one then the other. Barely peeling away from them, he turned to Miles, pointing his chin at the small building to his left. "You can stay in that cottage over there. I trust your woman will keep you warm tonight. I know mine will keep me plenty busy."

"So she will." Miles nodded. Judging by the wink and a grin the ruffian gave him, the village expected to hear sounds of love making all night. He would not disappoint them.

The group disbursed. The leader spanked the bottoms of both girls. His hands gripping the girls' rumps, he led them to his place, his roars of laugher reverberated off the stone houses.

Miles led Dobrila to their humble accommodations. He lit the candle on the windowsill, picked up the iron cast holder and turned the dim light toward the room. A narrow bed with wooden headboard and a wood plank doubling as a table surrounded by three stools occupied most of the hut's floor. "Small but clean."

Dobrila scowled. "How could you consider living in this cupboard? My chamber is two times bigger than this entire cottage."

"Dove, these people were nice to offer us a warm bed and food for tonight. The least we can do is to be grateful." He caressed her shoulders, pulling down the lace. "They expect us to make love and we shall not disappoint them."

She gasped and her face turned crimson. "You want to indulge them?"

"Why not?" He shrugged. "After all, this could be the only opportunity we have."

A sigh left her lips, but in the next instant a brazen grin appeared on her face, confirming she wanted him. "It's improper before we are wed, but my father won't have any choice if you ruin me. I waited years for this and those two shameless hussies should not be the only ones who will get their dose of their man tonight."

"Making love to me will not ruin you, only make you better." He cupped her face in both hands, brushed his thumb over her lips then crushed his mouth to hers. His tongue explored her soft and warm mouth. He teased her by plunging deep until her body tightened against his. She reached for him, snaked her arms around his neck, coaxing a groan out of him. He lowered his hands to the small of her back, pulling on the bodice of her dress, leaving it hanging loose on her waist.

She withdrew and gasped, covering her breasts. "I'm like a tavern wench."

"You're nothing of the sort." He cupped her nape and urged her back to his lips, while he struggled to step out of his boots. His feet rejoiced once freed from the stiff leather wear.

She returned his kiss and slipped her hands under his shirt. To his amazement, she pulled his tunic up and over his head, then glided her hand over his bare chest.

"So big, firm, and smooth." Her whisper was husky with desire.

Each of her kisses ignited white sparks behind his closed lids. She tugged on the waistband of his breeches.

He covered her small hand with his large one and helped her undo the knot. The pressure on his groin eased as the garment slid from his waist and legs. He crushed her to his chest. She arched against him, and their hips thrust. A fierce ache built deep in his gut.

He scooped her in his arms, and she gave a small shriek. "Oh my God, Miles, loving you freely is so beautiful."

"I told you the riches don't matter if we're not free." The bed squeaked as soon as he lowered her to the straw filled mattress.

She giggled. "The villagers will get their entertainment tonight."

"And every night from now on, I hope." He scrambled out of his loincloth and quickly covered her body. "I can't wait any longer. Can you?"

Her eyes darkened, and she pressed her lips to his. "Take me now, my love. I'm yours."

She wrapped her legs around his hips. In one slow motion, he glided his erection inside her moistness until her muscles sheathed him. She gasped next to his ear, making him groan.

The moment of their lovemaking consumed him. Her hands glided over his back and shoulders, her soft kisses on his heated skin, the whispers and gasps in the darkness, all mounted his excitement fast. They rocked on the rickety bed until her body tensed under him, and her hips bucked.

"Oh God—Miles—I can't hold on anymore," she panted before a long moan ripped out of her throat.

Afraid the beast inside him would awaken and urge him to hurt her, he fought the climax, but lost the battle. An immense orgasm built up and rocked his body. He groaned with her, pressing their laced hands deeper into the mattress.

Wave after wave of pleasure pulsed through his flesh, arching his back.

The tremors subsided and he collapsed over her, relaxing a hold on her hands. She panted while tending his lips with gentle kisses.

Leaving his legs tangled with hers, he slid to her side and spooned her. Overjoyed the monster inside him stayed dormant, he wanted to make love to his sweet Dobrila over and over again. Judging by her glossy eyes and relaxed brushing of her fingers on his arm, exhaustion was setting into her body. Now that he held her secure in his arms, he too succumbed to his fatigue, but he continued to circle his thumb over her nipple until it pebbled.

"We'll keep the village up all night if we carry on like this." He leaned in for a kiss.

"They asked for it," she said, laughing before meeting his lips.

*✺✺✺*

The vision behind his eyelids ceased and he blinked fast to get his eyes adjusted to the light of the lamp. Miles squeezed Kate's hands and cleared his throat. Her face was expressionless. Her shoulders rose and lowered with her long sigh before she opened her eyes.

"Well," she gasped. "That was quite something."

"I worried if I should show you the first time I made love to Dobrila, but you took it pretty well. Though I must admit, I didn't show you every detail." He gave a quick tilt of his head. In fact, showing more details could turn into some strange porn and he didn't want Kate to see him in a different light. He waited for Kate's reply, but she only nodded, staring into the space. She must be overwhelmed by remnants of emotion left by the vision and the love it conveyed for Dobrila. "Some things are better left undisclosed." After another pause, he got to his feet. "Now it's getting a bit late."

She grabbed the bedding from the chair. Her hands trembled while she tried to get the fitted sheet around the edges. Maybe he shouldn't have shown her the vision. She was going to have enough trouble sleeping with Amanda's threat.

He covered her hand with his. "I can sense your unease. Lay down with me and, for one night, forget about this world."

She froze. Only a blink indicated she still paid attention to him, but by her expression, she wasn't appalled. "I'd gladly lay with you. I better change into my nighty. Oh, wait. I don't have a nighty anymore. Amanda shredded it." She left for her bedroom. What would she wear when she stepped out of her room? It would be near impossible to contain his desire if she wore a negligee. She reappeared in her oversized T-shirt, and he expelled a breath of relief.

"I need to get something from my car."

With the bed made up, he grabbed the keys from his coat pocket and stepped out of her apartment. The crisp spring evening air enveloped him as soon as he set his foot out of the building.

He shivered in his cotton shirt and took longer and faster strides to his car, grabbed the two pieces of green fabric from the back seat, and rushed back to Kate's apartment.

"Hey, I have this spare toothbrush. It's still in packaging and it's yours if you want it." Her voice drifted from behind the closed bathroom door.

"Sure," he threw over his shoulder, stripping off his clothes in haste then pulling on the cotton pants and top.

The bathroom door popped open and she stepped out, toothbrush in her hand. She gave him a once over, then burst into laughter. "Are you getting ready to perform a surgery?"

"Laugh all you want. The scrubs are very comfy to sleep in," he said, keeping his gaze at the drawstrings of his bottoms, but her bare, long legs entered his vision.

He flipped the cover, lowered to the bed and tapped the empty spot next to him. She gulped and lowered onto the mattress. Coils dipped under their weight.

"There's no need for uneasiness. You're safe here. We're friends." He drew the blanket over her and pulled on the string of the lamp on the side table, leaving the room in a dim light of the digital clock.

With his arm draped over her hips, he gathered her closer. Gazing into her eyes, he urged her mind to relax. "Sleep now."

Her lids lowered. She drew in a long breath, then another and her steady breathing continued. The rigid hold of her hand on his shoulder loosened and her hand slid off. He laced his fingers with hers then pressed their joined hands to his chest.

# Chapter 16

Through her lashes, Kate stared at the low ceiling of her apartment. She yawned and turned toward Miles. His side of the bed was empty, but the warmth of his body lingered on the sheets and pillow. Running water echoed in the shower, a sign he hadn't left. Good thing she used sea scented bath products. He wouldn't come out smelling like fruit or flowers.

Sleep fuzzed her head, calling her back to slumber. How had she fallen asleep so fast and so deep? Normal shuteye would have been a faint snooze and she would have awakened when Miles left her side. Why didn't her senses register the shift? It was almost like she'd passed out.

The bathroom door popped open and humidity flooded the room. He stepped to the bed and placed his hand on her shoulder peeking from the covers. His lips thinned into a funny frown and he tsked. "Come on, sleepy head. I thought you'd be up and dressed by now."

She moaned, because she wanted him back in bed, not because he was pestering her to get out. "A few more minutes, please."

"You used them all up. Come on. Out of bed." He sat

on the couch armrest and towel dried his damp hair.

Propped on her elbow, she drank in his muscular arms, shoulders, and chest, trimmed to a narrow waist, his hips wrapped in her best pink towel. What would happen if she leaped at him and pressed her lips on his? The flare of heat faded. He would refuse her and she'd feel embarrassed and awkward.

He halted and peeked at her from under the towel.

She gulped. He must've heard her thought or *read her*, as he had put it. Better play dumb and pretend nothing happened.

"Okay." She rolled onto her back and kicked off the covers. "I'm getting up."

"That's not it." He bent, picked up his shirt from the floor, and shook the garment. His gaze narrowed while he slid his arms through the sleeves, giving him the predatory appearance. "Hmm…"

Oh, no, she didn't like the sound of his hesitation. Heat rushed to her cheeks. "What are you pondering?"

"Whether to indulge you in one kiss, but I'm afraid it would lead to other things." He buttoned his shirt. His casual tone changed to lecturing. "Kissing leads to touching and…well, you know how it usually ends."

Her mind spun. He had read, perhaps even heard, her unspoken words. It gave her the creeps. She licked her lips, yearning for his tongue to do the same. "Come on, Miles. We slept together. The kiss can be just that. Nothing more."

"We shared the bed," he said, turning away from her. His belt buckle clinked while he pulled the trousers over his legs and his taut butt. "Better go get dressed."

"Okay, I get it. You're acting like a jerk because you want to distance yourself from me so when it is time for you to leave I will say good riddance." She regretted the words before they left her lips. Of all people, he didn't deserve this kind of treatment. Still, with every word he said, he buried a dagger deep in her heart. "I'm sorry. I didn't mean to hurt you." She tugged on the hem of her shirt, stretching the cotton closer to her knees. "Guess the saying is true, we hurt the ones we love the most."

"No, Kate. Don't speak like that. I'm sorry. We're going back and forth on this issue." He approached with slow steps. His mesmerizing gaze captured hers. She couldn't blink or look away, only chew her bottom lip. His arms snaked around her shoulders, and he pulled her to him. The warmth of his body wrapped her close. He leaned back, cupped and tilted her chin. His sharp jaw tightened. "I suppose one kiss won't hurt."

Her pulse quickened and she had enough time to close her eyes before he crushed his lips to hers. Relief flooded her and her spirit soared, he wasn't angry at her hurtful words. His bottom lip coaxed her mouth to open and she met his demanding tongue. Heaven. He was kissing her like he owned her. Her heart swelled with love for him, the one person who befriended her in the most unusual way and took care of her when she needed it most. If he granted her one kiss, perhaps she could entice him to do more.

Alas, it would not happen. Their love could never be, at least not now, not for a long time. The realization was like a cold slap to her face. She trusted him with her heart, more than she had trusted anyone in a very long time, but kissing was bad idea.

She broke the kiss and smiled. "Thank you for this."

"No," he whispered, closing his eyes, his luscious lips slightly open. "Thank you."

Silence hung heavy and she searched the apartment for something to focus on. Green numbers flashed 8:15 on the digital clock on the stove. "Oh my God, is that correct time? I better get ready or I'll miss my bus." She eased out of his embrace and headed toward her bedroom.

"I've been urging you to get your tush in gear, haven't I? Hurry up, and I'll drive you to the campus." His playful voice reached her before she shut the bedroom door.

Oh—h—h God, she could die in his arms. She plopped on the bed and cradled her forehead in her palm. A dark shadow eclipsed her heart. Last night's vision replayed in her head, only she imagined his hands caressing her body, his lips planting those hot kisses on her neck.

She shrugged off the fantasy and grabbed a long tan skirt and button down burgundy shirt. Couldn't appear before Amanda and the student council like she had just rolled out of bed, even if she had. Out of her nightclothes, she dressed in haste and clasped on silver neckless with a tiny crimson rose pendant to complete her outfit. Dyane's farewell gift always brought her luck. It was one fancy thing she had and only wore on days she needed good fortune on her side.

Maybe her witchy friend breathed some kind of magic into the piece of jewelry.

On her way to the bathroom, she caught a glimpse of Miles on his cell phone. After running a brush through her hair, she scooped the thick bundle in a low ponytail. A rinse of her face in cold water would have to do. She lifted the blouse and sprayed body mist on her stomach and wrists. Jasmine scent filled the small room.

A glance in the mirror confirmed her invigorated appearance. The deep sleep Miles had somehow inflicted on her had recharged her body and mind. She no longer feared Amanda and her cronies. Still, her stomach squeezed. The conniving twit would have a dirty trick up her sleeve, for she never played fair.

Ready to face the world again, she tugged at the bottom of the shirt, straightening the creases around her waist, and then opened the bathroom door.

He went still, his hand halfway to his coat pocket. "Wow, you look sharp. I'm sure you'll do great today."

"God, I hope you're right." She grabbed her purse and jacket. He held the apartment door open. She stepped through and spun the keys in three locks.

"I know I am. You wait in front, and I'll bring the car around." He rushed up the stairs and out of the building.

She reached the first landing at the same time Miller shot down the stairs. "Hey, Kate."

Anger seething, she pointed at him and frowned. "Don't you hey me."

His steps faltered, the rucksack swinging on his shoulder. "What?"

"Did you and Amanda have a good laugh at my expense?" She expelled a hot breath through her nose, her chest heaving.

He shook his head, and scowled. "I don't get it."

"Oh—h—h, you don't?" She curled her fingers into tight fists. "It must've been hilarious. Now that I helped you get your grades up, you continue your sick pranks. Instead of Potter, you have Amanda to taunt me."

His eyes widened, while red color flushed his face. "I swear, Kate, I have no idea what you're talking about. And for the record, I never wanted to be mean to you." He hung his head as if in sudden fascination with his feet. "I was hoping you'd notice me, that's all." He shrugged one shoulder. "You didn't."

Nothing but sincerity infused his tone. Maybe she'd been wrong about him and he wasn't involved with Amanda's threat. She lowered her fists to her sides and swallowed to steady her voice and racing heart. Never before had she stood up to a bully. Her new-found courage dried up her throat and mouth. "Did you give Amanda the key to the laundry room?"

His mouth hung open. "Shit! That's where my key went. I've been looking for it since she spent the night at my place." He narrowed his eyes. "Why? Has she done something?"

"What do you think?" Kate flung her hands in the air. "She's threatening me to clear her name before the student committee and say that I lied when I accused her of cheating on the tests."

"Crap, man. I'll go with you and confirm she did cheat. I saw her with crib notes too." He pulled the zipper of his hoodie all the way to his double chin.

Her initial anger toward Miller deflated, replaced by the hint of compassion. "No need, she'd just ruin both of us. I think I can convince the committee of my innocence."

"Be careful. She can be vicious, like a feral cat, when she's threatened." Miller turned his head toward the glass entrance door as Miles's sleek, black vehicle pulled up by the curb, fluffy clouds reflected in its tinted windows.

"I see your *friend* is here. Good luck today. I'm sure it'll all work out." Acid laced Miller's tone. He squared his jaw. A frown of disgust scrunched his nose.

With his hand on the door handle of the building entrance, he halted and glanced at her over his shoulder. "I never took you for a gold digger. Guess I was wrong, after all." He stormed out of the building, his head hung, before she could say a word.

She jerked her head backward so hard, her ears hurt. Miller liked her and wanted her to notice him and, therefore, he'd chosen to go along with Potter and play mean pranks on her. Yeah, she'd noticed him all right, only not the way he had wanted. And now he resorted to calling her a leech. Nothing she did or said could prove she, in fact, was not sponging off Miles, but what did it matter? She didn't owe any explanations to anyone and certainly not Miller.

She squared her shoulders and pushed the door open, then strutted to the passenger door. Soft instrumental music came from the speakers. She settled on the seat, appreciating the feel of leather caressing her backside. Yet another thing she'd miss once they parted ways. The idea to continue on without him in her life had sunk in—she could barely stand the thought—but she must be strong and learn to endure loneliness again.

"Did I see your pupil storm out?" Miles's voice jerked her out of her reverie.

"Yeah, I kind of feel bad," she said, buckling in. "He didn't know Amanda took his laundry key, and I accused him of being in cahoots with her." She flipped the visor down and inspected her face. Wow, a restful night had done wonders. Or maybe being in love had brought this glow to the surface. So what if she couldn't have him? She could pretend he was beside her, but she'd be talking to herself and not to him. Still, there had to be a way for them. No, she would admire and love him from afar, and wait for him to throw a few crumbs of affection her way.

God, she got handed her great-great-grandma's unfulfilled destiny. The one he couldn't bring himself to execute on her ancestor and therefore had secured her future by marrying her off to a crippled man. Kate's heart squeezed. Now he would leave her in a few weeks since the story was close to finishing. Hope was all he would leave behind after he vanished from her life.

Miles pulled up in front of the Greek restaurant they'd dined in last night, breaking her train of thought. "Why are we stopping here?"

"I ordered us some breakfast." He cut the engine and eased out of the car, but left the keys in the ignition, leaving the weep of a violin to drift from the speakers.

"We don't have time for breakfast," she shouted before he closed the door.

He hurried on toward the restaurant entrance and slipped in the black doors. She eased back into the firm seat. After a few minutes, he emerged, a large paper bag in his left hand and in his right a cardboard tray with two tall paper cups.

He sipped on his beverage before opening the car door, then slid behind the wheel and handed her the bag. "The rest is for you."

"Thank you, but you shouldn't have." She grabbed the bag and dove inside.

"Of course I had to. Your fridge is barren." He dropped his drink in the cup holder, then started the engine and pulled out from the parking spot.

She placed her cup next to his, lining the opening with his. At least their cups could meet where their mouths touched. In a way, she would get a small piece of him next time she took a sip. Paper crinkled under her fingers and she found a golden bagel with a generous portion of cream cheese in the middle. Her stomach growled and she took a big bite.

"Mm-mm, this is delicious. How come you're not eating?" She spoke around the bite. Miller's accusation brought bitter bile to her throat. Maybe she was sponging off Miles. Since she'd met him, he'd taken care of her in every way.

"Not hungry in the morning." He checked his side mirror and changed lanes. His grip on the steering wheel tightened and he gave her a side glance. "Miller's wrong. You're not sponging off me. It's my pleasure to take care of you."

"Someday you'll have to let me in on this secret of reading my thoughts." She took another bite, savoring the bagel and soft cream cheese. The fact that he knew her every thought had not phased out any more. By now, she was convinced she couldn't hide a thing from him.

He rolled a low chuckle. "Perhaps someday I'll teach you how to read others."

Crumpling the wrapper, she swallowed a mouthful, then reached for her coffee. She popped the lid and blew on the steam curling from the dark surface. "You can teach me any time. Why wait for someday?"

He pulled up at the curb in front of the main campus building. "Not today. When can I see you next?"

"Whenever you want." She replaced the lid on her coffee and gathered her bag.

"This weekend then." He nodded. "I ordered dinner for you, at the restaurant. They'll deliver it to your door at seven. Are you going to be home by then?"

Stunned, she stared at him. He had ordered her dinner? "Yes, but—"

"No buts, you need to eat." He gave her a reassuring smile and pointed at the digital clock on the car's control panel. "You better go now. And don't worry, you'll win this thing."

"Okay, I believe you." She smiled, but butterflies rose in her stomach. With her fingers on the handle, she cast one more glance at him. "I'll see you this weekend."

"I can hardly wait." His wink sent those nervous butterflies to flutter again, only this time they spread over her entire body.

She stepped onto the curb, then stared at the taillights until he turned onto the main street and disappeared from her view.

Time to face Amanda. With slow steps, she approached the entrance of the campus building. Andrew paced the hallway back and forth, chewing on his nails. He dropped his hand to his side and his shoulders relaxed. "I was afraid you wouldn't show up." He fell in step with her.

"And let Amanda win? Never." She increased her pace. "She isn't the only one who can play the game."

"I'm coming in with you. If they're allowing her to bring along her entourage, then you should have one person on your side." He spoke fast, keeping up with her pace and pulling his baseball cap off his head.

Kate halted and turned to him. "Thank you, Andrew."

"Don't mention it." He squeezed her hand. "You stood by my side every time I've gotten picked on for being gay."

"Hey, that's what friends are for." She tapped his arm and cast a weary glance at the office door. "Let's face them. Shall we?"

Amanda perched on a desk, black shirt loose over her long skirt, a large crucifix chained around her neck. Kate snorted. Goodness, the girl lacked a wimple and coif to complete her pious nun's costume. Her expression mimicked those of angels depicted on church icons. Would this committee fall for her sudden devout appearance? It wouldn't be much of a surprise. After all, she bamboozled her way through the entire teaching program.

Kate took her seat in the chair farthest away from Amanda and her cronies.

Andrew joined her on her left side. He leaned closer, cupped his hand over his mouth, and whispered, "Can you believe the nerve of her?"

"She looks ridiculous." Kate bit her lower lip to stifle her chuckles. When Miles got wind of this, he'd roar with laughter.

An older man entered, followed by two more teachers—a stern-faced middle aged woman, and a younger male in jeans and T-shirt who closed the door. Silence fell over the room while the trio took their seats behind a plain desk. The woman tugged on her dark suit jacket, passing the stacks of paper to her two co-workers.

"Since we are all present, I believe we'll begin." The man with graying hair spoke, lifting his wintry blue eyes from the papers in front of him. A grimace settled on his wide face as if he stifled laughter. "Miss Fournier—" He pointed at Amanda and cleared his throat. "Why don't you start by explaining how you obtained over a thousand signatures on your petition to have Miss Rokov expelled from this institution?"

A wrecking ball punched Kate in her stomach. The bagel threatened to come to the surface. Wait. What? Amanda had done what? No, no, she must've heard that wrong. The vile girl hadn't had time to collect that many signatures in one day. Unless…oh, God! She must've accumulated them over time. When had she started?

The fake cross swung on Amanda's ample chest as she rose. "Students practically begged me to sign the petition."

Simone snorted. "Yeah, right. We all know how you got those signatures."

Kate snapped her head up at Amanda's exploited crony's interruption, her eyes widening at Simone turning on Amanda. But she shouldn't be surprised, the girl finally got that Amanda and her group had used her.

Amanda spun on her heel, her wide eyes turned at the girl. "Shut up, Simone. No one's asking you."

The young committee guy put his hand up, cutting Amanda off. "No, miss. Do come forth if you have something to say."

Simone sprang to her feet, sending her glasses askew. "She asked people to sign a petition to have a vending machine placed in the cafeteria, not to have anyone expelled."

Amanda's eyes narrowed, warning written on her face directed at the turncoat on her brigade. "From now on, go hang around your fat mamma, not us."

Simone crossed her arms over her flat chest and pushed her thick framed glasses tight to her nose. "You cow, so now you'll resort to fat mamma jokes. My mom died when I was little. My aunts raised me. Wanna poke jokes about that too?"

Amanda flashed a tight-lipped smile and wobbled her head, but said nothing.

Simone wrinkled her nose and shook her head. "Remember this when you don't have money for an extra-large coffee and a danish."

The small-framed woman behind the desk lifted her head from the papers she'd been writing on and addressed Amanda. "So, this is really about a vending machine?"

Amanda's lips quivered, her murderous expression replaced by confusion. She looked to her cronies for support, but one by one, they averted their gazes to the floor or their fingernails.

"Miss Fournier, we're still waiting on your answer." The woman's lips thinned to a pink line on her skinny face.

"Well, yes." Amanda hung her head. "I didn't mean to…err…" She broke into a high-pitched giggle.

The hell she didn't. Kate expelled a tight breath. Now the committee needed to prove Amanda did cheat on the tests and this meeting would come to an end.

The older man cleared his throat and addressed the room. "The committee reviewed your tests and concluded you need to retake three of them."

A loud, collective gasp echoed in the room. Andrew rubbed his hands. "The witch is dead."

The same man held his hand in front of him, cutting

the audience from premature clapping. "Consider your-self lucky. Some of the teachers believe you earned the grade on your own merit. This meeting is adjourned. Miss Fournier, please stay behind for further instruc-tions."

Kate stood up, but couldn't bring her feet to move. That was all? She had fretted and, if not for Miles, she would've spent the night tossing and turning. She wanted to approach Amanda and slap her, scream, and curse at her. No, she was better than that. She swung her bag over her shoulder and left the office.

"This is far from over, rock ass." Amanda's growl reached her at the threshold.

No, it wasn't finished. When it came to Amanda, she had to keep humiliating someone every chance she got. Kate glanced at her enemy. Amanda's face flamed red and her eyes glared.

"For the record, my last name is Rokov."

# Chapter 17

While most students sweated final exams, Kate's diligence during the semester had earned her an exemption. Inside the campus library, she headed for her favorite table tucked beside the shelves of cataloged books. For the next two periods she planned to catch up on Miles's story.

She scrolled through the music library of her laptop and settled on a country tune. Due to the *Quiet, Please* signs plastered in every corner, she made sure the volume wasn't loud enough to seep from her headphones. A click on the icon of her taskbar brought a fresh blank page on the screen.

Every nerve in her body clamored with excitement. She scratched her temple, shifted in her chair, cracked her fingers, tapped them on the tabletop, and stared at the books' spines on the nearest shelf. Why couldn't she concentrate? How she wanted to talk to Miles, but most of the day he'd be in meetings. Would he think of her? Those few moments before she'd fallen asleep in his arms returned to her mind. If only he would hold her like that every night. She quit daydreaming. The cursor flashed on the white background, each word she'd typed deleted. She closed her eyes and placed her fingers over the keyboard. Now, what had he shown her? Oh, yes, the first time he made love to Dobrila. The soft kiss Miles planted on Dobrila's lips. Her image replaced Dobrila's. His mouth descended so slowly on the tender spot of her neck, his hands caressed her own body. Heat pooled in her core. She crossed her legs tight, imagining his muscular body pinning her naked to the mattress. If only. Those tender moments, his soft whispers of endearment, gasps and caresses were not meant for her.

Her fingertips tingled. The sensation increased to a painful burn and traveled up her hands. She opened her eyes and wiggled her fingers. The searing became unbearable. What the hell?

She frowned. Pressure that had built at the back of her neck eased, and she forced her shaky hands onto the keyboard. She slowly typed the flow of words as the fantasy replayed. The keys clicked faster and louder with the culmination of the vision. She perched at the edge of the hard chair and squeezed her thighs against the strong tightening of her core, however pleasant, but the action only increased the sensation. Heat roasted her cheeks. She glanced around. Squirming in her chair like a horny teenager was a sight best left unshared.

Damn it. Writing this scene in a public place wasn't the greatest idea. But writing it in the privacy of her home might tempt her to take care of her own itch, and with Miles's ability to block her from seeing him, he could be there watching. No more visions of lovemaking with Dobrila. A girl could take only so much.

She scanned through her typing, the heat inside rising with each word. A bit of tweaking here and there, but some good work. If she reacted to her own written words this way, she'd nailed the passion between Miles and Dobrila. She'd love to watch him reading this passage.

Would he laugh or squirm like her? Yes, the entire story was about him, but describing his actions in this particular scene without sounding silly proved quite challenging.

A tap on her shoulder had her jumping in her seat. She flipped the headphones from her ears and turned. A skinny girl carrying a bulging backpack stood behind her. Thick glasses made her dark eyes appear huge.

"Excuse me," she said, slipping a crisp white paper under Kate's nose. "The librarian said I can find this book in the teaching resource isle, but it's not there. Can you help me?"

Kate glanced at the reception desk. No librarian. The woman rarely minded her post, anyway, and when she was there, she had her nose in a book. "Maybe the book is taken out. That librarian wouldn't bother to check."

The girl shook her head, sending her wispy bangs to fall over the rims of her glasses. "I asked her and she said the college copy is not to be checked out and that I can find it here. I really need it for my assignment."

The pleading in the girl's voice jarred Kate's pity. Poor, lost first-year student. Rookies were not likely to find much sympathy from the experienced students, let alone a member of a graduating class.

Kate saved her work, minimized the program and lowered the lid on her laptop. She stood and stepped toward the shelf. Unattended things often went missing in this college, but she'd keep her eye on her stuff. Besides, she'd only be a few steps away. "I know which book you're looking for. Everyone used it during the first semester. You can copy the pages you need. So at least you don't have to sit here for hours and write things down."

"I appreciate your help," the girl droned, trailing behind her. "I'm fast tracking through summer, hoping to end this torture sooner."

Smart kid. Pride filled Kate's chest. The fear of being away from her home for the first time had filled most of her first year, she'd still remember those days with fondness. The girl reminded her of her own eagerness to hold her diploma. At the beginning of the program, graduation seemed far away. The two summer courses she'd taken before third semester had eased the load. "You won't think the same when you graduate."

She ran a finger along shelved titles. Everything except the one the newbie needed. "Sometimes students misplace the books."

Kate stretched her neck to glance at her stuff. Still there.

The girl crouched and examined the low shelves. "Can't find it. What does it look like? The books on this shelf are mixed up." She pulled a tome out. "Look, this one's 'Economics 101' in the area for teaching resources."

"Just leave that book out on a table and it will get shelved where it belongs." Kate rounded the corner. Bingo! Familiar book with big, dark letters. "I found it."

"Oh, thank you." The girl sprang up and flew to her, grabbing the book from her hands. "I don't know what I'd do if you didn't find it."

"Hey, don't mention it. It's my pleasure to help you. Good luck with your assignment and everything else." Kate nodded.

The girl scooted away, taking her seat at the small table tucked between two shelves. Kate pivoted to return to her place. Her heart dropped to her stomach. The laptop was missing.

Crap! That was what she got for helping others. Amanda had to be behind this. Probably hid her laptop as a prank. The twit.

She pawed through her bag and searched nearby tables. Nothing. What the hell? She'd left her computer right here, it couldn't have flown away. The librarian was back at her desk. Perhaps she'd seen something.

Kate gathered her bag and headed for the librarian. Stacked books covered the surface of the long, sand-colored desk. "I'm sorry to interrupt, but did you see someone take the laptop from that round table?"

The woman's lips curled down and she shook her head. "I was away from my desk and I'm not a keeper of student's personal things."

Loud laughter drifted through the wide open double doors. Students gathered around Amanda while she read from the screen of an open laptop. Her laptop.

"He took her in his embrace and sealed her lips with his. Ooh." Amanda's mocking voice boomed over the collective laughter.

Kate's gut clenched, but she tightened the grip on her bag and hurried toward the circle, elbowing her way to the ring leader. "Give it back, Amanda."

Amanda lowered the laptop, revealing the stupid grin on her face. She'd traded the silly outfit she'd worn at the meeting for a low cut top and a short skirt. Instead of a crucifix, a long necklace with large beads hung over her bosom.

"And if I don't? What then?" She flicked her eye-brows and returned her attention to the screen. "Oh, classic. Listen to this! 'He lowered her to the mattress and covered her naked body with his.'" Once again she yanked the computer down and smirked. "Pfft, as if you'd know anything about sex. You probably wear grandma's boring flannel nighty in bed."

"Why don't you write volumes on the topic since you have extensive experience? You should know what I wear in bed. You shredded it last night along with my other clothes." Kate bit hard on her lip. "Give. Me. Back. My. Laptop. Now."

Loud cheers and whistles erupted from the crowd. A few curious onlookers pumped their fists and chanted, "Fight, fight." Others, males mostly, joined in the lilt.

Kate filled her lungs to push down brewing rage. The last thing she needed was to act on impulse and indulge the crowd in their frenzy for catfight.

"Come on, Amanda." Miller's deep tone turned heads in his direction. "Don't be such a bitch."

"What's it to you, Miller? You got a soft spot for a frump girl too?" Amanda flipped her bleached hair over her shoulder and puffed her large chest. "I don't get it. All of the campus guys have the hots for her. What the hell do we need her for? She just takes up space. Think of all those who couldn't enroll in college because of these foreigners. And when they graduate, they'll take our jobs." Amanda extended the laptop toward Kate. "Come and get it then."

Miller lowered his gaze at his sneakers, shook his head, then walked away. So much for his help.

Focused on Amanda, Kate stepped for her computer. She avoided further provocation by ignoring Amanda's comments. Every college offered enrollment to students from other countries, she had not taken anyone's spot. Nor would she take anyone's job. Applying to advertised positions was open to all who qualified, so let the better person win.

Amanda grinned, flipped the computer over her head. "Catch."

The blue case flew across the crowd, landing in someone's outstretched hands.

"Got it." A young male at the back of the crowd called.

Kate ran to rescue her laptop. Too slow.

Amanda ripped the computer from the young man and sprinted for the railing. She held the laptop over the banister of the third floor balustrade. "You want it, come and get it." The laptop in her hand tethered and she flashed her yellow teeth stained with red lipstick.

Kate took a tentative step, her hands trembling. *She won't dare.*

Amanda loosened her grip and the laptop slipped out of her hand. "Oops, clumsy me."

Onlookers rushed toward the railing and leaned over, letting out loud gasps.

"No." Kate gulped. Her heart stopped as her computer plummeted toward the hard floor of the campus foyer.

The fast descent of the blue case halted mid-air and the laptop spun, hovering above a wide-eyed student's head. He slouched and scurried away, and the laptop eased to the floor in a gentle movement. Curious spectators oohed and aahed at the phenomenon.

"What?" Amanda shrieked like a rabid cat. "How is this possible? It defies all laws of gravity."

Kate tore down the stairs. Potter followed on her heels, shoved her aside and stomped with all his might on the lid. Plastic cracked. Amanda cheered.

Miller rushed Potter and pulled him away. "Stop this, you moron."

Potter struggled against Miller's hold, but managed to stomp on it several times and kick the laptop against the wall.

Kate's heart stopped for the second time. Something had prevented the computer from crashing to the floor, but would it survive Potter's damage?

Two campus security guards broke through the crowd. She flew toward the broken laptop. *Please, don't let it be totaled.* She picked up the cracked and busted piece off the floor. Components rattled and bits spilled out of the broken frame.

The wide-open foyer spun, and she staggered toward

the main door. Her chest squeezed. She could live without most of the things her computer stored, but not Miles's story. Stupid of her not to back up her work. She should have skipped a few meals and saved up for a memory stick. Her sob hitched and made her hiccup. She pressed the computer to her chest. The security guards escorted Amanda toward her. She didn't care. Her world was already shattered.

The trio stopped in front of her.

"Miss, do you want to press charges?" The guard's words barely reached her through the fog around her brain.

She nodded. It was time to stop people like Amanda and Potter who mistook kindness for weakness. She'd let them walk all over her for far too long.

"You also need to charge Mason Potter." Miller pushed his way through the throng, holding onto Potter. Resolve filled his expression while Potter jerked against his grip. "He jumped on her computer."

"You asshole," Potter sneered.

The other guard nudged Amanda forward while his counterpart took hold of Potter's shoulder. The twit stuck her tongue out at Kate. "Let's go, you two. Security office. Police are on their way."

"Kate!" Andrew skidded to a halt in front of her, the rucksack bouncing on his back. "I heard what happened. Shit! She has gone mad."

"The story, Andrew." She forced the words out. "It's lost forever. All my hard work."

Andrew flashed a half smile, insecurity in his eyes. "Data from the hard drive can be extracted and restored."

"This isn't an episode of CSI. It doesn't work that way, and if it does, I'd need a forensic team to recover anything from this wreck." Her throat tightened and her last words came out as a high pitch squeal.

"It's been done. Don't despair." He put his arm around her shoulders.

"What am I going to do with data with no laptop or computer to use it?" She didn't know where to look. The pity on Andrew's face bothered her, but not as much as students in the lobby halting to point at her and form circles to whisper. Yet none approached her to offer help or a kind word.

"I'll talk to students. Maybe we can collect money for a new one." Andrew's casual tone coaxed a half snort out of her. No one would part with their money for her busted computer.

"No. No. I'm nobody's charity case." The words came out sharper than she intended.

"Don't be like that." The light went out in Andrew's eyes. "I just want to help."

"I'm sorry. I didn't mean to be rude to you. Still, I rather you not start a collection basket for the poor." She managed this long on her own and wasn't about to slip now.

He hung his head, but in the next moment leveled his eyes with hers. "I'm sorry too. If I was with you, this wouldn't have happened."

"You can't be with me always. Besides, you had to take the test." For the first time she dared to glance at the busted laptop gripped in her hands. "You think there's hope to get the data from this?"

He shrugged. "A tech guy would know. Unfortunately, I don't know any. Maybe Raul does. He's got connections everywhere."

The glass wall of the building, revealed the bus pulling up at the stop.

'Go home. Go to Miles.'

That same female's soft voice echoed in her mind, filling her with longing for her sanctuary. "I'll go home.

Don't know what am I going to do there, but that is the place I want to be now."

"Do you want me to come with you?" He zipped up his bag. "I'll come up with an excuse later for not taking the exam."

"No, it's okay. The college may not give you another chance to take the exam and you don't want to flunk because of this. Let me know about Amanda and Potter. God, this time they've done it. I couldn't let them get away."

Maybe others would come forth now that she'd stood up to the bullies.

Andrew placed his hand on her shoulder, his lips lingering somewhere between a smile and a frown. "The good thing is karma is only a bitch if they are. She'll catch up with them."

"Right," Kate whispered.

Fate could take decades to catch up with anyone, if it ever caught up at all. She'd rather see the two of them get what they deserved now. Nothing mattered but to forget this day in Miles's embrace.

Andrew rubbed her arm. "If you don't need me, I'll go to the next class. Can I call you tonight?"

"Of course." She hurried for the bus stop.

"Kate?"

*Miller.* She paused at the bus's wide-open door, but climbed the two steps and flashed her monthly pass at the driver.

"What do you want, Miller?" She trailed down the aisle for an empty seat, but the bus was overcrowded, so she opted to hold onto a bar in front of the exit door.

"To apologize." His meaty fingers wrapped around the same pole, above her hand.

"No need. I guess I should thank you for seizing Potter."

The bus pulled away from the curb and she widened her stance to keep her balance.

"It's the least I could do." Miller hitched the backpack higher on his back, gave her an awkward smile and coughed into his free fist. "Ah...this is awkward, but I have to say it. I like you and, for what it's worth, I'm sorry. I realize it's too late and that I've lost any chance when I got carried away and played sick pranks on you."

Kate slid her hand down the pole, increasing the distance between them. He liked her? Was she blind the whole time that she couldn't see it? No, it was his way of treating her. Not the best way to show his admiration.

"I like you, too." His expression changed to hopeful with her words so she continued before he got any wrong ideas. "As a neighbor, of course."

"I like you a lot." He averted his gaze toward the window, but not before his face fell. "And I get it that I'm not your type. Can we at least be friends?"

"Let me think about it, okay?" She tweaked her head. Hell, she may be a sucker if she accepted his offer, but friends were in short supply. Still, a fake friend was worse than an open adversary. At least she knew who her enemies were.

For the rest of the ride, she stared out the window, trying to avoid his gazes. She contemplated whether to be his friend. The bus pulled up in front of her building. She lined up at the middle double doors, but Miller remained clutching the pole, his fingers white.

"Sure, we can be friends," she said, returning her gaze to the front. The door opened with a loud hiss and she stepped onto the sidewalk. God, befriending him better not bite her.

# Chapter 18

Midday sun cast lines through the blinds at the resume in Matthias's hand. He ran his thumb over his eyebrow, while another young doctor delivered the well-rehearsed deadpan lines. Of all candidates who had come through his office since morning, the thin man seated across from him at least had the decency to wear a suit, unlike the person before him. At the request to remove his multiple piercings and cover his tattoos during work hours, contestant number thirty-seven had grimaced and declared his personality had every right to shine through.

And a potential employer had every right not to hire him. What kind of world did they live in? Everyone wanted a paycheck that came with a job, but couldn't bother to show some love for the profession.

Rubbing his eye, he tilted the sheet of paper to get the words in focus. Why hadn't he left the hiring process to someone else? No one seemed truly interested in the anesthesiologist position, but the candidate seated in front of him was the last interviewee and had the most impressive resume.

Strange weariness replaced Matthias's earlier victorious surge. He kneaded his sore neck, but the sensation only increased.

'*Kate needs you,*' Emina's ethereal voice echoed in his mind.

He straightened his back and gripped the papers in his hand, crumpling them. '*My dove, what happened?*' he replied through their special telepathic channel he'd believed lost forever with her death.

'*I tried to help her, but there were too many. I sent her home to wait for you. Go to her.*' Emina's voice faded with her last words.

His insides tightened and twisted. He swallowed down the brewing rage and stepped to his desk, then gripped the thick edge. Pain stabbed his eyes and he blinked fast, fighting to keep the beast under control. In the next moment, the agony ceased, and he glanced at the man sitting across from him. His eyes, shielded by thick glasses, held the same uninterested expression, no indication he had noticed anything unusual. All the same, urgency pressed on Matthias's shoulders. He must end this meeting.

He cleared his throat and leaned over the desk. "I'd like to bring you in for a second interview. The estimated opening date of the clinic is set for mid-September, providing everything goes as planned."

The subject pushed his frameless glasses up his nose and sniffed. "That's six months from now."

"Yes, I realize that." Matthias extended one arm out, palm facing up. "It gives you time to get experience until then."

"My internship will be done by then." The man bobbed his head on his skinny neck. "I'll try to perfect my skills as much as I can. There's nothing I wouldn't do to work with you, Dr. Zrin. Your reputation precedes you."

Matthias arched an eyebrow at the man's sudden change of tone. Maybe he'd been wrong about the interviewee.

Matthias nodded, getting up and offering his hand. "Concentrate on getting more experience under your belt and you'll do fine."

What kind of doctors would come out of these new generations? The personal touch and caring seemed to be a thing of the past. To memorize data from the textbooks and recite the lines was one thing, but to have great bedside manners was something entirely different. Whatever the outcome, he would breathe some character into this man and shape him into the best anaesthesiologist. The man returned Matthias's strong handshake. There was hope, after all. Much of a man's character could be told from his handshake.

Now he must run to Kate.

Matthias yanked the cell out of his pocket. Nothing, no missed calls or messages from Kate. Maybe she emailed him. He returned to his chair to check. A few new messages in his inbox displayed in bold, but none from her. Too proud to ask for help, no matter how badly she needed aid.

At the push of the button on his desk phone, the fast dial tone filled the silence. Six ring tones later, her recorded voice asking the caller to leave her a message chirped through the speaker.

"I know you're there. Pick up the phone." Only crackling of the static came through. "Kate, pick up the phone." More static met his demand. "Okay, you're not up to talking. Sit tight, I'm on my way."

He ended the call, grabbed his car keys from the desk, and threw his jacket over his shoulder. On his way to the car, he fished out the cell from his pocket to dial Fortuno, changed his mind, and shoved the phone back into his trousers. The best way to reach his friend was through the shared mental connection. After all, immortality was good for something.

'*Get me the college dean on the phone.*' He pushed the mental message through to Fortuno. Whatever had happened to Kate, he'd bet anything in this world it had something to do with the recent developments at her school. And he'd make sure those responsible got the maximum punishment.

'*Are you enrolling in yet another program?*' Curiosity laced Fortuno's voice and boomed in Matthias's head. Damn it, in over a century his friend still had not learned to control the volume of his voice when he got excited.

'*No, I meant Kate's college. And while I've got you, transfer some money to her account.*' Matthias tossed his jacket on the passenger's seat. The weather had changed so fast and it could turn again. At the moment, clear sky replaced the morning lingering clouds. He got in the car and slid the key into ignition.

'*How much?*' Fortuno asked with business-like voice.

Matthias tilted his head, inserting the key into the ignition. He'd love to pay off her entire loan. Anyone in the world would jump at the opportunity. Kate however, would jump down his throat. '*Half of her student loan.*'

'*Give me ten minutes. You'll have the dean on the phone ready to eat from your hand.*' Fortuno ended the connection, easing the noise in Matthias's head. If anyone could pull the administration strings and intimidate the big wigs, it was the ever-resourceful Fortuno.

The phone rang as Matthias approached the highway ramp. The unknown caller flashing on the small display screen meant Fortuno had come through. Though disappointment prickled his chest. Kate hadn't returned his call.

He pushed the talk button on his mobile, the chiming stopped. "This is Dr. Zrin."

"Yes," a deep voice droned through the earpiece. "This is James Sterlton, dean of the Ryerson's College, your, err, assistant I believe, said you demand a word with me, hmm?"

"Mr. Sterlton," Matthias said, pausing to check his blind spot before merging onto highway. "I need to speak with you in regards to an incident involving students, Miss Kate Rokov in particular."

"Ah, yes. That was an unfortunate accident. Hmm." The dean coughed. "Miss Fournier and Mr. Potter ensured me they didn't mean to carry it so far. It was supposed to be a joke. Perhaps Miss Rokov overreacted and they retaliated. Things escalated from there. Hmm."

Miles gripped the steering wheel so hard his fingers hurt. If the dean said hmmm one more time, he'd snap. He'd be damned if he let this man flip the blame to Kate. Typical to convince the victim of misunderstanding that it was all meant in good, old-fashioned fun. "An accident? A joke? Truly, Mr. Sterlton?"

Matthias would get the truth out a little at the time. And he had nothing but time, providing the traffic moved at the regular pace. The trip to Kate's place would take about an hour.

"It was meant as nothing more than a prank, and I'm sorry for the damages done. However, I can assure you, Dr. Zrin, the perpetrators are dealt with. Now, as for Miss Rokov's laptop, there's nothing me or the college can do. If Miss Fournier and Mr. Potter would find it in their hearts to pay for the damage done, it is up to them, but they cannot be forced to do so. Hmm." The dean's stern voice was odd.

*Their hearts? And where would those be found?* So that was it. They wouldn't let her be until they broke her prized possession, her laptop. Nothing he couldn't replace if Kate allowed him, but dammit, a crime was a crime. Pressing Potter for money would be as useful as trying to squeeze a stone, and Amanda and her conniving ways would wiggle out of obligation to pay out a penny. Poor Kate, she must be crushed. "How did you deal with the two instigators?"

"They now have a permanent record and the disciplinary committee will review their actions and determine if they'll be awarded their diplomas at this time, hmm. However, we cannot keep them from graduating if they meet all the requirements."

"Is that the best you can do?" The dean's explanation lacked satisfaction. A record? No more than a stain that would get buried deep in the mountain of red tape administration.

"I can understand your frustration, but this is the extent of my power. May I ask what your interest in Miss Rokov is? I was informed the foreign student has no family here. Hmm."

"I am her benefactor." Matthias wriggled. Perhaps he pushed the issue too far.

"Her benefactor, hmm?" The dean dragged the words out, giving them a whole different meaning. No doubt, the man took him for someone who would stoop so low. Matthias half expected to hear "Is this what you call it nowadays?" Better to end this call before he got accused for perversion.

"I appreciate your call, Mr. Sterlton. I understand joking in good humor, but when it goes too far, bad things happen, people get hurt, and private property gets damaged or destroyed." Matthias pressed on the gas pedal as he rushed the words out.

"Our campus prides itself on providing a safe and secure environment and acceptance for all. Diversity is important to us and students are encouraged to embrace it, hmm. Furthermore—"

"Yes, yes, I'm glad to hear that, Mr. Sterlton." Matthias was not in a mood to listen to the dean reciting well-rehearsed lines he most likely didn't believe in. "Keep up the great work."

He ended the call, not letting the dean utter another hmm. Neither had he bothered to hide sarcasm from his voice. Kate had not been physically hurt, but her laptop was damaged and she was ridiculed, and the dean hid behind school policy and regulations, trying to sweep the act of animosity under the rug of joking and pranking.

It wasn't fair to Kate, but life was what it was and she must toughen up against the world. He had failed her. Amanda was trouble and he should've been there to protect Kate. Now all he could do was to lessen her pain.

He arrived at her place on auto-pilot, parked the car, and headed for her unit. A set of cement stairs led him to the building's basement. No sound came from Kate's apartment. He rang the doorbell. She didn't answer. He rang again. Still nothing. He tried the door, but the entrance was locked. She was in there, her heartbeat loud and clear in his ears.

Damn it, he hated mentally forcing the locks on the door to open, but he must get to her. Since the night she'd accepted his presence, he hadn't entered her apartment this way. He placed his hand over the first lock, and the soft click ensured him the latch gave in. The same happened with the other two. He shoved the door open. Staring straight at him, she hugged her busted laptop to her chest and rocked in her chair. The rickety legs squeaked in time with her deep yelps.

His heart broke, seeing her so crushed. The door closed behind him as he headed straight for her. He knelt beside her and caressed her shoulder, trailing his hand down her arm. "Kate, love. It's okay. This is not the end of the world."

Her gaze snapped to him, and she choked a sob. A single tear slid down her cheek and hung from her chin. He ran his thumb over the droplet. "Let me see the laptop."

He tried to pry the computer from her hands, but she wasn't letting go. "No, Miles. It's done, they won. Your story is forever lost."

"Honey, the story is not in there." He tapped the broken frame. "It's in here." He moved his fingers to her temple and then to her chest. "And in here. I made sure of that."

Her lips stretched in a half smile, while tears freely raced down her face. "Why do they hate me so much?"

"Out of jealousy, nothing more. You represent everything they can never have. Come on now." He nudged her chin. "Let me see that beautiful smile of yours."

At last, she released the laptop in her grip and wrapped her arms around his neck. "What do they have to be jealous of? I have nothing."

He tightened his hold around her waist, pulling her out of the chair and onto his lap. "You're beautiful and smart, and…and, did I mention beautiful?" The watery smile she gave him loosened the knot in his chest. "Much better," he murmured into her ear.

She pulled back and stared at him through her puffy and red eyes, but at least the tears ceased. He swallowed thickly, pushing the desire to claim her lips with his. In the next moment, she pressed her lips onto his.

Caught by surprise, he didn't fight his desire and deepened the kiss, tasting salt from her recent tears. His tongue met hers and she gave a soft moan. His mind spun, he closed his eyes as ardor slammed into his groin, hardening him in an instant. Thankfully, she ended the kiss with a nibble to his lower lip that only fueled his fire.

"I'm sorry. I couldn't stop myself from kissing you."

"Don't be sorry," he whispered, pulling her closer to him. "One great kiss deserves another."

He seized her lips with his, staking his claim. Damn it, he couldn't stop from advancing on her. This wouldn't end well. What if Emina was watching? She wanted him to love Kate as he loved her, but his heart harbored love for only one woman.

The thought of his dead wife deflated his yearning. He pulled back and pressed his forehead onto Kate's. "Feeling better?"

A stupid thing to ask, but those were the only words that reached his fogged brain.

She nodded and rewarded him with her winning smile. "You're right about the story being in my head and my heart. I'm living it with you."

"See, no one can take that away from you." He reached for the broken computer. The loose parts shook inside. "I'll take this and see what can be done about it."

"Nothing, just look at it. It's a wreck." Her tone changed for a cheerful one. "Strange thing was, Amanda dropped it from the second floor, and just before it hit the hard surface, the computer somehow hovered and lowered to the ground in a slow motion. I knew it wasn't damaged, until Potter stomped on it several times."

Matthias flipped the case upside-down, ignoring her remark. Telling her the spirit of his deceased wife lingered around would be too much, given her current state of mind.

A new anger brewed in him. It had to have been one strong and deliberate hit to smash the sturdy plastic. "The frame is cracked, but the hard drive may be intact."

"And what am I going to do with a hard drive?" She threw her arms up and slammed her thighs. "It's not like I can shoot lasers from my eyes and read the data on it. I planned to get a memory stick, but they are so expensive."

"I have a laptop I don't use. It's been sitting in its box for two years now. It's yours if you want it." He gauged her reaction. At least his offer made her forget he ignored her remark about the laptop landing softly on the floor.

She puckered her lips. "Was it your wife's?"

He shrugged one shoulder. Damn, she was good. "Dobrila never took up to the technology. I tried to teach her but she had a hard time. She saw it as a necessary evil. You probably wouldn't believe me if I told you she only got her driver's license in the last five years."

He lowered his gaze to the laptop in his hands. Resurrecting memories of his wife brought nothing but sadness. "Anyway, I'm sure she'd love it if you put the computer to good use."

Kate crossed her arms over her chest, tapped one foot on the linoleum floor and chewed her lip. Her eyebrows drew closer, forming a deep crease shaped like letter V between them. Finally, her expression eased and she pushed her breath through her nose. "Thank you." He opened his mouth to say she would not regret it, but she stuck one finger at him. "Only because Dobrila would want me to have it."

A short chuckle shook his chest and he placed a kiss on her temple. He had planned to continue with the story later in the week, but this unexpected turn of events presented him with a new opportunity.

"How about we get out of here? It's a nice day and some fresh air would do you good." He got to his feet, pulling her up with him.

"I'd like that." She rubbed her palms together. "You know, there's one thing I must say. No matter what they did, or how much they hate me, I will never put this behind me if I don't forgive them."

Her words froze him, and all he could do was to stare at her. Emina had always said the same, forgiving was the attribute of the strong, not weak.

"I did mention you're smart, didn't I?"

"Yes, you did." She opened the apartment door, but halted, pointing at the busted laptop in his hand. "Maybe leave that here for now. You never know if the Prima Donna's lurking, and if she sees you putting it in your car, who knows? She may break in to get it."

He placed the broken device on the table. "You're right. It's not worth risking it. I'll get my friend to pick it up while we're out."

"How would he get in? I'm not leaving the door unlocked." Her ponytail shook with her head, but it was her big eyes that showed her sudden new worry.

"Same way as me, he taught me the trick. You can relax, no mortal can do this and locks are left intact. Even CSIs wouldn't find a single trace of forced entry, because it's not forced." He relaxed his shoulders as creases on her forehead smoothed, but her lips remained crooked.

"Hmm, so can you enter any building in this way?" she asked, locking the door.

"No, it doesn't work on doors wired into computers with security systems, like banks for example." He gave her a sympathetic shrug. The few mortals capable of psychokinesis would never be able to replicate the trick of forcing the locks open.

She turned for the stairs and paused on the first step. "Interesting, you can read minds, open bolts, make yourself invisible. I wish I had some special skill like that."

"You do, your eagerness to help is one."

"Ha! Whole lot of good that got me. Stupid me, I left my laptop unattended when I went to help a new student find a book." She continued up the steps, but halted and spun to face him. "No more Miss Nice Girl anymore."

"Love, you learn from your mistakes, but you are what you are. I wouldn't want you any other way. Now, where are you taking me?"

"There's a park within walking distance. We can sit on the bench and watch the lake."

"Sounds good." He took her hand. "After our walk, I'm taking you to dinner. Patios are open, I'm dying to eat al fresco."

"You dying? No way. Wait, didn't you pre-order a dinner for me?" Her mocking tone tickled his insides and he rolled a quiet chuckle.

"My friend can drop it off too, when he comes for the computer. I'm sure the food will keep for a few days." He held the building's door open for her.

Angry voices drew his attention. Miller towered over Amanda next to his rusted coupe. "I used a condom. It can't be mine."

Amanda slapped his already red cheek. "You jerk. Condoms break."

He grabbed her wrist. "It didn't break. I'm positive," he shouted. "I'm not sure what your game is, this time, but I'm sure you're playing one. The truth will come out sooner rather than later."

Kate's mouth hung open and her eyes widened. Matthias urged her onward. "She's up to her old tricks, and this is none of our business."

# Chapter 19

Various cars lined the parking lot of Kate's building, equally spaced out for her to meander behind Miles. She rounded the corner and stepped onto the sidewalk. Sun, still high, bathed the street in shimmering light and plenty of warmth. Passersby had shed winter coats for shorts and T-shirts. If only she had time to spare on getting her legs and toes in shape for shorts and sandals.

Typical for Southern Ontario climate, yet the sudden arrival of summer weather never failed to find her unprepared. Oh well, a pair of capris and cloth sneakers would have to do.

"So where are you taking me?" He took her hand in his.

Her heart fluttered, but she stilled the wild beats. His quirked eyebrow brought a smile to her. She chuckled, pointing ahead. "The park's a few streets over."

He fell silent.

His eyes stayed fixed on the cracked sidewalk, one hand in his jeans pocket, the other holding hers, their fingers laced. Just like a couple. Only they weren't a couple, not as in lovers, but a couple of friends. Yet, they held hands all the time. They even kissed. So what were they, if not a couple?

She groaned inwardly. They'd been down that road before and solved nothing. He must work through his grief and she got to live it up before she settled down with a man. She straightened her back. When the parting came, she must remain tough and not show her sorrow. If she could stay with him, she'd jump at the opportunity to settle and forgo the living up part. At least he'd promised a life together was in their future, but how sincere was his oath?

He squeezed her hand lightly. "I'd ask you what you're thinking about, but I already know." Grinning, he bumped her shoulder with his, making her giggle.

"Really?" The tremor in her voice betrayed her attempt at indifference. "What was I thinking?"

"You wonder how sincere I was when I promised we'll be together one day." His smile vanished. He continued in a hurt tone. "After my solemn promise you're still questioning if I'll come through."

She stopped, her heart squeezed. "Oh, Miles, I want to believe you, but…I don't know how long I'll be able to hang onto your promise."

"Don't hang onto it. You will do fine, I know you will. Live your life, and when we're both ready, destiny will bring us back together again." He nodded, tugged on her arm, and continued along the sidewalk.

She window-shopped, but the sting of tears blurred her sight. She blinked them away. He'd keep his promise. Perhaps she was *that* naïve to believe him. However, once again the sincerity in his voice convinced her. He was more than just a friend, the one person in the world who knew her better than anyone else. That someone who made her stronger, dare she think of him as her soul mate. No matter what happened, she'd always love him and nothing would ever change that. The knot in her throat loosened with a hard swallow. *God, don't let my voice come out squeaky.* "We'll turn left at the next street."

Amanda and her predicament would help her forget the fact her time with Miles was coming to an end. "What did you mean by Amanda is up to her old tricks?"

The corners of his lush lips—lips that had kissed her not long ago—tugged upward.

"The truth will come out soon." He tightened his hold on her hand, causing her to halt on her toes at the edge of the sidewalk. "Make sure it's safe to cross. That biker's speeding. Well over the limit on the residential street."

The bike whooshed by, its engine revved, sending vibrations through the pavement. Miles tsked and shook his head, staring after the biker.

"Come on." She nudged him forward. "He's just a youngster, must be his first bike, and he's proud to show off. So what you know about Amanda is nothing but a hunch."

"I smelled a rat when she approached me. Enough about her." He dismissed the issue with a wave of his hand and a head shake. "Let's hope that 'proud biker' doesn't end up in a hospital or six feet under, or put someone else there."

He shaded his eyes against the afternoon sun and scanned the park area before them. Children's laughter and shrieks of delight echoed from the colorful climber and swings. When the narrow path cleared of joggers and cyclists, he crossed to the grass in a few strides. "Do you come here often?"

"Whenever I get a chance. I like to watch Lake Ontario." She pointed at the blue water spread in the distance, then pivoted to face him. "It's not like our Adriatic, but it's a close second, and in winter the frozen sur-

face glistens in the sun. You'd think it's covered in diamonds."

He shivered, rubbing his arms. "Couldn't get me out
here in the middle of winter, burr."

"The trick is in thermal underwear." She swiped her
hand down her body. "From head to toe, keeps you warm
and toasty in sub-zero temperatures. Plus, I even took up
skating. Can you believe it? Before I came to Canada,
I've seen snow twice, maybe."

"Hmm, thermal underwear, hey? I'll keep that in
mind if I want to watch you skate. I'm not the one for
winter sports. Tried skiing once. I'd rather sit in a chalet
and sip on a brandy." A tattered ball landed at his feet. He
picked up the baseball and tossed the ball from hand to
hand.

"Over here!" A young man stretched his arm over his
head, waving his butterscotch colored baseball glove.

Miles swung his arm in a circle, releasing the ball
straight at the man's gloved hand.

"Thanks, man." The ball player doffed his blue cap,
displaying TFD in white letters, and nodded at Kate.
"Hey."

She granted him an equally quick nod and a smile
before he turned and jogged back to the baseball back-
stop. His gray breeches were stretched tight over his firm
backside.

A slight smile lingered on Miles's lips. "Do you
know him?"

"No, not really." She shook her head. "The guys
from the local fire station gather here once every few
weeks to play baseball. He nods at me or waves sometimes. Today was the first time he's said a word."

Miles snapped his head toward the baseball diamond.
The young firefighter swung the bat over his shoulder,
kicked the red dirt and glanced their way then back at the

pitcher. Miles's smile widened, the corners of his eyes crinkled. "I have a feeling he'll be saying a lot more than just 'hey.'"

"How can you be so sure of it?" She took a step back, headed for a picnic bench nearby. Could she go out on a date with another guy? Miles wanted her to experience life without him, but in truth she could not let anyone else in her life. A relationship would diminish the memory of Miles. She'd sit at home and wait for him.

The weather beaten bench scraped against her pants. She brushed away dry pine needles covering the seat and lowered to the hard wood.

"I'm not sure of anything, but you should give the man a half decent chance. Loneliness is hard. At least promise me you will go out and make friends and not sit at home waiting for me." He joined her at the bench, wiping his hands on his trousers, dark fabric stretched over his muscular thighs.

"What I will do with my life after you leave is my business." She would follow him anywhere if he but asked, without any doubt. But she would not grant him his wish to love another man. The conversation was heading toward the dangerous territory again. She must end it now before he got vexed at her stubbornness. Filling her lungs, she let the air seep out of her along with her tension. He was right of course. She should get out more. "Let's go on with the story. That's why we came here after all, not to fight."

"We're discussing, not fighting, but yes, let's continue." He took her hand, gave her a slight squeeze, then placed her hand on her thigh. "I want to try something different today."

He didn't want to hold her hand during the séance. Was he prepping her for an easy parting? "How will we establish the connection?"

"That is what I want to test, if we can connect without physical touch." His fingers trailed her cheek, and she lowered her eyelids. "You still need to close your eyes, though. No peeking and no questions before we start. I want to show you everything."

A breeze from the lake carried his sandalwood aftershave toward her, and she licked her lips, reminiscing in their latest kiss. He kissed like a God. "What about all those months you whispered in my ears or during my exam?"

"I've only spoken to you, couldn't project images into your mind." He bumped his shoulder on hers.

True, her stubbornness must have something to do with his inability to penetrate her mind. "How will you know I'm entering the vision?"

"Well, you'll have to tell me when the pictures start to play behind your eyelids."

She nodded. "Let's begin."

For a few long moments, only darkness lingered. She drew several breaths and exhaled loudly, shaking her head. This was hopeless. Why was he doing this the hard way?

His hand landed on her fidgeting fingers. "Concentrate."

Her fingers instantly wrapped around his. "It's hard without holding onto your hand."

"I know. It's hard for me too, but do try." Once again, he let go.

"Okay," she whispered, shutting out all sounds from the park and relaxing her shoulders. In the next moment, red sparkles flashed behind her lids. Soon the dots turned to squiggly lines. The vision changed again to a fuzzy meadow where lush green grass swayed in the warm breeze. The picture sharpened and she eased into the experience.

"Children are running around a blindfolded Dobrila, her arms stretched straight in front of her. I think they are playing a game." Kate waited for Miles's confirmation.

"Yes, children accepted her as their playmate. Now continue without speaking or you'll break the concentration."

*e⁄ɔℰ⁄ɔ*

Dobrila's melodious laughter bounced above the children's. She pivoted, grabbing onto a boy. "Aha, who did I get now?"

The child's black curls shook with his jerk, but his giggling never ceased. He freed his arm from her hold and ran off, his dirty soles kicking high behind him. Miles chuckled and stepped in front of her. Her hands reached to his face. "I've got someone," she shrieked.

"Guess who?" he whispered, pulling down her blindfold.

She smiled and he pressed his lips to hers. The taste of sweet wine she'd sipped on at lunch, lingered on her lips and he deepened the kiss.

She broke away from him and licked her lips. "Miles…" she whispered behind her cupped hand. "The children are watching."

"Ah—h—you kids had her long enough. She's all mine now." He mopped sweat off his brow on his sleeve, scanning the unkempt bunch of curious onlookers. With a swift plunge, he wrapped his arms below Dobrila's hips and swung her over his shoulder.

"A little while longer, please, Miles."

Children's complaints followed him on his way to their meager cottage.

"Not today." He clutched a giggling Dobrila tighter. He ended each day and started a new one by making love to her. On some days they'd break the midday monotony by spending hours exploring each other's bodies, finding what pleased them. Today would be one of those afternoons.

In the distance, the huff of horses approached. He halted and shielded his eyes against the sun. Two roan beasts carried riders toward the village. The red banners flapping in the wind identified them as messengers from his and Dobrila's castles. Damn it, their six weeks of blissful living among these ruffians and their families came to a hasty end. But he'd expected this.

"Why is my father sending a messenger? Put me down, Miles." She tapped his shoulder, but it was the worry in her voice that vexed him.

Villagers rushed out of their huts. Some carried pitchforks, but they all had grim faces. The horses snorted, coming to a halt in front of him. One rider mopped his forehead with a silky kerchief before handing over a scroll with the house of Vitturi seal.

Miles took the rolled paper in his hand and broke the wax. He read the elegant calligraphy, but the words didn't sink in.

"What does it say?" Wide-eyed, Dobrila took the scroll and lowered her head to read. Her mouth slowly opened while her eyes widened more. "My father offered the hand of peace to yours and he accepted for our sake. After so many years, our houses will cease the feud and let us join in marriage." Her face lit up, and she threw her arms around his neck. "Oh, Miles!"

He grabbed her wrists, unhooked her arms, and walked her a few steps away from the prying ears of the two messengers. "Dove, this could be a trap."

She shook her head, setting loose strands to flutter. "No, Miles. My father has finally come around as I always knew he would. He just needed time." After gripping him in a tight hug, she rained kisses on his face. "We're going to be married. Married, Miles. Our families couldn't have given us a better present than granting us our love."

After all these years, their families made peace. Why now and not sooner? There had to be a snitch among the villagers. Someone leaked the information to Conte Vitturi. The conte must know his plan to have his imminent son-in-law killed hadn't come through and the young countess's virtue had been compromised. No doubt, in her father's eye, she was a loose woman no other man of good standing would want. Her grin and glimmer in her rounded eyes couldn't be ignored. How could he deflate her spirits? He relaxed his shoulders and pulled her close.

She broke away from him and bounced in front of the horsemen. "Yes, we accept. Please tell my father to send a coach at once for our return home."

"The coach is awaiting at the road, young countess." The man extended one gloved hand toward the steep hill while gripping the reins with his other. The horse shook its head and snorted, pounding hoofs on the cracked earth. He patted the animal's neck. "Easy, easy."

She extended her arm, her smile reached her eyes. "See, my love? My father has thought of everything. Let's go."

"Dobrila," he scolded.

She threw him a sharp look.

"We lived among these people for six weeks. They fed, clothed, and sheltered us. Don't you think they deserve a decent goodbye from us?"

She swallowed and redness replaced her stern expression. "Where are my manners? I do apologize. My enthusiasm got the best of me." Then she turned to the village leader and placed her hand over her chest. "Gratitude."

Grabbing onto the fabric of her skirt, she lifted the tattered hem above her ankles. "I want to get out of these rough peasant's woolens and into my silk gowns. I'll go say goodbye to my little friends."

He wrapped his arm around her shoulders, but his gaze connected with the village leader's. The same man, who'd spared his life on that dark and hopeless night, now had a worry line marring his always grinning face.

The leader approached with slow steps. "Are you sure about this? Her father commissioned us to kill you."

"I'm not sure about anything." Miles extended his hand to him. His gut clenched. "I will never forget your hospitality."

The man took his offered hand and gave it a firm shake, then hugged Dobrila. He tapped Miles's shoulder. "Take care of her and do be very careful. I don't trust that man. Neither should you."

Miles nodded, but a lump formed in his throat. It was Dobrila's future that worried him the most. "Don't worry about me."

Trudging behind Dobrila, he started toward the road and the awaiting coach. The young women frowned, some sniffed and wiped their eyes at their departure, but their mothers smiled, waving eagerly. Children ran after him, many begging Dobrila to stay and play once more. She grinned and patted their heads.

Two mules harnessed to the coach grazed on the lush grass at the side of the road. Dobrila quickened her steps. The coachman jumped from his post and held the door open for her. She leaped into the carriage, sprawling on the burgundy velvet seat. "Oh, how I missed this."

Miles took the seat facing her. He twirled his hair to ease bad premonition pressing on his shoulder. "Dove, we left in haste. I feel awful for abandoning those people."

The whip cracked and the coach rattled down the dirt road, the pounding of hoofs and creaking of the carriage filled the silence.

She scrambled to her knees in front of him. Two lines formed on her forehead, but glee danced in her eyes. "Just think, Miles. In a few days we'll be a husband and wife. Doesn't that make you happy?"

He granted her a quick smile. "It does, dove. It does."

"Oh, Miles," she said, taking the seat beside him. "I want all bells ringing from the steeples. Let the world know you're marrying me. I waited for this my whole life."

He couldn't help but chuckle, then kissed her temple. "And you shall have it."

Soft, loose strands of her braid fluttered in the cool wind gusting in through the open half-door. She lowered her head to his shoulder and closed her eyes. "And I want to carry the biggest bouquet of red roses, and my gown shall have the finest lace and silk, and…"

He wrapped her in his embrace, closed his eyes too, and let her plan out the day she waited on her whole life. He half-listened, a worry knot forming in his neck. What prompted this sudden change of heart in both his and her fathers? Miles rested his head on the cushy seat. His theory of Dobrila's ruined reputation held a lot of merit. He ruined her, so he now must make her his wife. He would've done so years ago if she hadn't been under strict supervision.

The rocking of the coach and the heat lulled him. He blinked fast, trying to stay awake, but he lost the fight, and dozed off.

The carriage jerked to a stop, and Miles woke with a start. Conte and countess stood in the Vitturi's castle courtyard under the middle arch supporting the lower balcony. Tendrils of green foliage swayed over their heads.

Dobrila smiled, but fear flashed in her eyes. She took his hand and gave him a reassuring squeeze.

He kissed her fingers. "Let's face your parents."

She swallowed and nodded. "My mother doesn't look pleased. Neither does my father."

"Don't worry. I'm sure deep inside they are very happy for us." He suppressed a snort. Her parents reminded him of two vultures ready to swoop down from a branch and pluck his eyes. What he wouldn't give to squeeze the living breath out of that lanky man who'd marked him for death and paid the highway robbers to do the dirty deed. However, violence wouldn't solve a thing.

Her mother's face contorted in a grimace as Dobrila crept closer. "Despicable. Look how you are dressed. Do you take yourself for a peasant? A serf perhaps?"

Dobrila lowered her head and gripped her wrist with one hand. "No, Mother."

The woman squared her shoulders and her jaw. "Well then, our fears are confirmed. It is obvious you have fallen from grace. For all we know you could be with his bairn." She glanced at Miles. "I cannot bear to look at you."

He wrapped his hand around Dobrila's elbow, not granting her mother the satisfaction of addressing her further. "Come, dove. You're welcome in my house. It's your house, too."

Dobrila nodded and slowly turned to follow him, but her father's angry voice stopped them in their tracks. "You will not inherit the castle, lands, or the wealth. It will all go to your uncle. I cannot strip you of your title, it's yours by birthright, but believe me if I could I would do it in a heartbeat."

"My gowns!"

She gasped and threw a worried look at Miles.

He shrugged. He preferred her out of those heavy layered dresses anytime.

"We have seamstresses. Better than in your father's employ."

"I suppose I don't have a use for your wardrobe, so it'll be sent to you along with your hand maiden. The wench is good for nothing," her father growled, swiping his hand as if swatting a fly, then left in haste. His hurried footsteps echoed through the stone paved corridor.

Miles led her toward the double wooden gate. A slow grin stretched his lips as joy rushed through him. Still, he would prefer if their families agreed to their marriage, instead of discarding their daughter to him as an act of riddance.

Dobrila halted and spun to face her mother. "Goodbye, Mother. Try to smile once in a while. Your mouth is set in a permanent frown."

Old Countess Vitturi's eyebrows shot up while her frown deepened. "Such rudeness. What can be expected of an impudent child who hid amongst ruffians? Be off."

Miles took Dobrila's hand and pressed a kiss to her palm. "Come, dove. Let's leave this place as lovers who'll be married in a few days. No more hiding, no more forced separation. I'm yours and you're mine."

She cast him a lopsided smile. Tears glistened in her eyes and a shaky breath left her lips. "I'd hoped they'd come to their senses. Now I see they never will. Why must it be this way? Don't they want to see their grandchildren? When they arrive, that is."

Grandchildren? How would he tell her there wouldn't be any? The fault would be all his, but the society they lived in always blamed the infertility on a woman. His footsteps faltered and he turned to her. "I too wish our families were accepting of our love. You always believed your father would come around. Perhaps it's not too late."

He continued on to his castle. People they chanced to meet lowered their glances at their joined hands. The gossip was sure to follow. Why not give them something to talk about? He pulled Dobrila to him, wrapped his arm around her waist and kissed her on the cheek.

Her eyes widened and her shoulders froze. "Miles, people are watching."

"Let them watch." He placed another kiss on her lips this time. Then he pulled back, his arm still around her waist, and faced the people. "Let it be known to all that our houses will join though marriage."

"Miles." Scolding laced her hiss. "The officials are to make that announcement."

"No, dove. Your family will not recognize our marriage through officials. But they cannot deny it before God." He nudged her onward, but she stood frozen, staring at him. "Do not be afraid." He tucked lose strands of her hair behind her ear. "I am here for you to love, serve, and protect you. You're my lady."

Her warm palms sandwiched his hand and she placed a kiss on his fingers. "And you are my lord."

An elderly man approached, offering the crimson rose to Dobrila. "I was the late contuses's gardener. She loved my roses. I hope you will too."

Dobrila lowered her gaze to the blossom in the wrinkled man's hand. "Thank you. If all of them are like this one, I'm sure I'll love them."

The man nodded, his weary eyes closed for a moment, and he released a long breath. "I planted the bush in the courtyard just for her. With God's grace I'll plant one for you."

Dobrila smiled, pressing the petals to her nose. "I'd love that."

He returned her smile and trudged away.

"See?" Miles laced his fingers with hers and faced west. "People like you already."

The dipping sun touched the pine covered hills in the distance. "Come, it'll get dark soon. My father will have supper on the table. We'll have a good night's rest. Tomorrow wedding preparations can start."

೧೨೧೨

A gentle squeeze on Kate's forearm jerked her from the vision. The clink of a metal baseball bat hitting the ball catapulted her back into present. The young firefighter who had greeted them ran backward with his gloved hand outstretched. She blinked a few times until she got her bearings back.

"Why did you end the vision here?"

"Because I'm hungry and I thought to spare you boring wedding details." Miles brushed his knuckles on her arm. "Am I wrong to skip that part? I mean, maybe you'd like to see Dobrila's dress fittings, arguments with the cooks, carts delivering food, entertainers trying to line up the next act—"

His grimace and flailing hands tickled her insides. She let out a loud chuckle. Darn it, she should've guessed he'd read her thoughts. "As if you need to ask. Besides, I'm sure your servants bustled around, running the chores."

"Wasn't sure your thoughts weren't clear on that, but now that you confirmed, I guess I'll skip over it. And yes, servants did all the grunt work. Still, I wanted everything to be perfect for our day."

He stretched out his long legs and got to his feet. "Let's eat. There's a nice restaurant offering Mediterranean cuisine, the owners are Croatians. Are you in mood for some calamari or black mussels or even grilled squid?"

The mention of delicacies from her native cooking caused her mouth to water. She sucked the moisture gathering over her tongue and swallowed. "I'd love all of it."

He pulled her to standing. "Then what are we waiting for? Before I forget, you must be looking forward to your convocation?"

She frowned and shrugged. "I neither look forward to it nor do I care."

"Why is that?" Astonishment crept to his tone.

"Because I'm not going."

"Why not?"

She shrugged and lowered her head. "All students will have family and friends attending. And I have no one. I can use the time better looking for apartment and a job. I have to move out. The building is for students."

"And what am I, if not a friend?" His penetrating gaze cut her to the core, but it was the sincerity in his questions that convinced her to grant his wish. Though she'd love it if he was more than a friend. *Someday...*

"Okay. If you want to attend my graduating ceremony, I'll invite you." Before he could utter another word, she pointed at him. "It comes with a condition, though."

He quirked an eyebrow. "What kind of condition?"

Would he agree to her request? There was no way she could wait another week or a day. "You show me the rest of the story tonight. There couldn't be much of it left."

"You're right, there isn't. Can't wait, can you?"

"Tonight, after dinner," she demanded.

With his hands propped on his narrow hips, he chewed on his lower lip, his stare fixed at the ground. "Fine, you win." He leveled his eyes with hers. "However, I want to try another thing. I asked you not to hold hands to see if we can establish the link without a touch, and it worked. Now, I want to test the distance the link spans. I'll contact you sometime tonight."

She raised her eyebrows. *Establish a connection without physical touch and how far it spans*? What was he up to? "If this experiment of yours doesn't work, then you're calling me on the phone."

"Persistent, I see." He jutted his chin. "Fine, as long as I get to see you pick up your diploma next week during the ceremony."

"Why do you want to see me in the black gown and a funny, square cap with tassels?"

Tilting his head, he took hold of her elbow. "So I can treat my favorite graduate to lunch."

# Chapter 20

The warm breeze carried freshness from Lake Ontario and ruffled the curtains on the wide-open patio door. Matthias lowered to the lounger on the veranda. The golden liquid in the snifter tucked between his fingers swirled with his lazy wrist movements. He brought the glass to his nose and inhaled the potent fragrance of the single malt. The brandy's heady aroma tempted him to gulp his drink. Instead, he sniffed its oaky bouquet and placed the glass on the side table. Then leaned against cushions and gazed at the starry sky.

The established connection with Kate called for a celebration, but he'd commemorate the occasion solo. After he tested the span of their bond. He glanced at his iPhone. Digital numbers displayed 11:00. She would be up, waiting on him to make the contact and he shouldn't keep her waiting. If their connection worked over great distance, he'd be able to stay with her even after he parted from her. Opening the mental channel toward her should take no effort—he couldn't stop thinking of her and that was all he required.

'Kate, can you hear me?'

"Um, what?" Her shout thundered through his head.

He cringed.

*So all that speech wasn't make believe.* "I hear you, loud and clear." *God, this is awkward and cool at the same time.*

He snickered. A first time attempt at long distance telepathic communication could be confusing and Kate was not immune to beginner's mistakes. Nonetheless, hearing her melodious voice pulled on his heart. How he wanted to be with her.

*'Kate, love, your thoughts and spoken words are a jumbled mix. Use one, not both. Your internal voice preferably.'*

"Like this?" Her voice came as a whisper.

*'Yes, just like that, only think of what you want to say, but don't say it out loud.'* A smile crept to his lips. She was a fast learner and got a hang of the unconventional telecommunication fast.

*'How is this possible? I mean…well, you know what I mean.'*

*'We always had a special bond. All I had to do was open up the pathway and connect. It's hard to wrap one's head around this, but believe me this is best I can explain.'*

*'Wow, not sure if I could get used to this. Don't let phone companies find out about this trick.'*

*'No trickery, I promise.* He scrubbed his hand over his face. *Let's see if we can share my memories across the distance. Ready?'*

*'Um-hm. You can start anytime, but first is there any hope to resurrect my computer?'*

*'I'm afraid it's dead. Good news, my friend extracted the data and loaded it all into your new machine. He'll drop it off at your place tomorrow. Now, get comfy and let me know when you get the first visual.'*

He leaned his head on the firm mattress of the lounger and rewound his mental chronicles. '*I suppose you'd like to see Dobrila's wedding dress. It was a sight to see.*'

'*Yes, I'd love a glimpse.* Kate's joyful reply confirmed his guess.

'*Okay, I'll start just before I unburdened her of the gown.*'

Her snort followed by loud chuckles was sure signs of her breaking the concentration. "Unburdened her? Is that a fancy word for get her nekkid? Don't show me the entire scene."

'*You're speaking out loud again, and laughing. Please focus and don't worry.*' He struggled to keep his chuckles from erupting. His old-fashioned word choice must be hilarious by today's standards.

She cleared her throat, but giggles erupted from her end. '*Sorry, lost it there for a moment. Go on.*'

'*Here it comes.*' He projected the images fast so she couldn't break into more snickers.

ભ્યભ્ય

He wrapped one finger around the loose end of the cord criss-crossing the back of Dobrila's bodice. The silk string came undone at his tug and the dress opened, sliding off her milky shoulders.

'*Miles, Dobrila's dress was exquisite.*' Kate's dreamy voice entered his memory. '*The lace, pearls, embroidered flowers at the top of her shoulders, real work of art. But I'd rather you don't go too deep into the love making scene on your wedding night. I hope you'll understand.*'

'*Yes, I do. The one scene I showed you was more than enough.*' It still had hard impact on Kate. He shifted, leaning on his right arm. It wouldn't be fair to send images of his first wedding night to Kate. As the story neared to its end, sadness crept into her eyes. '*I'll fast forward it to the morning after.*'

"Miles!" A holler seeped through his sleep.

Miles blinked into awareness. *Who the hell—*

Judging by the birds chirping, the sun had barely emerged.

"Miles! Get out here, Goddam it!"

Miles rolled to his side and placed still-sleeping Dobrila on the pillow.

She stirred and moaned. "What in God's grace is that ruckus?"

Miles pulled his breeches on. "It's nothing. Go back to sleep."

"Miles, come out here," the drunken voice slurred. "I've got your wedding present."

Miles rushed toward the open window and pushed the curtains aside. Conte Vitturi stood on the stone bridge spanning the moat to the castle. What on earth did he want? The man hadn't had the decency to show his face at their wedding.

"Keep quiet, Conte. I'll be down in a few minutes." Miles grabbed the shirt off the chair, placed a kiss on Dobrila's nude shoulder and, careful not to step on her crumpled wedding dress, left the chamber.

Cold stones of the castle's floor soothed his bare soles. Only a handful of servants greeted him on his way down the marble steps and through the courtyard. They had all worked extra hard to make their day special. The least he could do was to grant them a day of rest.

Miles pushed open the heavy wooden door separating castle's courtyard from the rest of the world. Conte Vitturi stood a few steps from him, one arm behind his back, the other hugging a wine flask to his chest.

"You should go home, Conte. The wedding present can wait—"

A shot from the flintlock pistol deafened him. Hot lead grazed his temple and he wiped the warm blood oozing down his face.

A deadly gleam entered the conte's eyes. He dropped the pistol and flask.

The thunder of Miles's heart pounded with the blaze of agony at his temple. Thank God for wine, single shot pistols, and bad aim. Another inch and he'd be a dead man.

Conte stepped closer. He pulled out another weapon from his waist band and cocked it with a hair-raising click.

Miles froze. Too far away to grab it from his hand, too close not to miss, drunk or sober.

His finger squeezed the trigger. Gunpowder ignited with a dull bang.

The bullet hit Miles square in the chest and knocked him onto his back. He blinked at the sky, trying to catch his breath.

Conte leaned over him, spat and kicked him in the ribs. "You thought I'd let you win. You thought you'd play fire with me and not get burned. No one beats me."

People surrounded him. Dobrila's muted screams reached him. She flew to his side, kneeled and pressed her hand over his, clenching his chest. But his blood oozed through their joined fingers.

"Miles, love. Stay with me." She panted. "Get a medico! Now!" she shouted, pressing harder on his chest. His blood smeared her shift.

Conte's voice drifted to Miles, dripping with anger. "Get dressed, pack your bags, and go home."

"Never. I belong here. With my husband." Her crumpled face entered Miles's fast-narrowing vision field. She rained kisses over his forehead. "No, Miles, no. Open your eyes. Stay with me, my love."

He blinked, struggling to keep his eyes open, but his senses were abandoning him. Searing in his chest increased and drawing in another breath became excruciating. "Don't you fret, my dove, I don't feel any pain."

She raised one bloody hand and smoothed his hair. "Don't go. Stay with me. Please. Please. God, don't take him."

"I'll be fine, dove. Just hold me now and let it be." He panted, while sharp pain ripped his chest with each laborious breath. "Wait for me. I'll come for you."

If this death was like all others, the beast would bring him back to life and he'd return better, stronger. Only, this time his death was not by his own hand, but by a hot lead bullet. Something he never tried before. A tickle deep in his guts ensured him his old friend wouldn't let him stay dead for long. However, this time his death was witnessed by many and he couldn't return from the dead. An opportunity to get Dobrila the hell away from here. Start anew someplace else, where no one knew them.

Dobrila sobbed. Tears left clean streaks through the blood smears on her face. "W—what are you saying?"

"You'll see." He managed to brush her lips with his hand. "This is not the end."

He fought to keep his heavy lids from closing, but strength was draining out of him. In the next moment, his hand dropped and so did his eyelids. The last beat of his heart reverberated and mixed with Dobrila's long wail. Then his world shut and darkness engulfed him.

*ⴄⴄⴄ*

Matthias closed his eyes. Reliving the last death was just as painful three centuries later as it was then.

Kate sniffed, sighed and sniffed again.

'*Are you crying?*' She knew the story well and his

shooting should not come as a surprise. It had to be the way he presented it that got her.

'*No.*' Another sniff followed by a sigh. '*Maybe—yes. Just a little. I didn't think I would, but seeing it all unfold before my eyes is heart wrenching. Conte Vitturi didn't just end your life, but Dobrila's too, and he ultimately wiped two powerful names from existence.*'

'*But he also ended a century-old feud.*' Miles reached for his snifter on the side table. The liquid now turned lukewarm, yet the aroma intensified. Still, he raised the glass to days gone by, to the life that used to be.

'*Will you show me the rest? There couldn't be much left.*' A blowing nose mixed with her voice.

'*Yes, I want you to have it all written down before your graduation ceremony. Promise you'll stop crying.*'

'*Already did. Let's continue with the story. You were buried in the same chapel you were married a day ago. I know the inscription on the gravestone.*'

'*The inscription* Peace to Lovers *was chiselled into the stone after Dobrila's body was put to rest over my coffin. Watch the rest of the tragedy, as I call it, unfold.*'

ℰℋℰℋ

Miles hid in the shadows of Dobrila's room inside the convent of St. Nikolas. A few simple pieces furnished the small chamber. She kneeled at the low bed, rosary wrapped around her clasped fingers. No words came from her lips, but he read her mind. She prayed for death to take her. He had remained dead longer than he anticipated. With each awakening, the beast lost a bit of its power, the urge for blood diminished.

She lowered her hands and slowly turned her head in his direction. Her eyebrows drew closer. The light of the half burned candle couldn't reach the corners, but she must've sensed him.

If luck was with him, she wouldn't scream if he showed himself. He took a tentative step toward her, but retreated when the door flew open and a nun entered.

The young nun stepped aside, holding the door wide open with one hand and a candelabrum in her other. "Mother Superior seeks audience with you."

Dobrila dropped her rosary and got to her feet in slow motion. "At this late hour?"

"Yes." The nun jerked her head at the doorway. "She is waiting in her chamber."

"Fine, give me a moment." Dobrila grabbed the leather pouch and stashed his letters inside.

"You can leave those behind." The nun urged her, waiving her hand.

"I'm not leaving my room without them." Dobrila pulled the wilted rose from the drawer. The same flower a gardener had given her on the day their marriage was announced.

"We can leave now," she said, following the nun out the door.

Miles followed, staying in the shadows. A few nuns waited by the Mother Superior's quarters. They nodded and ushered Dobrila inside, then closed the door behind her. Hard as he tried, he couldn't hear what transpired inside, but in the next moment Dobrila shot out of the room.

"No, I don't care for my father's wishes. I will not get ordained. Miles will come back for me. I know he will. He promised." She still clutched the pouch with his letters. Her thumb pressed hard over the thorn on the rose's stem, blood dripping down her finger.

Mother Superior's stubby form appeared at the doorway. She pointed up. "You're to marry Him. Like all of us here. We are devoted to our one Lord and Master until the day we die and join him in eternity."

"I am already married to a man of flesh and blood. You can't make me take the oath of silence," Dobrila snapped, her face turning red.

"He's dead, child. I understand your longing for him drove you insane. You will find peace and sanctity here. Take the vow of silence and spend the rest of the days good Lord has granted you in devout prayers." Mother Superior stepped toward her.

Dobrila scooted backward until her backside hit the balustrade of the first story.

Mother Superior turned to the nuns. "Seize her and strip that ridiculous wedding gown off her. Three months is long enough. Cut her hair and put her in a nun's habit. We must proceed with the ordaining ceremony."

Nuns moved in, surrounding Dobrila. Two of them gripped her by her arms.

"Let me be!" she shouted, struggling against her restraints. She broke free. In a nimble jump, she climbed the railing. Eyes wide, her face contorted and resolve filled her voice. "You'll have to ordain me in my death."

"No," Miles whispered, reaching out. She wouldn't. "Don't do it, dove."

Before the words left his lips, she stepped off the railing. Letters from the leather pouch came loose, twirled in the air, and slowly descended over the stone courtyard. Nuns rushed down the steps and surrounded her.

The anguish of grief swamped over him. He couldn't step out of the shadows. His heavy legs wouldn't carry him. Instead, he bit his arm to stop a wail from ripping out of his throat and punched the stone wall, but could not feel the pain. Damn it, he should've changed into a priest's clothing and fooled the nuns that he came to listen to their confessions. He expected to find the convent dark and peaceful, all occupants long asleep.

"Place her body in the infirmary. We'll bury her tomorrow. It's getting late now. Let us retire." Mother Superior's flat voice drifted from the first landing. Her large body swung as she took the steps up to her chamber.

"Mother Superior," a nun called from the bottom of the step.

The heavy woman halted. One hand on the stone balustrade, Mother Superior addressed the nun in the courtyard. "Yes, Sister Mary?"

"What shall we say to her family? How did she die?"

The nun's shoulders rose and fell with her heave. "She died of a broken heart, of course."

"Can one truly die from it?"

"She did. Ensure the cobblestone is scrubbed well from all that blood." Mother Superior pivoted and continued up the stairs, then wobbled. The door of her room closed behind her with a loud squeak.

When the last of the nuns left Dobrila's body placed on the stone table, he rushed to her side, pausing only to pick up the wilted rose off the floor. "W—why, dove, why?" He kissed her still warm forehead and pressed the stem into her curled hand. "I failed you. I'm so sorry."

A deep chuckle trailed from the dark corner. "Because she loves you. Wants to be with you."

Miles raised his head in the direction of the voice. "Show yourself."

With slow, deliberate steps, a tall, pale-faced, and red-eyed man came into the moonlight climbing in through the small window.

Miles tightened his grip on Dobrila's wrist. "I know your kind. What are you doing here, vampire?"

The man jutted his lower lip and shrugged. "My kind? What makes you think I have a kind?"

Miles straightened and took a step closer to the man. "I met a vampire or two before. Now, once more, what are you doing in a convent?"

"Lechery, what else? However, other intentions brought me to these parts. I tracked that bitch of your stepmother to your house." He growled, voice deepening as he continued. "Not to mention her weird daughter who turned me. Only to find out you terminated them."

Miles sneered. Conversing with the vampire was the last thing he wanted under the circumstances. "I didn't terminate them. They burst into flames all on their own."

The vampire's slow steps echoed on the stone floor. "Rumor had it you summoned the angel who set them ablaze. Then she stopped you from turning into a full vampire. You're envied among us."

Rumors about him circled the vampire's world. Have they been watching him? Fear mixed with confusion. What would they want from him? "Envied? Craving blood but not having fangs to sink them into a vein is nothing to envy."

"You have the best of both worlds. Do you have any idea what I, or any of us, would give to be a day walker? Or to enjoy the food like mortals do?" The vampire lowered his bloodshot eyes at Dobrila's lifeless body. "She's not dead. Her heart is still beating."

"It's barely palpitating." Miles's last words came out as a whisper. He shook his head to dislodge the fact she was gone.

"To a vampire, that's still a beating heart. She committed suicide. If you believe in all this nonsense, her soul is destined to Hell."

"What are you implying, bloodsucker?" Anger shook Miles at the vampire's suggestion that Dobrila was going to Hell, fear that it might be true, disgust that the vampire was proposing to make Dobrila into one of them.

His unexpected visitor spread his arms wide. A casual frown appeared on his long face. "You deserve an eternity of happiness." He lowered his arms to his sides. "And I can give it to you both."

*An eternity of happiness.* Yes, by God, he and Dobrila deserved such bliss. Elysium. Was there a place like that, down here or in Heaven? But a taste of it was something the vampire could provide. "Do you think I'd curse her with immortality?"

"Ah, my dear friend." The vampire waved his finger. "Every mortal would kill for it. It's a gift you don't throw away."

"I'm not your friend." Miles swiped at the vampire's still waving finger. *An eternity of happiness.* Damned words wouldn't stop echoing through his head. "Her soul will go wherever it is destined to go."

"You misunderstood me, my friend. She'd be like you, not a vampire. Your angel made you immune to the venom when she drew it out of you. Suck the poison out after a few seconds exposure. Long enough to start the change, but not to complete it."

*An eternity of happiness.* Those damned words again. He leaned over Dobrila's body and cradled her head in his arms. "Nonetheless, she'd have a beast inside her to conquer. I cannot damn her with such a destiny."

The Vampire landed his heavy hand on Miles's shoulder. "Don't we all have our own phantoms to tame? You'll guide her through, she'll be fine. My fiend is mild mannered. I imagine hers will be, too."

He pointed at her lifeless body. "This is her final minute. What will it be?"

*Miles and Dobrila together forever.* No matter what he chose, the guilt pressed heavily on his gut. Presented with this unexpected chance at second life, no matter how beastly and inhumane at times it could turn, he couldn't let her die and lose her for good. He brushed his lips over her forehead. "Forgive me, dove. I'll guide you when your demon takes over your mind and body. You'll be fine and, in time, you'll learn to control the beast's urges." He faced the vampire. "Do it fast and be gone."

The vampire smiled slyly and took Dobrila's hand. "It'll be a shame to mar her beautiful neck. Her wrist will do."

Miles closed his eyes and pressed a long kiss to her temple, trying to block sound of her skin breaking under vampire's fangs. Remorse tore through him. It was wrong to doom her to immortality. Her soul should be allowed to pass into the light. Only, her soul would not go into the light, it would go into the perpetual darkness where she'd burn in the pits of Hell especially designed for those who took their own lives. He couldn't let her go there.

"All done." The vampire's deep and calm voice pulled him out of his moral battle. The tall man stepped to him and tapped his arm. "Levant is my name, remember that. I'm honored you let me sire your wife."

Miles glared at him. Why did he despise the man who gave him the last chance at happiness for all eternity? Dobrila faced years of hardship and struggle to tame her demon. No doubt, there'd be days she would wish she was dead. Only time would tell if she'd curse him for making this decision for her tonight.

The vampire put his hands up and tilted his head. "I wasn't expecting gratitude from you, but a simple thank you would be enough."

"Get lost, vampire," Miles growled.

The man took a long step back. "One day you'll thank me. I know you will."

He gave one quick nod and backed into darkness.

Seconds later Miles grabbed her wrist, placed his lips over the swollen area surrounding two puncture marks and sucked out all the bitter bile until the metallic taste of her blood filled his mouth. He brushed his knuckles over her cheek. Her expression appeared oddly relaxed and at peace. Was she trying to tell him he had made the right decision?

He curled up next to her on the cold slab and scooped her into his embrace. Smoothing her matted hair, he listened for any sounds, but only silence taunted him until morning bells.

Receded in the dark corner and secured behind the heavy curtains, he waited for nuns to prepare Dobrila's body for the funeral. A plain casket encased her corpse. Two stout men carried the coffin onto the cart pulled by one scraggly mule.

Keeping to the shadows, he followed the carriage to the chapel where they'd married and where his body had been laid to rest. The men left the double door wide open to let the air in during the hot summer day. He slipped behind the statue of the Lady of Sorrows. They grunted and raised the flat stone covering the grave to the right of the altar, lowered her casket and replaced the cover. They took off their caps, made the sign of the cross and stood over the grave for a few moments. One of them said amen then they left and closed the heavy door, filling the small interior with screeching of the hinges.

Darkness surrounded Miles. Days blended into nights but he would not leave her grave. He lay there, listening for any sounds of Dobrila coming to life. Yet only scratching of a scurrying church mouse broke the silence. Had the damn vampire lied? No, the creature of the night would not feed from the corpse. She would awaken. He must be patient.

Her heartbeat came in so weak he almost mistook it for a mouse's, but the sound grew louder and stronger. Joy swirled through him.

She'd come back to the living.

He spurred onto his feet and pushed the flat slab, opening the grave. His fingers worked fast to loosen the nails holding the lid to the coffin.

She clawed at the wood, struggling to breathe.

He pulled the coffin open and helped her to sit up. "Thank God and all deities, you are awakened."

Her mouth hung open while she stared at him, but at least her breathing steadied. "Do my eyes deceive me?"

"No, dove. Eyes cannot deceive."

She scanned the church's interior. "Are we in Heaven? For it looks an awful like Earth."

"We're not dead—if that is what you're asking." He swallowed down the fast forming knot in his throat. The hard part of explaining what exactly they were was upon him. "We are alive, but a different kind of alive."

She shook her head and a deep crease marred her beautiful forehead. "You're not making any sense, Miles."

"There's a lot I must explain and I will in time, and time is all we have from now on." He wrapped his arm around her shoulders and lifted her out of the grave, then replaced the cover over the gaping hole. "There, let them think we're forever buried here together."

He dusted his hands off and wrapped his fingers with Dobrila's. "I've secured us ship's passage to another town where no one knows us. Still we must abolish all ties to our families and live as ordinary citizens, not as nobilities. Can you do this for us, Dobrila?"

She nodded, but her breathing sped up. "Where are we going?"

Under the cover of the night, he led her out of the chapel. "To the town in northern Dalmatia, Di Zara."

"Oh, Miles, so far away from home." She halted and cast one long gaze over the sleepy village, then faced him and smiled. "There never was any future for us here. Let our new life begin."

The dark surface of the Adriatic Sea glistened under the full moon. Holding her hand, he headed for the tip of the long pier jutting into the water where a dingy bobbed on the gentle swells. Anchored at the foot of the bay Master Rokov's ship swayed with the movement of the sea.

Once they were aboard, the anchor was weighed, the dinghy was hoisted. The ship drifted away. Miles stared at his sleepy town until the cluster of red-roofed houses was nothing but a speck in the sea. The majestic sails slowly glided along the masts and expanded as wind filled the sheets.

# Chapter 21

The images behind Matthias's lids had ceased, leaving him in darkness. He blinked, adjusting his eyes to the dimmed patio lights. The breeze on his face he'd confused as the one from his vision, ruffled the curtains of the open sliding door and confirmed he was back in this lifetime. Knowing his tale had ended, the tightness in his chest eased a notch, but a different ache replaced it. The time to part with Kate neared and he would have to stay strong for both of them. The sadness inside her grew with every passing day, no matter how hard she tried to deny or ignore it. Her eyes have lost some of the glee that lit them when she'd turned to look at him.

He cleared his throat, making sure his visual connection to Kate had ended. A long inhale came from her, followed by a stretch of silence.

'*So now you know the entire story.*' He waited for her reply, which wasn't forthcoming. '*Kate? Are you still with me?*'

'*Yes, I'm here. Why did you choose Di Zara or today's Zadar? You could go to any other city along the coast.*' Her voice carried a hint of accusation.

'*There was a medical school and a hospital where I found employment. But the main reason was, I'd sent your great-great-grandmother there. Not in the city, but on the island in the city's archipelago. I hoped to see her once more. I never did. Or maybe I did, I'm not sure if the woman was her so I kept my distance.*' Would he have approached her if he'd been certain the woman was her? No, nothing good would ever come out of reopening old wounds.

'*Couldn't let her go, could you?*' A sigh followed Kate's reply.

'*No, no I couldn't. I had my Dobrila, but there was always a void I couldn't fill. I just wanted to see for myself if Kate was happy. I was stunned she had never gotten over me.*'

'*Yeah—she couldn't let you go.*' A long yawn came from Kate's end. '*It's getting late.*'

'*Your yawn is my cue to disconnect. Next time I see you it'll be for your graduation ceremony. Getting excited?*' He had doubts if forcing her to attend the convocation proved a best maneuver, but she'd regret not going. After all, this could be her only graduation so why pass on it?

'*I am now. I'll see you in a week then.* Kate uttered an audible moan. '*Goodness, I'm so tired. Can't wait to hit the pillow, but I'm sure I'll dream about you and Dobrila. By the way, how did she take the news?*'

'*Much better than I'd predicted, though there were days she cursed me. It was harder on me to see her struggle to control the beastly urges.*' He shook his head, dispelling the memories of his wife's agonizing moments. Damn the vampire and his mild-mannered fiend. Dobrila had shredded her silk gowns to free her body from restrains of tightly laced corsets. She'd pull out clumps of her beautiful hair. Her inhumane screams would forever echo in his mind. He'd had to restrain her to wash her heated and sweaty skin in cold water, but the sponge bath brought her no relief. It wasn't until he carried her into the sea in the middle of the winter and immersed them both, that her convulsions eased. Minutes after, they'd make mad love, right there on the secluded beach and he knew she could go through 'her incurable illness' as she had referred to her condition.

Kate yawned again and he returned his thoughts to her. '*Go to sleep, love. Conversing this way is draining, especially the first time. Sweet dreams.*'

Kate would fill his dreams, like every night, for a week until he saw her again.

෴

A sparse applause broke through the college auditorium as Kate's name was announced over the speakers. Matthias snapped picture after picture while she crossed the parquetted floor and climbed the three steps. She shook hands with the dean and others from the assembly, took her scroll, stepped down from the stage, and headed back to her seat.

He relaxed his trigger finger and sat down. The homely woman next to him flashed him a smile, but after a second returned her attention to the screen of her phone in her thick hand.

The announcer called the next graduate to step on stage, a person whose last name begun with S. Thank God, only seven letters of alphabet left. By the quick head count of those in line at the right of the stage, some twenty people waited for their call.

The dean's address had taken the most of the ceremony. The man's deep, monotonous voice had put the attendees in a trance. Matthias had a hard time controlling his yawns. Mr. Sterlton should record his speeches to cure insomniacs.

Class valedictorian stepped up to the microphone and delivered the invitation to join for a snack in the college hall.

Nothing made the people from the audience hurl toward the two exits faster than the announcement of treats.

He remained seated. No point trying to squeeze through the throng bent on getting food. Once the crowd cleared, he went in search of Kate. He found her under the banner displaying Class of 2006. Her gaze met his and her face lit up for a brief moment.

"Thought you'd never find me in this swarm." She pointed at the long table. "Didn't take them long to clean up those trays."

"Don't worry about cheese and crackers. I'm taking you to a nice lunch. Ready?"

"I have to pick up my real diploma." She shook the scroll in her hand. "This is just a blank sheet of paper. I can't believe someone in the past kept the cap and a robe as a memento, so now college is forced to make us return these in exchange for our documents we worked so hard to get for years."

"I'll wait here." He leaned on the wall behind him.

She spun in the direction of the door, but faced him again. "Oh, and I have to make a pit stop. I had to go hours ago."

He pushed away from the wall. "Speaking of which, I must excuse myself too. Where are the boys' restrooms?"

"That way." She pointed at the blue sign hanging from the ceiling. "They may not be to your liking, though. Just warning you not to expect to smell roses in there."

"In my three centuries, I've seen my fair share of

gross privies. I learned to hold my breath." He chuckled and tapped her arm with his fist. "Hurry back."

The restroom stood empty and quiet, but God Almighty, what a stench. He pulled the door shut, filled his lungs and took the closest stall. Seconds later, the door popped open and female giggles echoed off the tiled walls. Two sets of feet entered the booth next to him. One in platform sandals, the leather straps dug into meaty feet, and the other in worn, red cloth sneakers.

A belt buckle clinked, and trousers dropped around the guy's hairy ankles. The girl dropped her purse on the floor, raised one foot then the other, slipping panties over her sandals.

Her date groaned and shoved his foot under the thin divider. The girl placed her foot next to his as she straddled him.

Matthias pressed his lips together, stifling snickers. Who knew he'd be treated to a restroom sex scene? Ah, college life, he missed it.

He took care of his business. There was no need to stick around and witness two young students scratch their need.

He unlocked the door to leave.

"Stop." The girl's sharp tone broke the man's moans. "Do you have protection?"

The guy's hard breathing ceased. There was a moment of silence. "Why? Miller already knocked you up. You can't get pregnant again."

"You moron," she snapped and sprang to her feet. The red sneaker moved back. "Do you think I'd let myself get pregnant by Miller?"

"But—"

"His dad is a school principal, and he'll get me a job. Then I'll suffer a sudden miscarriage and we'll all be happy." She stomped her foot. "Once I graduate, that is."

Her voice dripped with anger. "All because of that stupid foreign bitch who ratted on me."

The guy pulled up his pants. "You're wicked, Amanda."

"A girl has to do what a girl has to do." She picked up the purse off the floor. "Now no glove, no love. Bag it."

"I don't have any condoms on me. Let me ask around. Meet you in the lobby." The door lock clicked and red sneakers stepped out of the stall.

When the two unexpected lovers left the bathroom, Matthias walked out. Despite the urge to wash his hands, he left the restroom and filled his lungs with clean air. He'd have to sanitize his hands with the gel inside his car.

Kate headed in his direction. She'd traded the black gown for a large manila envelope.

"Hey, Kate. Wait up," Miller called after her. "I want you to meet someone."

She halted and pivoted in his direction. "I'm in a hurry."

"Won't take long." He tapped the shoulder of a tall, skinny man behind him. "Dad, come meet Kate, the girl I told you about. She helped me graduate."

A man in a dark suit lowered his rimless glasses to the tip of his narrow nose and scrutinized Kate. He stepped closer and shook his index finger, ignoring her offered hand. "I know foreign girls want one thing, to marry for a visa." He threw a sharp look over his shoulder. "Boy, you're lucky that nice girl Amanda got you before this one. Now, where's your bride? I have a contract for her to sign. Ah, here she comes."

Extending his arm, he wrapped Amanda in a hug. "You taking care of that grandson of mine?"

She grinned, and sugar laced her voice. "Oh, Mr. Miller, how do you know it's a boy?"

"Millers only make boys." He slid his hand into his suit pocket and extracted a white envelope. "Here's the job offer. All you need to do is sign on the dotted line. And, you can call me Dad."

Miller Junior's expression soured, terror crossed his wide eyes. "No friggin' way." He turned to Kate. "I'm sorry."

"Amanda, where you've been? I've got it." The young man in red sneakers raised his hand, wrapped condom between his fingers. He winked. "Still in the mood?"

"Moron," she shrieked, a grimace contorting her face.

Red sneakers frowned and shrugged. "What? You said you weren't knocked up."

Miller's frown stretched into a victorious grin. "I told you, Dad. She's lying." He turned to Amanda. "The campus had enough of your bullshit and your lies. All you managed to accomplish is animosity among the students."

"What is the meaning of this?" Mr. Miller pulled the envelope out of Amanda's hands. "Not so fast. Explain yourself."

Matthias caressed Kate's shoulders. "Had enough drama for one day?"

She angled her head at his and smiled. "Oh, yes. Let's get out of here."

Amanda lowered her gaze to her feet, her face paled. She scrunched her lips and shook her head.

Miles laced his fingers with Kate's and nudged her along. "Come, we have reservations at a nice restaurant. The same one we ate at the last time. You enjoyed the food."

"It was a real treat to find Dalmatian cuisine in Toronto."

She matched his strides to the car with a bounce in her step.

Over the course of lunch, her demeanor changed from bubbly to inhibited. She pushed the food around the plate, but didn't taste it.

"Are you up for a nice dessert?" he asked, waving to the waiter for the bill.

She shook her head, not meeting his eyes.

"I know what's bothering you. The story is done and I'll leave you alone. Need I remind you, we made a deal. And a deal is a deal, after all."

She blinked fast, grabbed her purse from the back of the chair, and pulled out the three-ring binder. "Let's not talk about it right now. I finished typing the story and printed it out. Here it is. Would you read it?"

He took the folder and smiled at the title. "Rose of Crimson, it fits. I'm sure you did a great job, it'll be my honor to read it."

"What do you want me to do with it?" She rested her chin on her curled fingers. God, her lips were so inviting from that angle.

"It's yours to do with as you wish." He signed the receipt and got to his feet. The sadness in her tone sliced his heart. He wasn't looking forward to parting. "Let's go to the park we visited on our walk."

On the narrow foot path, his footsteps faltered and so did hers. He stopped and faced her. She swallowed audibly and glanced away.

Their parting would crush her, and she already barely held herself together. There was but one thing he could do to ease her sorrow, and despite his moral dilemma he would do it. Seeing her like this squeezed his chest.

"Look at me," he demanded, cupping her chin and forcing her head toward him.

Her face crumpled and, in an instant, tears poured from her emerald greens. "I told myself I'd be strong and not fall apart when the moment came, but I can't help it."

"No, love, please don't. Understand this is not good-bye, but until we meet again. I'll watch over you always." He locked his gaze with hers. She was under his spell. Now was the perfect moment. "I'll be there with you. Always," he whispered, reaching deep into her mind and wiping it clean of him.

She would not have any recollection of him other than what she'd learned about him in the legend. The look in her eyes changed from sorrow to indifference, to no recognition. Before he released her from his mental hold, he stretched out his arm grasping the folder in her purse and pulled out the novel.

"In a second, you'll wake and the pain you felt will be gone." He crushed her to his chest and took one last opportunity to inhale her jasmine scent. In a swift motion, he jerked away from her and dropped the pages, releasing the mental hold. "I'm sorry, miss. I didn't see you there."

"No, I'm sorry. I don't know where I was walking." She slapped a hand to her forehead.

Wind rustled the pages of the open folder. He bent over and picked up the sheets. "Here you dropped this."

"Thank you." She smiled, taking the binder in her hand. Her eyes held neither love nor recognition for him as they had only minutes ago.

Pain ripped through his heart. But this was what he wanted, to see her at peace. He had taken her sorrow and would suffer for them both.

She took the seat on the same bench he'd shared with her over a week ago. Her attention turned to the pages of his story. He retreated to the low wall behind her. A folded newspaper lay on the wall, the Toronto Star. He spread open the paper and hid his face.

"Hey!" A skinny guy jumped onto the bench beside her.

She cringed. "Jeez, Andrew you startled me."

"You left so fast you didn't hear me calling you." He leaned toward her. "What're you reading?"

"A story I wrote." She kept her face at the pages on her lap.

Andrew leaned closer, lowering his face at the pages in her lap. "Wow, it's done. You mentioned this book before Amanda and Potter broke your computer. I didn't think you'd have it finished yet. Can I read it?"

"A strange urge pressed on me to complete it and have it ready for today. I can't explain. It's a true tragic love story that happen some three centuries ago, but there are details in it, details no one could possibly know. I swear, if feels like I lived it myself." She hugged the binder to her chest and directed a smile at Andrew. "It was nice of you to get the students to donate coffee money for my new laptop. I still can't believe you convinced them. Most wouldn't let me sit with them at the table in the lunch room."

"This world doesn't hate you, Kate. In fact, many students like you. Simone donated the most. How could she not? Your trial before the student committee helped her break away from Amanda's grip on her wallet. And you were the only one brave enough to confront Amanda." He tweaked his head. "I wish you'd understand that. By the way, did you find a new apartment?"

Her slow nod was barely noticeable. "I do understand. My days of being shy and alone are coming to the end. And, no, I haven't found anything yet. I've just started looking though. Why do you ask?"

"I'm moving in with Raul and my mom doesn't like to be alone. Would you mind staying with her? At least for a while until she gets used to the idea I'm gone. I'll drop by as often as I can."

"That's a generous offer. I'm afraid I wouldn't be much of a company to your mom. However, I'll consider it. I've received a letter from the government stating my loan is reduced due to my academic merit. I still owe half of my student loan to the bank. Most of my money will go to pay it off." At the sound of a horn, she turned. Her gaze paused on Matthias, but continued toward the car parked by the curb.

"Raul is impatient. We're late for a party. I have to go." Andrew stood and tapped her shoulder. "See you soon, and hopefully you'll move in with my mom so I can read your book when I visit."

She nodded. "I'll think about it. Say hi to Raul and have a great time at the party." She dipped her face at the rustling papers on her knees. Andrew ran off toward the honking car.

Matthias kept his steady gaze on Kate for a few minutes then stood to leave. His plan had worked better than he expected. Not only didn't she have any memory of him existing, but all she came in contact with during their time together remembered things differently. The false government letter convinced her she had been granted loan forgiveness due to her exemplary grades. Fortuno was quite an artiste. She'd be fine. Sometimes he wished he could erase his mind too, but memories were all he had to hang on to.

A soccer ball rolled up to her feet and two small boys halted in front of her. "Can we have our ball back?" the taller of the two asked.

"Of course." She dribbled the ball in her hand and extended her arm to him. "Here."

"You guys." The young firefighter ran up to them. "I told you not to disturb her. The lady was reading."

"But, Uncle Craig," the same boy said, turning to the man in the baseball uniform. "You told us to do this."

He smiled sheepishly and shrugged. "Guilty." He then scratched his neck. "Ah, this is awkward. My crew goes for a pint after every game. Would you like to join us?"

"I don't know." Kate shook her head. "Beer's not my kind of drink."

"Oh come on," the boys whined. "We don't drink beer either."

She snickered, gathered her things, and rose from the bench. "Well, since you asked so nicely."

With the firefighter and his two nephews, she walked away and disappeared around the corner.

Damn it, he should run after her, take her in his arms. Tell her he had made a terrible mistake. But his feet stood rooted. He did the right thing by setting Kate free. She would return to him and he'd be ready to love her. These few months together were but a test for their future. Though he had not felt beast's stirring inside him for weeks, he had to be certain the entity was accepting of her. This Kate was stronger than her ancestor, but would she leave him if he turned violent? He would sooner sever his own arm than hurt her.

'*Do not despair. When two souls are meant to be together, eventually they find their way back.*' Emina's soft tone instilled much-needed encouragement.

He set on his lonely way, until Kate entered his life again for good, he'd keep his watch over her.

# *The End*

## About the Author

Zrinka Jelic lives in Ontario with her husband and two children. A member of the Romance Writers of America and its chapter Fantasy Futuristic &Paranormal, as well as Savvy Authors, she writes contemporary as well as paranormal with a pinch of history. Her characters come from all walks of life and love comes in many colors. With a love for her native Croatia and the Adriatic Sea, you will find her characters in mostly good weather, but some rain must fall in everyone's life.